LAST NOVEMBER

A SURVIVOR'S STORY OF THE NUCLEAR HOLOCAUST OF 1983

The Bus to Fort Kobe was not air conditioned, I was wearing a pair of jeans and a black T-shirt, and both were soaked through with sweat before I recovered my duffle and garment bag at the airport. It has been a long, but sleepless flight from Fort Benning, Georgia to Panama City, Panama. My Airborne School class had gone almost entirely to Fort Bragg, North Carolina, except for three guys going to Vicenza Italy, and me. The one poor schmuck who when sitting in the recruiter's office thought Panama sounded exotic and volunteered for this.

This was not what I had envisioned, of course, nothing in the Army was. I thought my buddies from High School would enlist too, but in the end they all chickened out. Basic Training looked kind of cool, but in the end it was a lot of running around shouting, getting shouted at, and freezing my ass off. By the time I got to Advanced Individual Training, I took a bus across fort Benning to another falling down barrack, less yelling, and a lot more sweating. Though I had cursed the chill in the air in the cold Georgia nights, I would miss it as the summer heat came. Not only did we sweat from sun up to sun down, but the bug made a feast of me. The ticks were bad, the humiliating 'tick checks' they inspired out of the fear of Rocky Mountain spotted fever. The mosquitoes where worse, there was nothing for them. The swarmed you, buzzed into your ears, up your nose, never letting you rest or sleep, and God help the Private that scratched or swatted on! The whole Platoon would have been killed if this where Vietnam! By the judgment of our Drill Instructors the battlefield must be littered with slaughtered Platoons of grunts, where one man had swatted, a mosquito, scratched an itch, or any other of the millions of sins Privates were prone to. I would have showered in ticks, and washed them off with mosquitoes if only the term Chigger had never become part of my vocabulary. Invisible insects from the deepest pits of hell the crawl upon you and gather where your uniform it tight, around the tops of your boots and under your belt being their favorite. One they are in place the burry themselves deep in your skin. What they do there is a matter of much debate among the Privates of Fort Benning. The most horrible, hence the theory I believe is that they lay eggs under your skin, then die. As their tiny bodies decompose in your flesh you are overcome by the most maddening desire to scratch imaginable. Drill Instructors screaming, you don't care, the Platoon, will die, you don't care. You will die, good! I have seen many a young troop, myself included scratch themselves bloody. When you are done there as small open holes that weep a yellow fluid. One hole for each chigger. I had the company record of 62 in a night. The fluid leaks and when it dries it sticks to your uniform so when you move the scab it torn off. It takes more than 6 weeks for a chigger bite to heal.

The road quickly turned to a one lane dirt road, jungle crowded in around us. I imagined this must have been something like Vietnam had looked like. Like all young soldiers I knew, I felt cheated that I had missed that, which was certain to be out last real land war. The last US forces has pulled out of Vietnam 10 years ago, Saigon had fallen 7 years ago, and these had not been much since. The Hostage Rescue Attempt 4 years ago was a disaster, reminding Washington how little Politician could stomach the sight of blood. When Reagan was elected and I heard my teachers fretting that he would get us into World War Three, I have to admit that, it did not have the effect on me they had hoped. I hoped they were right.

We passed brightly painted ram-shackle huts with corrugated tin roofs. I stared up into the trees hoping to spy a monkey, and down into the stagnant water looking for gators, or caiman. I was shocked well into the journey when we skidded around a corner and there is the middle of the jungle, tower high above the trees sat an enormous luxury ocean liner. A wave of chatter went through the handful of troops on the bus. I remember someone humming the theme to 'the Love boat'.

When we pulled into Fort Sherman a fat Sergeant in a sweat soaked set of BDUs got on the bus, he had the look you would expect of a corrupt Southern Sheriff. "Alright, listen up!" He bellowed, if you orders are to Fort Sherman get off the bus. If your orders are to Fort Kobe, stay on the bus!"

A thin black kids called from the back of the bus, "What about Fort Clayton?"

The Sergeant looked as though a vein would burst in his head. "If you are going to Fort Clayton, you are on the wrong Fucking bus!"

Troops began wrestling there gear off the bus, after a long time, it was just the Fort Clayton kid and myself. He looked pleadingly at me, as though I would know what to do. He stepped off the bus like a man going to his execution. A few moments later he came running back to grab his gear.

The Sergeant lumbered back on the bus. He pointed a fat finger at me. "What the fuck are you doing still on the bus?"

I stammered, "Fort Kobe, Sergeant" and he turned his attention to the kid grabbing his gear. His attention to the other kid, and loosed a sting of profanity laced instructions as he chased him off the bus. The door closed, it was just me and the driver. He was did not say a word as we pulled away.

More jungle and a long bridge over the Chagress River marked the rest of my journey. I started to get nervous. Should I put my uniform on? If not now, when?

The gate guards waved the bus though and we pulled off in front of the 1st Battalion 87th Infantry Headquarters. I turned to ask the driver a question, but the driver closed the door and drove away. I stepped into the door, and cool air hit me. Among the recruiting posters and peeling paint I saw the sign for the latrine. I rushed in and stripped, throwing on my class A uniform.

With jump boots firmly laced and my red beret tucked under my arm, I felt a bit of confidence, returning. My blue infantry cord, jump wing, and Army Service Ribbon where like talismans making the invisible the fact that I was a skinny kid six months out of High School, thousands of miles from home, and scared to death. I pulled the folder containing my orders and records out of the bottom of my garment bag. Steeling myself for what was to come I headed upstairs towards where the signs said S1.

I found a counter, an old fragmentation grenade with the number one hanging from the pin say on a 'complaints department take a number' plaque. A fat bearded black Specialists barked, "Sign in!" at me. I glanced around for the sign in sheet. "There!" He pointed. Massive black Sergeant with a gold tool lumbered up to me. "PFC, are you giving my Specialist grief?"

I snapped to Parade rest, "No Sergeant!"

"Who the fuck are you?" He shouted at in my face. I was taken aback by this, this was the sort of treatment one got in Basic, and Airborne School, but it was not supposed to happen, in the 'real Army'.

"Private First Class McGill, Sergeant." I barked.

"Why the fuck are you dressed like, John Fucking Wayne?"

I looked at him seeing a skinny confused white kid reflected back in that gold tooth. "Sergeant?"

"Sergeant what?" He shouted, I noticed his troops where all gathered around enjoying the show. "What the fuck are you trying to say?"

"Sergeant, I was ordered to report in Class As"

"Get out of those ridiculous ass boots, faggot ass beret, get a God-damned garrison cap on your head, and report in like a real fucking soldier!" He shouted. "Now! Move it!"

I darted down stairs. Scraping the back of my fingers blood digging my low quarter shoes and garrison cap out of the duffel.

They were scuffed up, and looked like shit. I raced back upstairs, the Sergeant had been laughing with a group of black troops. He came around the corner, chewing me up and down. I was sweating, my trousers where wrinkled from having been stuffed in my jump boots.

After an interminable ass chewing, I was told to report to First Sergeant Hoefmeir at Alpha Company. I dragged my gear down the stairs, already exhausted. The Alpha Company Headquarters was less than a block away, by the time I got there I was soaked in sweat.

I came into the office like a wounded buffalo, the company clerk looked at me, like you might a bit of road kill. He was a skinny white Specialist with a long nose. "Where are your jump boots troop?"

I was slack jawed, and stammering. He smiled, and said "Get'em on." I rapidly dug them out of my bag. "Alpha is the only Airborne Company in the Battalion, and they hate us." He explained, as though he was talking to a slow child. "Battalion is the enemy, never forget that."

I spent the next hour filling out paperwork, mail cards and the like. The Specialist was helpful and annoying at the same time. The last thing was to report to First Sergeant Hoefmeir. He was a fire plug of a man, white, covered in tattoos. He looked me up and down, I stared straight ahead, waiting for ass chewing to begin. "Third Platoon." He said and picked up his pen.

The Specialists grabbed me, and pulled me out. "Don't look so stunned. First Sergeant is not a big talker. Except when he is drunk, and then stay the fuck away from him. "He flopped down at his desk. "Want a coke?"

"Sure, please" I answered.

He threw some change on the desk. "There is a machine out back. I buy you fly." I looked confused, "I pay for both, but you have to get them genius."

When I came back my future fire team leader, Specialist Bill Collins was standing by the clerk's desk, thumbing through a newspaper. "Hey Hall," he said to the clerk, "did you hear the Russians shot down a Korean Airliner?"

"That newspaper is over month old, genius." He said without looking up.

"Is everyone on board still dead?" Collins asked with a smirk, he looked at me, "New guy, you just came from the world, are those folks all still dead?"

"As far as I know, dead and frozen in Siberia somewhere." I answered as they each snatched a cold coke from my hand.

"Ok, if the brain trusts is done, get the fuck out of here. I have reports to do." Hall said sounding somewhat like a school marm.

"Bill Collins, I am going to be you Fire Team, leader." He said shaking me hand.

"Bill McGill. " I answered drawing a laugh from both of them.

"Bill, Bill, and Billy that is quite a team you've got there Collins." Hall laughed

"No, Bill, Bill, Billy and Pedro!" Collins corrected him. He shouldered my duffel bag. "Come on Bill let's get you locked on over at the barracks. "

We were all in one room, I was given the top rack by the door, Pedro had the bottom rack. He was a diminutive Puerto Rican kid who always looked on the very of falling asleep or crying. Bill and Billy has the rack furthest in, and closest to our communal latrine. Billy Orson was a scarecrow think kid from Georgia, with thick glasses and a loud voice that he used constantly.

I was unpacking and putting my stuff in my wall locker, while Pedro listened to a headset and Billy sharpened a knife. "Hey Bill, when they gonna make you Corporal?" He asked angrily.

"I dunno Billy." Collins answered without looking up from his book.

"You been the Team Leaders for months now!" He insisted.

"Yeah," He sounded annoyed "I fucking know that."

"Well it's bullshit!"

"I know!" Bill said tossing his book aside. "I fucking know! What do you care?"

"Shit! Everyone else has an NCO for a team leader, so we keep getting' fucked with the bad details. "He squawked.

"NO! Everyone else has a Sergeant. You will still be fucked." Bill said with a bit of a smirk.

"First Platoon has a Corporal." Pedro chimed in. "'Corse he's black."

"What does that have to do with it?" I asked before I remembered not to speak.

"Man!" Pedro sat strait up. "That S1 is racist!"

"Yeah, no bullshit! If you ain't a Nigger, you're fucked!" Billy piped up.

"Hey!" Bill jumped up waving a finger at Billy. "What the fuck did I tell you?"

Billy grasped the combat knife menacingly. "It is!"

Bill looked apologetically. "It really is. If you are not boys with Sergeant Jones, you get nothing done up there." His face hardened, as he turned to Billy. "We do not use that fucking word though do we?"

"Fucking Yankee." Billy spat as we went back to sharpening his knife.

"We had some unpleasantness at the Fourth of July picnic, and we have to watch that shit. " Bill explained.

"Unpleasantness? It was a race riot!" Pedro said excitedly.

"Billy here used to be a Specialist to, as a matter of fact so did Pedro. Had I not left a little early I supposed I would have been busted to. There were only four guys in the Platoon that didn't get busted! "

Pedro smiled, "The line for Office Hours went around the block!"

"Yeah, no shit. " Billy laughed.

"By the time they go to the end, we had guys going down as heat casualties in line." Bill added with pride.

"That did not slow down the Axman!" Billy said we glee. "He gave them their right laying on the stretcher with the IV in their arm!"

That night I slept the sleep of the righteous. I had no doubt I was a fucked up soldier, in a fucked up unit, but I seemed surrounded by fellow fuck ups, and that would be good enough. The next morning, was Friday the company run. Our Company Commander was a small man with a long Italian name, he looked like a boy next to the First Sergeant.

Normally Company runs are designed to raise the motivation, they are not very fast, and everyone sings loudly. This was not like that, we were third in line, of the third Platoon, and so we were way back in the formation. When we right faced we were barely moving, the next thing I knew we were sprinting to catch up. Then I nearly slammed into the guy in front of me as 'the slinky effect' kicked in. This went on for miles.

After about a half an hour, Pedro started falling back. "Come on man, you can do this." I said to encourage him.

"Get your spic ass up here!" Billy shouted at him. "We are all hurting!"

"Come on!" Bill shouted at him, and that was how it went for another twenty minutes or so. In the end, we staggered back into the Company area and where dismissed.

I felt pretty good, I had survived my first company run in 'the real Army' and that was something. The rest of the day on the training schedule was 'weapons cleaning' and 'Sergeant's Time.' What that meant is that we went down to the arms room, after out showers and drew out weapons.

Once back at the room, I discovered my newly issued M16A1 was filthy, and I set to cleaning it. Billy was our M60 gunner, so he had a machinegun and 45 caliber pistol to clean. Pedro had an M203 grenade launcher on his M16 that he promptly set down and crawled under our bunk beds to go sleep.

Bill set his rifle in the corner, and picked up the bolter carrier group out of my rifle. "I have mine set to self-cleaning mode." He looked over the part, "Jesus what a mess!" He saw the confused look on my face. "Look Bill, here is the thing. Once we get these things clean, all they need is a light coat of CLP on parts that can rust, and they are good. Hall just puts weapons cleaning on the training schedule so we can hang out in the A/C, and the lifers leave us alone. If you are going to sleep you have to so it on the floor or in the latrine so when the Sergeants walk by the window they cannot see. We will keep this up until about 1600, then we turn our shit in and head down range"

"So, we do not take are weapons down range?" I asked sheepishly. The all laughed at me. I was terribly embarrassed, even though they were good natured about it.

After that evenings formation we all went back to the room, and changed into civilian attire. We were not fashion plates by any means. I got a chuckle out of Pedro's garish gold chains, and Billy's cowboy boots. We started by getting pitchers of beer down at the Enlisted Club as they were only a dollar a piece. It was a crush of soldiers tanking up on pizza and beer before heading 'down range.'

The town was as I imagine garrison towns had been since the days of Rome, street venders peddling every nature of trinket, fake and stolen goods, loud music coming from squalid bars, and painted whores trolling the back alleys. The fire team broke up getting off the bus, Pedro when with the Latino boys to the club. Normally the Puerto Ricans and Mexicans, I would later learn, would not mix, but the rules where a little different here, where there were so few of Americans. Back in New York the Puerto Ricans hated the Dominicans, but once faced with Mexicans they would band together. If the three groups when in the Company of Blacks, all differences where put aside until the common threat was gone.

Billy went off to the Country bar, where he and the Southern boys would dance and get wild, Bill explained that we, as Yankees where welcome there, as long as it was not to close to closing time.

Once drunk those boys liked to fight, and in the absence of blacks, or Latinos, Yankees would do. Without us, they would then fight, Texans, against everyone, South versus West, you name it.

We stopped at a bar called 'Peace Frog' it was maybe 30 feet wide, and decorated with Christmas lights in the shape of a peace symbol. They were playing a Doors song Bill liked so we grabbed a table on the sidewalk. "Normally you do not want to be on the sidewalk, but this place is just too damn loud inside!" Bill explained as he gestured for the waitress to bring us two beers.

I was pretty close to broke, just coming off of leave, but Bill insisted I not worry about it. It turns out he was from Buffalo, NY not more than 60 miles from where I had grown up. Like me he had joined hoping for some action, and thinking with the Marines in Lebanon the Army would not be far behind. "I don't know I hear the Marines are getting some action, but I also heard that they are peacekeepers and not allowed to do shit."

"Yeah, they have a club on the post called 'the can't shoot back saloon'. " I added and we laughed at that for a while. "I guess if we ever do get into it, they will have to send in the Army." I added weakly.

"Oh hell yeah!" Bill smiled enthusiastically. "Who ever heard of a War without the Army. Shit, they only have one Battalion there!"

A older Panamanian man with a spider monkey on his shoulder came up to our table, in a flash he threw the money on my shoulder. It shrieked and pissed on the table is he snapped a Polaroid photo. "You buy, you buy!" He waved the picture in my face, taking back his not angry monkey.

"Get the fuck out of here!" Bill shoved him away. A fat old Panamanian women came charging out of the bar with a broom that looked like a witch should be ridding on it. I thought we were in trouble, but she swung that thing at the monkey guys head like she meant to knock it off. He dodged it, to the great misfortune of the monkey that was sent flying. Being down with a piece of twine to the man's wrist it did fly far before his reflexive jerk brought it back upon himself, all teeth and fury. We laughed hysterically as the woman chased both man and monkey down the sidewalk, as they battled amongst themselves. Many passing GIs broke out cameras and got a good chuckle out of spectacle.

As we slowly regained out composure we looked at the urine table soak table, "I know a place where the beer is totally free on monkey piss." Bill said, sending back into hysterics, we had conducted a pretty through pre-flight at the E club, and where already pretty drunk. The old lady tried to convince us to stay, as she brought fresh beers, but Bill just shouted "We will be back later!" Snatching something off the ground, and handing it to me. It was the Polaroid of me with the monkey on my shoulder, and Bill attempting to snatch his beer out of the splash zone.

The street was crowded, "Make sure you keep your wallet in your front pocket." He said above the din, "these little geechees can pick your pocket while you are sitting down."

"What's a geechee?" I asked stupidly.

"Slang term for the locals, everyone uses it, so it won't get you in trouble with the Latin boys or anything. " He dodged a three wheeled motorcycle, set up as a taxi. "And do not keep you money together. Whatever you pull out of your pocket is what everything costs. Don't show them shit, until you have agreed on a price, " He pointed at me for emphasis. "nothing costs what they say. If you want a jacket and they say it costs $60 that means you can get it for $20, less if you are good, and maybe Habla a little. "

"We paid a buck each for the beers." I pointed out stupidly.

"Yeah, good eye. Beer is a buck, mixed drinks two bucks, everywhere all the time. If they charge less they get beat up, or worse. " He leaned close with a conspiratorial tone, only a drunk can truly pull off. "If you are a regular, sometime they take care of you, but normally that is when it is dead, like after closing. "

We stopped at what looks like it might have tikki bar with dried palm fronds, but the sign bore a poor likeness of a Viking ship. We entered the place, and there was a large Irish flag on the ceiling, and the wall was lined with dart boards. The bartender was a crusty old Asian woman, she smiled toothlessly at him. "Billiam! Where you been?"

"Oh, around" he said pulling up a bar stool. "A couple of the usual Ma."

She came back with 2 San Miguel beers. I had never had one

before, it is from the Philippines, cut with formaldehyde. It is not as bad as it sounds. "Who you're frien'?"

"Bill, this is Adjima." He gestured regally, "Adjima, this is Bill."

She cackled and shook my hand with what looked like a shriveled root, mumbled some pleasantry and scampered off. "I like this place," Bill opined, "I think it must be kind of like one of those places the guys used to go during the war. It used to be a whore house, most of the bars are. This is one of the few places that does not have 'buy me drinky girls'. It used to, from the Phillippines, but they got chased out. The locals did not like the competition, guess. Believe it or not those whores get annoying they want you to keep buying them expensive 'girl drinks' all night, and at the end of the night you still have to pay the bar fine to take them home. If you willing to risk it."

"They didn't send Adjima back to the Philippines."

"Naw, she's Korean." For some reason I found that funny, and we busted up laughing. Over many beers and games of darts, that became increasingly more dangerous to those around us, we at some point got into the great debate of if it was better to go to Ranger

School first, and then do to a Ranger Battalion or Vice Versa. My point was if you went already tabbed there was no danger of getting hurt, or not making it for some reason, and being that poor sap in the Ranger Bat that was not 'really a Ranger.' Bill's point was that if you made it through Ranger Bat's pre-Ranger course there is no way you would NOT make it whereas if you went from, say here. There is no way of knowing.

The cab ride back was quiet and rainy. We stumbled back to the room, and collapsed, I do not remember even climbing into my rack. What I do remember, and always will until the day I die, is the horrible sheik and anguish, pain and terror that awoke me around 0330 that morning. My eyes flung open in the dark as it sounded like someone was being raped and murdered by a gang of demons a few feet below me.

"Pedro!" Bill shouted from across the room, The screaming and thrashing continued. "Pedro! God Damn it!" Bill shouted. "Shut the fuck up!" Bill staggered from his rack throwing a pillow a Pedro, the lights came on, and Pedro was silent.

I peered over the edge of the bunk bed, Pedro looked bleary eyed up at me and shrugged "What?" He rolled up in his covers, "Shut the lights off, it is late."

"Fuckin' Pedro!" Bill cursed as he shut the light back out.

The next day I woke up feeling like crap. Billy came in around nine, still in the clothes he had on the night before, and covered in mud. He stripped cheerfully. "Hey fellas! How was your night?" He stumbled removing his boots. "Boy, I got fucked up!"

"You are fucked up." Bill growled pulling a blanket over his head.

"Where did you guys go?" Billy asked cheerfully, "I went to the silver spur, I tell you what there some girls in there was!"

Bill got up and staggered into the latrine. "Your dick is gonna fall off you keep messing with those whores."

"Naw, these were American girls." He protested to no-one as the shower came on in the latrine. Pedro rolled out of bed. "Those are somebody's wives man, you mess with them your dick is gonna get cut off!"

"Fuckin' lifers don't scare me none."

"Not even Hoef?" Pedro leered. It turned out everyone was afraid of Hoef. He was a Ranger in Vietnam, and was alleged to killed a guy in a Georgia bus station.

"Well I didn't see Mrs. Hoef anywhere." Billy answered evasively.

"Are you sure?" Pedro slunk over to him like a devil. "Would you know? No one has ever seen her. Any one of those country fried white girls could have been the Hoef's old lady." He said with a sneer.

"I heard she went stateside." Billy said wrapping a towel around himself.

The shower stopped and Bill, called in from the other room. "I heard she was fucking some young cook in the show hall, and he killer her. Took her out in the jungle and fed her to the gators"

"Yeah! I heard that too!" Pedro looked gleeful. "But, I heard he killed the both! He didn't feed them to the gators, though. No way, he chopped them up and fed them us!"

"You are a bunch old women!" Billy said making his way to the shower. "Like a bunch of old women yammerin' on about nothin'!"

Bill and Pedro gave me a wink. "I will bet it was in the stew last week." Bill said casually.

"No esse, it was in the gumbo!"

"Why the gumbo?"

"My bro Carlos over in second Platoon said he found a blond hair in his gumbo."

"Are you ladies still talking out there?" Billy asked annoyed.

"I don't know that stew was awfully gritty, like ground up bones." Bill and Pedro chuckled silently.

"Oh bullshit! Carlos told me that Specialist Hall at the Company Office found a toe nail in his gumbo."

"Shut the fuck up out there!" Billy squawked.

"It was painted!" Pedro giggled.

"I can't even hear you out there!"

Bill and Pedro where silently laughing to the point of tears. "Is it true," Bill forced through his laughter, "that on a fifty dollar bet...he"

"Swallowed it!" Pedro shouted. The sound of Billy vomiting in the shower sent us all into hysterics.

"You are cleaning that up!" Bill shouted when he regained some degree of composure.

After a very un-satisfying lunch at the mess hall, we where lounging around on the catwalk outside out room. Billy was talking about the Airborne tattoo he wanted to get, and suddenly remembered. "Hey ya'all want to go to the movies tonight, they go Star Wars."

We shrugged, "Sure," Bill said, "I have seen it a bunch of times."

"No the NEW one!" He said excitedly.

"Return of the Jedi ?" I asked.

"Yeah!" Billy almost jumped with excitement.

Pedro came out of the room drinking a beer, "What is Billy Bob all worked up over?"

"Return of the Jedi!" Bill said looking surprisingly enthused. "That is this week?"

"Yeah, Hall told me, you know what a geek he is."

"What is the big deal?" Pedro shrugged, "Carlos has it on VHS. Of course you can see people walking in front of the screen, and it has Spanish sub-titles."

"You've seen it?" He asked

"Sure."

"Yeah, I saw it at Airborne School." I added.

"Either one of you tell me a thing, I will fucking kill you!"

"What like Leia is Luke's sister?" Padro asked smiling.

"Mother Fucker!" Billy and I had to literally restrain Bill, after he slapped the beer out of Pedro's hand he seemed likely to kill him.

"What the fuck is up with white people and Star Wars?" Pedro asked slinking away.

I felt bad for Bill, he sulked the whole movie, apparently he had avoided all things Jedi until the film came to Panama. Afterward Billy and I took him to the club, and got a pitcher of beer. "So Leia is Lukes sister, that is fucking gross!" He lamented, then turned an angry I to Billy. "You they one thing about kissin' cousins and I will pop you."

"The speeders where cool." I said lamely.

"Hell yeah, they were cool!" Billy chimed in rambling on about the battle for Endor in embarrassing detail.

"And fucking attack of the Muppets at the end!" He slammed his fist on the table. That got some glances from the MPs, luckily Billy and I had the same thought.

"Let's get out of here, I need some real liquor!" Billy announced.

A short cab ride later we were at the Silver Spur, and I was staring into a shot glass of Jack Daniels sitting next to a bottle of Bud, wondering what I had gotten myself into. Billy raised his shot glass, "Here is to the Airborne!"

"Airborne!" We repeated downing our shots, and chasing them with beer. I shuddered from the after taste as I looked around the bar, a lot of tight jeans and cowboy hats. Stuck in the middle of it all, looking concerned was Specialist Hall, his expression was ferret like, and his neatly tucked in t-shirt seemed very out of place.

There was a ruckus by the pool table, Hall darted over to it disappearing from my sight. I heard shouts and breaking glass. The crowed parted as First Sergeant Hoef staggered bloody handed from the other room. Hall was behind him talking fast but so quiet only the First Sergeant could hear him.

First Sergeant threw a bloody elbow in Halls direction that he easily ducked. Hoef's eyes fell upon us. He lurched towards us. "Give these boys another round!" He barked.

To my surprise the bartender complied. First Sergeant Hoef picked up a shot glass, spilling half of it. "The big one's comin' boys." He slurred and downed his shot. We dumbly followed suite. He slammed his fist on the bar sending bottles and glasses flying. "Another God Damn it!" He shouted, slipping off the bar he fell, Bill and Billy scrambled to pick him up.

Hall looked dead into my eyes, as though he was measuring an experiment of some kind. 'What is the first thing I told you?"

I flirted with saying, 'to put my boots on.' It would have been funny, and accurate, and God knows there was no one in the Company who could not kick Hall's ass, but there was something that seemed to prevent it. "Stay away from the First Sergeant when he is drunk." I said meekly.

"Get the rest of the brain trust out of here, before the God Damned cops show up." I started to argue, but he cut me off. "Him! I can keep out of jail! You chuckle heads, on the other hand, I can't !"

We slipped away like cowards, and found our way to Ajima's, where we rounded out our evening of drunken dart throwing. It seemed I upon our return I had no sooner drifted into a deep sleep when the horrible shrieks from bellow me began again, only to be answered with "Shut the fuck up Pedro!"

Monday morning's PT secession was tough, a long run over the hills, but it was followed up by another wasted day in the barracks. On Tuesday Billy and I got sent up to the E club on detail to paint the doors, we were the lucky ones, some guys where re-tarring the roof. The weeks, and weekends flew by until the morning of 24 October, when I had just fallen back to sleep and there was a sharp knock of the door.

"What?" Billy shouted.

The knocker had already made it to the next door and was pounding on that one. Someone was shouting "Formation! Company Formation!"

Pedro slid wordlessly into his BDUs. Billy rolled over to go back to sleep. "Get the fuck ready, I will see what this is all about." Bill said putting on his shower shoes and headed out the door. I was lacing up my boots when he came back, "Hurry up and fall out!" He said throwing open his wall locker to fish out his BDUs.

We stood beneath a shroud of bug, on the airless moonless night, mumbling and cursing for what seemed an eternity. The First Sergeant marched out in front of Company and called us to attention. He did an about face and turned the formation over to the Company Commander. In a nasally voice he shouted, "When I give you the command to fall out. Fall out and form a school circle on me! Fall out!"

We rushed over to form a horse shoe formation in the grass, with the front ranks sitting, the middle kneeling and the last ranks standing. I always gravitated towards the back to avoid the chiggers that made their home in the grass.

"Alpha Company, a little over twelve hours ago a suicide bomber drove truck loaded with explosives onto the Marines Compound in Beirut Lebanon, killing hundreds. We do not know many, the casualties are more than anyone has seen since Vietnam. A Marine Battalion from Camp Lejeune North Carolina is already on the way right now. The First Sergeant will distribute a gear list to the Platoon Sergeant, any missing or broken items will be replaced, today. I want this unit ready to roll to the airfield in eight hours!" There was a moment of silence, followed by a lot of exited whooping and hollering.

Our NCOs herded us back into formation, and the Company dissolved back into the rooms. There was a lot of exited chatter, Sergeant Meeks called the Fire Team Leaders to his room, so Billy, Pedro and I were left to our own devices.

"Man, I hope we don't get left out!" Billy said excitedly.

"Man you are crazy. We ain't goin' nowhere. "Pedro said, giving voice to my fears. "They got every Mother-Fucker at Fort Bragg getting on airplanes right now! Plus the Marines have gotta be pissed! They are probably ready to Fucking swim to Lebanon for some pay-back!"

"While you guys are winning the war, what should we do?" I asked already getting tired of the nagging feeling Pedro was right.

"We will probably do a junk on the bunk inspection. " Pedro said as he started making his rack.

"I will be we do it outside on the poncho." Billy pontificated.

"It sucks more, but it makes the Captain thinks it's hard corps."

"Bro, if we do that it will rain." Pedro said sensibly.

"It don't matter remember before Christmas, it was sure as shit going to rain, and we set it up anyway. "

"Yeah, and what happened?" Pedro asked heatedly as he fluffed his pillow. "We had to drag all that shit in here!"

"Yeah, and that is what is going to happen again dummy!" Billy snapped excitedly.

Bill came in with Sergeant Meeks, who always stuttered when he spoke. "Oh, oh, okay. I n, n, need all ya'all, t t to get your shit. T t together!"

Visibly pained Bill interrupted him, "I am on it Sergeant. We will use the layout we did last time. Until it changes."

"Same same same as b, b before." Meeks stammered. "On the, b, b, beds 'cause it's a gonna r'r'rain." He stood uncomfortably close when he spoke. 'You r'r'r' gonna be th the example so, be be be quick about it!"

"Got it!" Bill answered trying to will Meeks out the door. He was rail thin, and chain smoked, he always seemed on the verge of panic, and his stuttering did not help. When he finally left we all exhaled.

"Jesus, was he worse than normal, or what?" Bill asked pulling the bunk bed away from the wall. "Get the racks quarter bouncing tight! Work in pairs just like in Basic."

"Hell yeah!" Billy said as they went to work on the rack. "I thought he was gonna piss himself."

"Probably wondering who is gonna frag his ass!" Pedro added with glee.

"I have to admit Meeks is not what I imagined an Infantry Squad leader to be." I said helping Pedro pull out rack away from the wall.

"That pussy panics every time we go to the field." Billy said folding the corners of his green Army blanket at a decent 45 degree angle. "When he shows up!"

"Yeah half the time he is sick, or has some kind of duty or something." Pedro almost spat.

"Afraid of every kind of bug, snake, and monkey in the jungle." Billy smiled.

"Monkey?" I could not help but asked.

"Yeah we had to keep moving our patrol base because of the howler monkeys. They sound like King fucking Kong, but they ain't bigger than 20 pounds." Billy said with disgust. "Maybe it is a family feud."

We all laughed, "Watch that shit Billy Bob!" Bill scolded without much force, just then a Corporal Glasgow from First Platoon came in.

There was a moment of awkwardness. "Bill you lettin' your redneck off his chain again?" He and Bill shook hands and gave a shoulder bump. They had been friends since basic.

"Yeah, he is getting ornery since Meeks took over the Squad."

"Oh Shit! That sucks, I wouldn't sweat it though, he has been fishing for an Office job at Battalion, and his going to fish a lot damn harder if he thinks we are going to combat."

Bill pulled a piece of paper out of his wall locker. "This is the only copy I have."

"No worried." Corporal Glasgow said pulling a notebook out of his pocket, and sitting down to copy the junk on the bunk layout down. "Did you see Jedi?"

Bill grunted. "Yeah."

"We finally get a black guy is Star Wars, and not only is he a fucking pussy, but he gets twenty second of screen time! What the fuck is up with that?" Glasgow said without looking up. "And, don't get me started on the Luke and his sister thing!"

"Have you heard anything from Company about this Alert?" Bill asked, not wanting to get on his Jedi soap box.

"Not really, you should ask Hall, I think he is sweet on you."

"Man, don't start that shit!" Bill rolled his eyes as he began folding his poncho liner. "I will grant you that is one weird dude."

"Knows his shit though. A monkey falls out of a tree, that dude knows about it before it hits the ground. He knew I was DA select for Corporal before anybody"

"Maybe he's sweet on you." Bill chided him.

"Well, I am a damn attractive man, but I do not think he likes the dark meat." They both laughed. "Okay bro, take care! Thanks for the info, I am sure it will change 8 times."

"Amen!"

It was about an hour later when we had out gear fully laid out on our racks, when the word came down that we would be conducting the inspection in the court yard. It was an hour later the rain started, and we had to drag out stuff back into the barracks. In the end we ended up with bottom racks doing junk on the bunk, and top racks doing ponchos on the floor. At 1300 we drew our weapons, and placed them on our displays.

As I recall, I did all right. My only gigs where that my tent stakes and entrenching tool needed paint. Three or more Gigs where a failure. Billy failed for his e-tool needing paint, and being rusty. Discoloration of his canteen cup, and dirty tent stakes. Pedro had so many gigs I do not recall, but after an incomprehensible ass chewing from Sergeant Meeks we all turned to getting Billy and Pedro ready for re-inspection.

Billy was raving mad. "Fucking bull shit! My tent stakes are dirty, we will lose the battle for sure! Oh my canteen cup did us in! Oh fuck no, there is rust on my e-tool, maybe because you Mother fuckers made be put it out in the fucking rain!"

Pedro found Billy's rants funny, I just thought they were annoying. "How is it, your shit looks like it has never been used?"

I asked Bill, hoping to shut Billy up.

"Simple, they never have. I got an extra E-tool and tent stakes. Hell Glasgow even has underwear that is only for inspections."

"That is just stupid!" Billy ranted. "It don't make no sense!"

"What doesn't make any sense is that we now have to go through this whole thing again at 1800!" Bill snapped. "You get that e-tool scrapped with CLP and dura-glit, dry it off and painted, same with you tent stakes, I will be checking them at 1730." He turned to Pedro. "You! What the fuck? You lost the guideline to you shelter half, and didn't tell anyone? The fucking underwear you put out is fucking dirty! Your whole display looks like ass!" He turned to me, "Get some 5-50 cord and make a guideline for Pedro."

Specialist Hall came into the room with a sneer. "Hey Bill, what is up with your boy's underwear?"

"Fuck!" Bill threw his notebook. "Pedro don't you have anything clean?"

"Those are clear!"

Hall chuckled, "We were confused by the skid marks."

"The other ones really are dirty!" Pedro pleaded.

"What the fuck does any of this have to do with fucking combat?" Billy seemed to explode.

"Shut up Billy!" Bill turned angry. "Get your ass over to the PX and buy 4 new sets of skivvies now, Pedro!"

"No good." Hall said with a shrug, "They are closed."

"Fuck!" Bill turned to me. "Do you have any extra?"

"Yeah, but they are marked with my name."

"Everyone calm down." Hall said coolly. "Get me your shortages, and I will see what I can find."

It was well after 2100 when we were re-inspected, after Meeks and the First Sergeant left our room we all collapsed. "What now boss?" I asked Bill.

"Pack it up." He said glumly. "Pack like you are going to the field. Get your H harnesses put back together, after we turn our weapons in to the arms room."

"Aren't we going to need our weapons in the field?" Pedro asked.

"Of course, and we will draw them back out in the morning." Bill answered patiently.

Mumbling endless complaints we turned to undoing our labors. It took hours to get everything turned in to the arms room. In spite of our instruction we just stuffed everything into our rucksacks, rather than water proofing it, as we would have for the field. My head finally hit my pillow around midnight.

Pedro started his night terror a little earlier than normal, and I was back to sleep when a knock came to the door. Pedro opened it, Hall was there in his PT short, "Guys, come down to the rec room, you are not going to believe this shit."

He was gone before we could ask him what was going on, he was gone. The rec room was already crowded, everyone was gather around the television. The graphic behind the anchorman was of paratroopers jumping out of a C-130. The word below it was "Invasion!"

"Where the fuck is Granada?" Someone asked.

"The Rangers and the 82nd Jumped in this morning, and the Marines are landing." Someone piped up.

"I hope they had on clean underwear." Pedro said sleepily.

There was some laughter. "It isn't clean anymore!" someone

added and there was more laughter.

"Shut the fuck up!" Bill shouted. "Where is all the combat footage?"

Hall came in. "They did not let the TV crew go in with them." There was more grumbling.

The story of Operation Urgent Fury slowly un-folded before us, and we fretted, here was our war, and we were missing it. We could have stayed home and watched the war on TV. Eventually people wandered to breakfast. By lunch we had heard the same thing a dozen times.

It was pouring rain outside when we finally meandered back to the room. Everyone was quiet, I climbed into my rack and tried to read a book, I couldn't concentrate and eventually fell asleep.

Bill woke me for chow, and we had a quiet dinner of greasy cheese burgers in the chow hall, until Meeks came running in screeching in-comprehensibly. We were rushed back to the barracks where formed up in Platoon Formation, and marched over to the Company Office.

The rain has slowed to a drizzle, and the work spread quickly, things where not going well on Grenada, they had run into Cuban Regulars, and Reinforcements were being flown in from Bragg, two Battalions so far.

When I got the Company Office I was issued a small American flag to sew on my uniform, 320 rounds of 5.56mm ammunition, and 2 fragmentation grenades. Like a crazed shopper with an arm load of bargains I ran the stuff back to the barracks.

I had to dig my H harness out of my pack and get it put back together. My heart was racing, this was really it! Loading my magazines with 180 round, and leaving the rest in the bandoleer I turned to the two black canisters that held my grenades, we had been told to leave then in the canisters, but they would not fit in the pouches.

Pedro came in next looking forlorn, he had been issued the same allotment I had, apparently there were no 40mm grenades, for his grenade launcher. He flopped down in a chair, not moving, "I cannot believe this." He mumbled over and over.

Billy came in next loaded down with M60 ammo, and a box of

.45 ammo for his pistol, he looked like a kid at Christmas, grinning from ear to ear. "Finally! We are gonna get to shoot some folks!"

We climbed into the back of the 5 ton trucks as the rain finally stopped, there was a lot of chatter as we rolled to the airfield. I remember looking up at the ominous sky and wondering if I should break out my rain gear, but since no one else was, I opted against it. The airfield was little more than an airstrip, we off loaded and dropped our gear in Company formation.

There were enough sewing kits around that we turned to sewing the flags on our right sleeves. I sat there watching Billy stitching his flag on, and shivered a little. Partly due to the fact that the rain was soaking through my BDUs and partly because it occurred to me that by this time tomorrow some of these soldiers would be dead. Our guys where fighting Cuban troops in Granada, I was not sure how big an Army Cuba had, but I knew it was pretty big, and there where Soviet troops in Cuba as well.

Bill came by with boxes of tracer bullets, we were told to make sure the last 3 bullets in each magazine where tracer so that we would know before we ran out in a fire fight. Of course for that 3 bullets to be tracers, they had to be the first three put into the magazine, so we set to emptying and re-loading our magazines, I was worried the plane would arrive before we were done.

As it darkened, I got the sewing kit and turned to sewing my flag on, Pedro's teeth where chattering, and I was getting cold. They started passing out MREs and heat tabs. Billy and Pedro made a circle of our Alice packs and set a heat tab in the middle. A heat tab is a one by three inch piece of compressed mystery material that looks like a sweat tart, and is flammable. It comes wrapped in tin foil and is designed so that you can spread the foil out and fight the heat tab on fire, it burns with a blight blue flame, and gives of noxious gas. The Army bought them for heating MREs, and they are excellent at heating one tiny portion of a meal while the rest remains ice cold. In the Infantry we generally used them for heating beverages or ourselves.

Billy was the first one to break out his poncho, and wrap himself up in it, which was a great relieve to Pedro and I who immediately followed suite. We huddled around the tiny blue flame by camouflaged ghosts. I tore open, my MRE dehydrated beef patty.

All around me the great exchange of MRE components started. Someone swapped a maple nut cake for cheese and crackers, another savvy trader got a chicken-a-la king main meal for a Ham and chicken loaf with the trackers and cheese included.

I pour water into the beef patty packet and looked around at the raged formation of lounging troops. Weapons where everywhere, no one seemed to be in charge, I wondered how long it would be before the lifers flipped out and had us stack our rifles.

The beef patty was like a giant bouillon cube eaten dry, with only the outermost layer soaking up any water. I on the other hand was soaking up water with the seat of my BDUs at an unpleasant rate. Bill came back from yet another leader huddle, and passed the word that we would start fire watch immediately with one man walking around each platoon.

As the rain came down harder I found it amusing to see 4 different guards, not more than ten feet apart marching around their prospective platoons. Thankfully, without being ordered, everyone just stopped doing that after about an hour.

Around 2200 hours, the word came down, no fires on the flight line. We here out of heat tabs, and everything was soaked anyway. I was cursing myself for not waterproofing my back earlier. I pulled out my wet poncho liner and sat on my pack Indian style with poncho and poncho liner forming a little cocoon around me. MY breath in the confined space warmed it enough that within a few hours I dozed off.

I awoke when the rain stopped a few hours later, both legs painfully asleep. I struggled to me feet, and still wrapped in my camouflaged shroud I stumbled around the Platoon. Soldiers where lying in every possible position, many snoring. Some smoking cigarettes and staring into the jungle.

The mosquitoes descended on us in clouds. I found myself wondering how anyone could sleep. As I paced around and the feeling came back to my feet Billy stood up, lighting a cigarette. He offered me one, I declined. It is funny now to think I was worried about cancer.

A horrible racket arouse from the jungle, I almost reached for my rifle, but noticed Billy did not move. The top of the trees shook as though a giant was rampaging towards up. A booming roar pierced the night, I could feel it in my chest, and it sounded like and enraged King Kong. "Howler Monkeys?" I asked a little hopefully.

"Yup." Billy said spitting.

"What's got them all riled up" I asked stupidly.

"Either it's gonna rain or the sun's comin' up." He said flatly. "I don't suppose they're comin'for us."

I knew he meant the Army. "No, I don't suppose so." I said as the false dawn started to glow in the East.

We spent the rest of the morning sitting on that airfield, around noon the heat became un-bearable and we started setting up poncho shelters in tree line. We were ordered to take them down, and hour later we were told we could put them back up.

We were treated to a marmite can meal on paper plates that evening just as the rain started. I think I got a mouthful before my plate collapsed. Our sun shelters became rain shelters, and failed us miserably. Water pooled in them, so we pushed it out with a rifle barrel only to have it soak us as it splashed in the mud.

The next morning around ten a company formation was called.

The First Sergeant called us in a school circle around him. Specialist Hall and the CO where nowhere to be seen.

"The Island of Granada is secure. " The First Sergeant said without emotion. "Nineteen Americans were killed, hundred and sixteen wounded. The American Medical students where all rescued. Twenty Five Cuban troops were killed, Six hundred and eighty captured. Forty Five Grenadian troops were killed and more than three hundred wounded. Operation Urgent Fury is over, and the trucks will be here shortly to take us back to Kobe."

Curses and shouts of joy echoed through the jungle, our war was over.

Wet and molding gear was flung everywhere and hung from the rails of the catwalk, the 'no drinking' word passed as soon we arrived back at Fort Kobe, and promptly ignored. Weapons and Ammunition had to be turned in, and God knew out weapons needed cleaning.

Billy was feverishly busting the surface rust of his M-60, and mumbling curses. Pedro had taken his M16 into the shower, Bill and I our scrubbed silently as someone blasted Led Zeppelin's 'immigrant song' on a boom box outside.

Meeks burst into the room sputtering and cursing that we needed to get our ammo turned in. More surly than I had ever seen him. Bill just stood up without a word to the Sergeant, and shouted 'Pedro get your ass out here!"

Meeks continued to sputter orders and shout and whoever was screaming along with Led Zeppelin. Bill looked around thoughtfully, "Billy you are on weapons guard, Bill and I will turn our ammo in and relieve you, once Speedy Gonzales gets gone humping the mirror just send him over to the Company Office with all his ammo."

We threw our h-harnesses on over our t-shirts and headed over to the Company Office. The line was at least 30 people deep. "Fuck!" Bill exclaimed. "This is going to take for fucking ever!"

"You know the wait time on a pizza is like an hour, let's order one before we get in line." I said trying to cheer him up. He looked at me with a piercing stare that suddenly reminded me he was my Fire Team leader.

"What are you fucking Rommel?" I stammered and he laughed,

"That is fucking brilliant! Go down stairs get us, two, no three pizzas! And grab us a couple of Cokes, I will hold out spot in line!"

We had a pretty good time just bullshitting and drinking our cold cokes while standing in line. By the time we got into the Company Office our Cokes were gone and we were starved. It was a round robin, we turned in our Grenades at the first table, ball ammunition at the next, then tracers, then M60 ammo, then 45, then claymore mines, then M72s rockets, then mortars rounds, then smoke grenades, then pop up flares, and out. We only needed to hit a few of the stations and were done.

When we got back to the room Pedro and Billy where tearing through wall lockers. "What the fuck?" Bill asked impatiently. "Pedro why are you still here?"

Pedro looked like he was going to cry. "I cannot find one of my grenades."

My stomach went cold. Bill balled his fist and looked like he was going to punch Pedro. "Who have you told?"

"No one, I swear!"

"Pedro you fucking moron, this is not a tent stake or a round, no one has a fucking extra one hidden!" Bill shoved past him. "This is an article 15 at least!" What he did not say was that Bill and Meeks would probably be fired for it. "Where were you carrying it?"

"In my pack like you told me!"

"Bullshit! If you did like I told you wouldn't have lost it!" Bill said punching Pedro in the stomach. Pedro doubled over, Billy and I pulled Bill away.

"Take it easy!" Billy said, "It has got to be somewhere! "

"Unless fuck-stick here dropped it in the jungle, or it fell out in the truck, some Geechee kid probably found it on the fucking road!" Bill raged.

"Wait, they did not check the serial numbers on our grenades. " I mused out loud. They all looked at me like I was stupid. As if to say 'so?' "We don't need Pedro's grenade as much as we need a grenade."

"I bet we could snag one from another Platoon." Billy said enthusiastically.

"No, not inside the Company!" Bill said, emphatically.

"The leg companies never got ammo!" Billy shot back.

"What about the ones that are already turned in? If one of those where to find its way out, Pedro could turn it in." I said hopefully.

"There is no way we are getting on out of there." Bill said angrily.

"What about Corporal Glasgow?" I asked.

Bill actually laughed, "We need something stolen, so asked the black guy?"

We all laughed and I blushed. "No, what said. You think Specialist Hall might help us out? "

"We'll tell him he can fuck Pedro!" Billy beamed.

Bill shrugged, "That seems reasonable."

"Oh man, that shit is not funny!" Pedro said looking pale. "This is serious!"

"It might be a tough sell," I added "I heard he likes 'em a little lighter."

"Yeah, but look at that little ass!" Bill said sizing up Pedro, "Hell, we might just have to give some to the First Sergeant to be safe."

Bill caught the look in Pedro's eye the same moment, I did. I can only call it horror, I think he was afraid he was going to be raped. When Billy started to say something, Bill just said "Shut up Billy."

"What the Mother fuck did I do?" He screeched.

"I will see if I can get Hall away for a moment. " I said not want to be in that room a second longer. The terrible possibilities of Pedro's night terrors filled my head as I walked over to the company Office. All I could think was, what the hell happened to that boy? I did not want to think about it, but there where all the horrors that could be dancing in my head. The door swinging open into and a drunken someone staggering into a sleeping boy's room. In a horrible flash I imagined a tiny Pedro clutching a blanket, flames all around him. Synthetic pajamas melting to flesh. I shook myself, I had always had a fear about burning.

It was still crowded in the Company Office, there was no way I could think about saying anything nefarious there in front of God and everyone. Hall looked at me like something he has scraped off his shoe. "What is it, Genius?"

I stammered was going to ask if he had eaten yet, but then the whole Company was going to think I was a fag. Shit! "We ordered some pizza, Bill wanted to know if you want in." I blurted out.

"Sure." He said non-committal. "Save me some." He turned back to the turn in. I stood there a moment too long. First Sergeant spotted me.

"McGill what the fuck are you doing here?" He barked. As I stood flat footed and slack jawed, Hall rescued me with, "He is relieving me so I can get some chow."

Billy came and relieved me watching people put bullets in boxes, and it was already dark, walking across the Company area I had those horrible thought again, and was glad to climb to our second deck catwalk. Hall is in my chair drinking coke, "Well, if it isn't the worst liar in the world!" He sneered.

"What's up?" I asked.

"Tell him genius!" Hall snapped.

"I was only issued one grenade." Pedro said looking forlorn.

"But," I started and Hall stomped on my foot. "Ow!"

"You where say?" He asked testily.

"Uh, yeah now that I think of it he was only issued one." I lied.

Hall stood up, "Come one Pedro, let's get your ammo turned in."

It was almost midnight when we got our weapons turned in and when my head hit the pillow I was out. My concern for missed martial glory evaporated with the feel of cool clean sheet and a roof over my head. The pounding of rain on the outside of the barracks made sleeping indoors just decedent.

The knock on the door came around 0200, and we were called out to company formation, they told us to hurry, and not worry about uniformity. Some guy where in just PT shorts, a lot where wearing showers shoes.

The water made it over the top of my shower shoes soaking my feet before they told us that the ammunition count was wrong and there was a missing Grenade. We stood out in the rain as every room was searched. I glanced over my shoulder, and saw the First Sergeant and Specialist Hall going through every room with the Police Sergeant.

It took hours, eventually we trudged back to our rooms tacking mud everywhere. No one was allowed to leave. The next morning instead of PT we did a complete cleaning of the barracks, and where inspected again. At the end of the day we were told there would be no liberty.

The morning of October 29th we did another Company death run, followed by a good ass chewing by the First Sergeant. No one was going to see the outside of the Company area until the grenade was found.

We did a complete junk on the bunk inspection that afternoon, and much to no-one's surprise the grenade was not in someone's gear.

On the 30th we removed trucked out to the airfield and walked up and down, on line looking for the missing grenade. We even got online where the poncho hooches has been, a canteen and flashlight where found, but no grenades.

We were sunburned, mosquito bitten and pissed off at formation that evening. When we were told there would be no liberty again that night we all stormed into our rooms. Refrigerators had long run out of illicit beer, and no one was allowed buy any kind of replacement.

Hall came by our room seeming a bit like a villain in a Bogart film, "Did you hear?"

"What." Bill asked annoyed.

"The Company Commander has been called up to Brigade! He might be relieved." He said dramatically.

We were all concerned, and I was afraid someone was going to ask him if he was getting scared, which I knew would piss him off. "Well, thank God it was not our Fire Team." I said un-convincingly.

Hall smiled a long slow, sick kind of smiled. "Yes, thank God for that."

After he left, Billy said, "Something about that guy gives me the creeps."

"Yes, he is like an under-taker." Pedro said.

"Hey!" Bill said sternly. "Everyone has a job, even the undertaker and he really saved our asses."

"Yeah Pedro." He caught what Bill was trying to say, "that creepy though he was, this guy had saved your ass and besides. Your friendly neighborhood under-taker keeps your street virtually cadaver free." We got a chuckle out of that.

The morning of 30th was quiet, there was a lot of grousing about the lack of liberty, and the rumors flew. The Commander was going to be relieve, the Commander and the First Sergeant where going to be relieved. My favorite one was Billy's when he came charging in with the breathless announcement that then entire Company was going to get busted down one rank.

The following morning we had a Company formation, with the new familiar threats and pleas to find the missing grenade, we then shuffled back to our rooms, for weapons cleaning.

I was sitting thumbing through one of Billy's tattoo magazines with my rifle is pieces on my rack, while Bill was reading a book, and Billy was sleeping on the flood, when Pedro came in excitedly. "They are going to let us go!"

"Bullshit!" Bill said without looking up.

"They are letting us go on account of Halloween!" Pedro chirped.

Bill laughed bitterly, "The Army does not give a fuck about Halloween."

"No, Carlos heard it from Glasgow!" Pedro said excitedly.

"How the fuck would he know?" Billy asked from under the bed.

"He is boys with the S1 shop!" Pedro said breathlessly. "Those guys are already on a beer run!"

Bill stood up purposefully, undoubtedly to go seek out Glasgow for the ground truth but did not make it to the door when formation was called.

That Halloween piss-up at the Enlisted will go down in history, or it should have. I remember two guy dueling with pool cures, one hearing his gas mask, and doing his best Darth Vader imitation, right before the MPs showed up. When they went to take the dueling Jedi away for fighting on top of the pool take, things quickly got out of hand.

Darth and Luke quickly turned their pool cures on the MPs to keep them at bay. The two MPs where quickly overwhelmed with shout of "Boo!" and "Attica!" as fusilladed of popcorn, and French fries. Initially there were only two MPs, a pair of young Privates. When the first bottle was thrown they retreated, to the jeers of the troops.

"We had better get the Fuck out of here." I said.

Bill agreed, and went to grab Billy, who was a little wide eyed. "Holy Fuckin' shit!" Billy kept saying.

"Let's get out of here!" I re-iterated as I saw flashing lights multiply in the parking lot.

"Where the fuck is Pedro?" Bill asked.

"Ain't seen him." Billy said, looking around nervously as a beer bottle shattered on the wall.

Bill looked thoughtful, "We have got to do."

Just then the MPs burst into the front door night sticks swinging. We bolstered towards the back of the bar. There fire alarm went off as someone got to the emergency exit before we did. In a blur I ran out the door. A handful of MPs where attempting to stem the human tide that rushed out the door. We rushed headlong into the woods, and down a ravine.

Within a few moments we were panting next to a steam, the three of us had made it. "I hope," I said gasping "They didn't get Pedro."

"No" Billy said collapsing on a green looking rock. "They had a big black guy, and a white dude in a cowboy hat, I think it was Brandon Fortnier."

"Is he your buddy from Texas?" Bill asked.

"Yeah, but he is from Tennessee." Billy said getting a handful of water, and rubbing it on the back of his neck.

"You know, if we follow this down to the fence line, we will come out just west of the front gate." Bill said thoughtfully.

"You think we could make it out in town?" Billy said hopefully.

"One way to find out." Bill said starting off. We walked in a silent ranger file down the ravine, the sound of the jungle night around us. We were silent, and it felt like a patrol, it occurred to me that I had not been to the field yet, since I came to the "real Army."

We got to the fence line and turned right, silently struggling up the hill when we got to the top we silently peered down on the gate. We watched as they MPs lazily waved traffic through. We slid away back down the hill. Bill whispered, "Ok here is the plan, we back it off a few meters, and come out of the tree line out of sight of the gate, and walk out like it is nothing."

We nodded dumbly and followed him. Where we came out of

the trees was a lonely stretch of road. We did are best to get all the different plant life clinging to us to let go, and started down the road. I kept hoping a taxi would show up.

The MPs at the gate might have thought there was something wrong, as we tried to act casual. A giant MP Sergeant with biceps the size of my thighs came out of the guard shack. In a booming voice he asked, "Are you going to WALK into town?"

"Yes Sergeant. " Bill answered coolly without breaking stride.

"Traffic is bad on the road, do you want to call a Cab and wait here?" The Sergeant asked.

"If tomorrow weren't payday." Bill said with a smile.

The Sergeant chuckled. "No need to waste beer money huh?"

We felt like conquering heroes when we got out beers at Peace Frog, we raised a toast to our great escape. We gloried in the grass and mud stains on or jeans and our cut up forearms. The old lady that ran the place came out without second round of beers and dropped a Polaroid photograph on the table, it was the one of me with the pissing monkey on my shoulder. I guess in the chaos of the broom beating the monkey man had dropped it. That sent us into another round of hysterics.

A group of the Latino guys came buy, Bill recognized Carlos. "Hey Carlos!" He called slurring slightly.

Carlos was a burley, but ugly fellow, kind of the anti-Pedro, where Pedro brought a Chihuahua to mind, Carlos made you think of a bulldog. "Have you seen Pedro?" Bill asked.

"No, man I have not seen that dude in weeks."

"What?" Bill answered a little too loudly. "Didn't he go to the club with you guys last weekend?" It was more like every weekend.

"No man." Carlos answered and then got into a quick discussion with one of his Friends it Spanish. "I think he has a girl down that the Love Club." He smiled, "Hey, I gotta run you boys have a good night, and watch out that the Axman don't get you!"

He gave Bill a quick handshake and took off.

"Fucking Pedro, the Love Machine!" Bill mocked. "No shit."

"Let's go down there and fuck with him." Billy piped in eager.

"That is right! We have been remise in young William's education." Bill opined, "He has not even seen said club of love."

"Well, that tears it!" Billy said slapping his knee. "We must go to the Love Club."

I was crimson, and did not know what to say. "I am broke."
Was all I could think to say.

"Then no pussy for you!" Billy teased.

"Shit brother, it is the day before payday everyone's broke. "
Bill said downing his beer. "It is free to look, though!"

Within moment we were ranger file cutting in and out of the
throngs of people, I looked above the street lights into the inky
blackness and wondered at the humidity, it was almost like the air
had weight to it. We were about half a block short of Ajima's bar
then Bill stopped and waited for Billy and me to catch up.

In the building have a plain white stone front, with a pair of
heavy wooden doors that looked like they belonged on a castle.
There was a small red illuminated sign that simply red 'Love Club.'

Billy dove right in. We were greeted at the door by an older
woman in business attire who asked how many we had with us, and
shouted something in Spanish to an attractive young Panamanian
women dressed as a nurse in a mini-skirt, white had all.

The room was a rabbit warren of deep dark corners with long

tables, boisterous groups of men, most Americans sat at tables surrounded by beer bottles, with costumed whores meandering bored between the tables.

After the 'nurse' took our drink order, we looked around for Pedro. A punk rock girl with a very bad red dye job, dressed all in black, except for the number 13 on a white disc around her neck, came up to me, kneeling down so I could see clearly down her leather top, "What is your name?" She asked.

I blushed, and Billy got to laughing at me, which of course made it worse. We made small talk for a moment or two and she asked if she could join us for a drink. I remembered what Bill had told me, I asked how much 'girl drinks' where. She said ten or fifteen dollars. I thought it was time to tell her I was broke, which got rid of her quickly

"Boy you are a smooth talker!" Bill made fun of me as a plump 'cheerleader' approached him. "Beat it we are waiting for someone. "

"Wait, maybe she knows him." I said stupidly. Billy giggled, "Yeah honey you ever see a little Latino fellow named Pedro?

Brown eyes, dark hair."

She laughed heartily, "All Latinos have brown eyes and dark hair."

"Not that girl!" Billy pointed to a blond bombshell in a prom dress.

The chubby cheerleader pulled a chair up next to Billy. She made a hissing sound, "That blond came out of a bottle!" We laugh and she introduced herself as 'Elena' and daintily shook everyone's hand.

"Our friend is a regular, I guess he has a girlfriend here." Bill asked while chubby and Billy rubbed legs under the table. I noticed she had a numbered disc necklace on as well, though she was number 23.

She laughed, "How about a drink?"

"Sweetheart," Billy said in a mock plea "I have nothing but love for you!" She stood up rubbing her tits in his face and kissing his forehead. She grabbed his cheeks like you would a child, "Then get a paper route, and come back and seem me. It is Elena, number 23."

As she left I noticed number 44, she was a very petite woman in a lime green mini skirt, with a translucent green top on, and I do not know what the hell she was supposed to be, with hoop earrings and green lipstick. She looked young, and bored, trailing behind her was a very upset looking Pedro.

"Hey Pedro, little buddy!" Billy shouted over the bad music. To my surprise Pedro bolted over to the table.

"Hey guy, you gotta lend me fifty bucks, please!" He pleaded.

"Oh, now Pedro!" Bill said in a Fatherly tone, "What would your Mother say?"

That seemed to sting a little, "Come on guys, this is serious!" He pleaded.

"You gonna give the money to her?" Billy asked gesturing to the girl in green whose hands where impatiently on her hips.

"That's my girl, man!" He said indignantly.

"Let me guess, she is a college student. Isn't she? " Bill asked.

Pedro did not answer. He glanced over his shoulder as she turned and headed towards a table of black troops. I recognized some of them from the Battalion, then I realized it was most of our S1 shop. "Come on guys, I will pay you back tomorrow!"

Bill kicked out a chair, "Have a seat son." He snapped his fingers, "Oh, waitress a beer for my grenadier please!"

Pedro sat but did not stop pleading. "Come on! If I do not take her home someone else will!"

"Yes son, she is a whore. That is how it works." Bill said as if explaining something to a child.

"No! She needs the money!"

"Well who takes her home, will provide said monies." Bill said with a cruel grin.

"Hell if I am given a whore Fifty bucks, I am damn sure fucking her!" Billy announced to the world and to my mortification. No one but Pedro seemed to mind.

"Don't you dare!" Pedro went crimson.

Bill leaned over and put a hand on my shoulder, "Pedro for the education of our neophyte here, how much does a roll in the hay go for around here."

He looked away.

"I promise, none of us." Throwing at bottle cap at Billy, "Will engage your lady friend this evening. IF you tell us the going rate"

"Sixty dollars." He mumbled.

Billy laughed, "You came to a whore house with ten dollars in your pocket!"

"That is pretty optimistic, Pedro." Bill scolded.

Pedro's girl was sitting on Sergeant Williams lap sipping a 'girl drink', I swear I saw Pedro shudder. "Come on!"

"Pedro." Bill said handing him the beer the waitress had brought. "Calm down."

"No!" Pedro leapt to his feet and bounded towards the table where his girl was deep kissing Sergeant Williams. I do not remember the word he used, but it is the Spanish version of 'nigger'. Apparently Williams knew the word as when he bolted to his feet Pedro's girls and the contents of their table when crashing to the floor.

Corporal Glasgow and Bill dove into the middle of the fray holding Williams back, Bill turned to us, pointing an angry finger at Pedro, 'Get him the fuck out of here!"

We grabbed Pedro and his feet did not touch the ground until his entire body hit the back wall of Ajima's. Ma came charging out from behind the bar shouting, "No fight! No fight!"

"Ma, it is ok. We just pulled our idiot friend here out of a fight over at the Love Club." I explained.

She gasped, "That a dirty place! You no go there! You get the clap!" She glanced around. "Where Billiam?"

"He told us to…" I tried to explain, she pinched my arm hard.

"You leave him?" She shrieked "You leave him?" She smacked me on the ear 'Get him now!"

I was stunned. "Now!" She repeated, and I darted towards the door, only to almost knock Bill over on the way in.

Once we collected ourselves we all sat at the bar, it reminded me of the last supper with a few less disciples and a very forlorn Puerto Rican Jesus in the middle. He kept rambling on about how she was going to come back to New York with him, and how the money was just a formality.

"Shit I would hate to think what Williams is doing to her right now!" Billy said cruelly. "Shit man you'll be luck to touch the sides!"

"Now Billy that is not going to cheer our man up." Bill said sipping his beer. "Pedro, our in-articulate Confederate cousin does have a point. Your fiancé is a prostitute in a third world garrison town. Not June Cleaver material."

"Who?" Pedro asked looking exhausted.

"You know, leave it to Beaver?" I asked.

"Leave that fuckin' beaver alone!" Billy chirped.

"Billy, Damn it!" Bill snapped, 'Give it a rest!"

"She was television's version of the perfect American housewife." Bill explained calmly.

"I liked Lucy!" Billy announced.

"Yeah, she had a thing for Latino guys!" I added.

"Ricky Ricardo was Cuban." Pedro said weakly.

"Ricky Ricardo isn't the point Pedro!" Bill snapped. "The Point," He continued calmly "is that once you are not in this Infantry fuck hole, you will find plenty of nice girls who do not get the bottom knocked out them for a living."

"There was something not right about Lucy though, "Billy pondered "She couldn't walk across the street without seventy different disasters happening to her."

"And what was the big deal about being in the show?" I asked.

"Hell I would have put her in the show to shut her up." Bill said, and like that saving Pedro was forgotten, and we spend the rest of the evening talking about the television shows we all grew up with. In the middle of it, Pedro sat silently.

The next morning to everyone's shock, out diminutive company Commander took charge of the run. Everyone had gotten extremely drunk the night before, and the formation reeked of booze. As soon as we stepped off into the thick morning air, I knew we were in trouble, maybe it was the grenade, or maybe the riot at the e-club but this was no standard payday run.

We bolted so fast out of the company area the NCOs stopped even trying to call cadence. The first puker was within the first ten minutes, when we hit the first big hill the formation stretched out. To my right Corporal Glasgow and Carlos where pushing a guy who was falling out, each had a hand on his back and where cursing encouragement.

I found myself slipping back, "Come on, brother." Bill encouraged me.

Billy came up alongside me. "You can do this."

We struggled up the hill Pedro was on my heels. When we got to the top I saw a guy collapse as if crushed by an invisible hand. "Medic!" The call went out as we struggled past. Normally you slow down after a hill and get the company back together. Not this time.

Billy started to struggle, "Come on, Billy!" I shouted, it seems nonsensical but such mindless encouragement can keep exhausted men together. It was somewhere in the third mile when Sergeant Meek stepped away to puke, it sounded like water being poured in the grass.

I started slipping back again, "Come on, Bro you can do it." Pedro said pushing me. Embarrassed I was able to find just a little more strength. That is how it went for about an hour when we finally reached the barracks and where told to 'quick time, march!' Which brought use back to a walking pace. Once we stopped Pedro collapsed unconscious, and I threw up, almost on top of Bill.

After the standard morning shower rotation, we all sat spit shinning our boots. Radio where not allowed during working hours, but Billy has a David Allen Coe tape playing, it was the 'You don't have to call me darling, darling."

"Billy," Bill asked rubbing a wet cotton ball on his boot, "how can you listen to a drinking song first thing in the morning?"

"It's a good damn song." He said as he buffed his boot with an old t-shirt.

"No one is arguing that, it is just this more like a close to closing time song." I said applying more boot polish to my cotton ball.

"Did you know," Bill said thoughtfully "That every human being on earth is genetically encoded to know every word to this song when drunk?"

Pedro and Hall came into the room, the both had a Band-Aids on their arms. "Look what I found at the aid station." Hall said caustically. "They put two whole saline bags in him."

"Looks like you got some yourself." Bill said a Pedro shuffled towards the bathroom. "I didn't see you fall out."

"I did not fall out, but I was pretty drunk this morning so I have Doc give me a bag before the run." He saw that we looked confused. "Alcohol dehydrates you, hence the cat shit in the mouth feeling in the morning. You blood volume does down, so you cannot get oxygen to you muscles fast enough, and you fall out of the run like a weak bitch. If, on the other hand you get you blood volume back up, well you get the picture."

"Did you see that brawl at the E club last night?" Billy asked enthusiastically.

"I saw a certain Fire Team run like rabbits at the First sign of trouble." He sneered.

"What the fuck?" Bill grumbled.

In a sing songy voice Hall sang, "When danger reared its ugly head they bravely turned tail and fled..."

"Do you WANT something, or is this a singing fucking telegram!" Bill barked.

"Yeah, there is free Gatorade in the rec room." He answered un-phased. "I guess the CO is feeling pretty generous after not being fired."

Bill gestured to me, 'Hook us up Bill."

I headed down to the Rec room in the center of the barrack, next to the pool table was a large cooler full of Gatorade. The TV in the corner was reporting on protests in England and Germany about the up-coming deployment of cruise missiles to Europe.

The rest of payday was pretty standard, everyone got haircuts, and lined up at the Company Office to have their checks issued. Anyone without a good looking uniform, fresh haircut, or bad shave was kicked out of line and sent back to square themselves away.

When I got to the head of the line, Hall looked down the list. "Sorry McGill, you are not on here.

The First Sergeant seemed to appear out of nowhere. "When is the last time you got paid?"

"When I left Fort Benning a month ago First Sergeant." I said snapping to parade rest.

He turned crimson. "Bullshit!" He practically leapt over the table, I thought I a dead man. He threw a heavy hand on my shoulder, "Come here!"

He stomped up the stairs like a storm trooper, flung open the door to the S1 shop and thundered, "Williams!" Two clerks sprang to their feet and snapped to parade rest.

The Command Sergeant Major, whom I have never seen before

was a giant of a man with skin as black as boot leather, he wore a Combat Infantry and Pathfinder badge, and a combat patch from the 25th Infantry Division. The whites of his eyes where horribly yellowed. He burst from his Office, "Who is disturbing my day?" He shouted.

First Sergeant Hoefmeir did not hesitate, "I want to know why my fucking troops are not getting paid!"

Those yellow eyes feel on me. "Troop! When is the last time you were paid?"

"Fort Benning Command Sergeant Major!" I replied with my head and eyes strait forward.

"That is a where not a when troop! When where you paid?"

"Upon leaving AIT a month ago Command Sergeant Major!"

He turned to Hoef, "Did he say 'upon? What kind of Company you running down there Hoef?" He then turned to the Clerks, "Get this troop a casual pay, and send a pay inquiry up to Brigade TODAY. Not a mother fucker in the Battalion is getting to step of Post until PFC McGill here has some of his money in his pocket, and if does not get his back pay on the 15th, these is going to be hell to pay!"

I would get my casual pay, which is a cash advance from the Army while they fix your pay. That 'hell to pay' prediction. The weekend was more of the same, Pedro flushed with cash disappeared and we went about our business. The only discernable difference in the world seemed to be that the nature of our late night drunken conversations had drifted from getting to the Rangers or Special Forces and toward college. In our guts we just 'knew' we had missed our war.

What we did not know was that a table top exercise in Germany called 'Able Archer 83' had put the Warsaw Pact on full alert starting on the second of November. No one alive will know exactly what happened on the November sixth. The thing I believe, I guess partially because it was a pilot that first floated the idea my way, and that I knew how exhausting alerts could be, was that the lead pilot of a flight of MiG-25s. They flight reached a checkpoint where they were supposed to turn north, instead they went straight across the border into West Germany. I wonder if the other pilots knew where they were and had great radio discipline, but after they got an embarrassing distance deep in German Air Space they were shot down by American fighter planes. Apparently the MiG-25 is damned fast, but turns like shit. Either way, they were shot down, either three or five of them, by two F-15 Eagles.

The shoot down obviously sent all of the NATO Air Defense folks on full alert, which made the Soviets even more paranoid. Back in Panama, we heard about the shoot down, and we went on our own 'Alert'. The upshot of it was that we were not supposed to leave post without signing out, and the Ammunition we had turned in to the Company Office, apparently did not get turned in any further.

On November Seventh we all trooped down to the duty desk and signed of post with our destination listed as 'the ville'. When we were sitting at Peace Frog it started to rain, so we went inside, we were surprised to see all the bar girls huddled around the television.

They news was showing protests in Europe, and stock footage of Soviet troops on the move. We ordered another round of beers, and waited for the rain to stop so we could make out way to Ajima's. Hall came bursting in looking like a drown rat.

"Hey Hall, it's raining." I said mockingly.

"Thanks genius", he said flinging water on me. "Have you see Hoef?"

"Oh shit you lost the First Sergeant!" Bill mocked, "Do you think he will survive without you?"

Hall looked disarmingly serious. "I have never seen him like this."

"What set him off?" I asked a little concerned, if this was worse than last time he just might kill someone.

"I don't know." He said despondently.

"Did you check the Silver Spur?" I asked.

"No, I'm an idiot. Of course Genius, Billy was there and told me you guys where here."

"Fuck, have a beer." Bill said more friendly than before. "They guy survived how many tours as a Ranger in Vietnam, he can make it through a night on the town."

"That's just it," Hall said sitting down and gesturing to buy all three of us around, "I am not sure he is in town. A few 5 gallon water cans and cases of MREs went missing." He gestured towards the television, "He really thinks the big one is coming."

"Must be the agent orange. " Bill said flippantly.

"Oh, he IS fucking crazy. He in his office and talks to himself."
He took a long drink of beer. "He gets into arguments in there, all
alone! I was cleaning the place up one time and you and you know
what I found in the shower drain?"

"Pubes?" Bill asked dryly.

"Yes" Hall answered and turned to inspect the bar. "What a
dump, this place makes the Silver Spur look classy."

"Well the sophisticated crowd does not come out until after the
polo match." Bill said haughtily.

"What the fuck are you two rambling about, what the fuck is up
with the First Sergeant's pubes?" Pedro asked a little too loudly,
drawing some odd looks from around the bar.

"No, shrapnel and lots of it." Hall answered.

"From where?" Pedro asked.

"Vietnam." Hall said coolly.

"I get that, but how is it still, you know, around?" I asked.

Hall took a deep breath, "Look, when a shell goes off millions of chunks of metal, dirt, rocks and what the hell else goes flying. A lot of that will do strait into anyone who is in the area. Some of it makes big holes, some of it you won't hardly notice. Once you are lugging all that crap around in your body, you make scar tissue around it, and your body slowly pushes it out. It will come right through the skin like a zit. The deeper it is the longer it takes. "

"Where does the First Sergeant live?" Bill asked off handedly.

"I don't know?" Hall said dramatically.

"How the fuck can you not know?" Bill didn't believe him, and neither did I.

"You have to have a recall roster of everyone not living in the barracks." I challenged.

"Yes, and his address is listed, actually as your room." He said with an evil smile.

"What?" Bill looked angry.

"He wouldn't tell me where he lived, and I needed to put something on the roster. It is not like he misses formation." He sounded like he was teasing us, but deep in my gut I believed him. Our First Sergeant did not want anyone to know where he lived.

The morning of the eighth of November we were debating going to the movies, when Hall popped into our room. "Looking for the First Sergeant?" Bill asked.

"No point." Hall said glumly "I take it you did not hear."

We all looked at him expectantly, and he said nothing. "Okay damn it!" Billy yelled, "Hear what?"

"The entire Warsaw Pact rolled out of their Garrisons."

"What does that mean?" Pedro asked.

Hall shrugged, "No one knows. They are not happy about the shoot down, and they might be trying to get us to cancel fielding the cruise missile in Europe."

"Ya'll going to the movies?" Billy asked already bored with the conversation. "Might want to see a movie before we spend another alert in the rain."

"What's playing?" Bill asked.

"Jedi." Hall answered.

Bill looked pained, "It's like watching someone fuck my sister!"

"You don't have a sister." I shot back.

He shrugged, "Then let's go to the movies. The popcorn will be good anyway."

NATO rolling out of their garrisons the next day was overshadowed in the news by a general strike that shut down most travel in Europe. Back in Panama we did not notice anything until President Reagan's Speech in Tokyo where we he called for calm, and said that as a gesture of good will the United States would not match the Soviet Reserve call up with by calling up our own Reserves, and he asked the Soviets to stand down.

On the 12th the Lufthansa Airline was shot down somewhere near the East German border, several hundred where killed. An Emergency session of the UN Security Council was called for the Next day Reagan flew back from Tokyo to attend.

We were all huddled around the TV in the rec room listening to Reagan's address to the UN at Three o'clock on the Afternoon of November 13th. He seemed to not be through with his thought when, he was hurried off the stage. The newscasters were prattling on about the interruption. Bouncing from live broadcast to live broadcast when we lost power.

We sat in the dark cursing for a few minutes and then wandered out on the catwalk. I remember going back to our room and trying to read, but it was too dark and with the air conditioning out it was soon stifling. We pulled our chairs out on the catwalk to relax but the sun was too intense so we went over to the E club.

There was no power, but the residual cool for the A/C was not bad, so when 1600 rolled around we ordered some beer. It is funny but we thought we were really flouting the rules. As we wandered back to the barracks after dark, everything seemed fine.

I climbed up into by rack and drifted off to sleep with the door open and the mosquitoes feasting on me. Pedro woke me around 0300 with his screaming. I went to the bathroom, was annoyed that the lights where still out, and then curled up with my poncho liner to get back to sleep.

The next morning was normal except after PT there was no hot water, and we bitched about the cold showers. The chow hall being closed annoyed us even more. We had a Company formation at 0900 telling us we were restricted to the Company area and to pack for a field exercise.

I could not help but notice that the First Sergeant was nowhere to be seen.

In packing this time we were meticulous in ensuring all of our individual items where in plastic bags and then everything was tight in our Army issue green waterproof bags. We packed our packs like we would be doing a river crossing although we were more concerned about rain that actually making the damn things float.

We ended up stacking our packs and helmets in the corner of the room, and getting MREs issued for dinner on the 14th. I ended up just having MRE cheese and crackers for dinner. When Pedro woke me with his screaming that night I was unable to get back to sleep due to hunger.

I gave up and headed out onto the catwalk to watch the sun come up. I watched the Company area slowly come to life. The gleam of the sun off the barrack made everything seem normal. I saw the First Sergeant drive in, he had a black jeep with a roll bar. He was already in PT gear, which reminded me it was pay day, and we would be doing a payday run.

I hoped we were allowed out in town, I wanted a hot meal, and this power outage was getting old. We fell out for PT and it was a nice easy run, as we shuffled back the barrack air was thick with rumors.

I slumped in my chair as Pedro got to the shower first. Since we did not have hot water, the showers went quicker. "How much longer do you figure this blackout can go on?" I asked off handedly.

"Depends on what caused it." Bill said throwing a sweaty shirt into his laundry bag. "I hope it gets fixed quickly, I need to get some laundry done."

"These damned MREs are not doing me no good neither. I ain't shit in two days." Billy gripped.

"I heard rumor that the thing with the Soviets went nuclear." I confessed my concern. "That is why the pulled the President out of the UN in the middle of his speech, is they detected incoming ICBMs."

"Now how could anyone here know that?" Billy asked annoyed. "Why would the light be out here if the States got nuked?"

""I do not know." I confessed it is just a rumor.

"It does kind of make sense." Bill said glumly. "Except for the lights being out here."

Sergeant Meeks came in, "Hey g' g 'get you w' w' w' weapons cleaned this morning. P'p'payday form'm'm'ation is at 1300. "

"Any hot chow?" Bill asked hopefully

Meeks shook his head. "Three MREs e' e 'each." As he turned to leave Hall came in. He glanced around looking conspiratorial. After Meeks left he sat down on Pedro's rack.

"You want the good news or the bad new?" He asked me annoyingly.

"Good news." I sighed.

"You are getting paid the same as everyone else today!"

"Shit, that is good news." I said feeling encouraged.

"No," Hall smiled devilishly "it isn't."

"Jesus man! What the fuck are you talking about?" Bill snapped.

"No one is getting paid." He said in almost a whisper. I am not sure why, but we all believed him immediately.

Billy say up from sprawling on his rack, "What the hell?"

"Yeah seriously." Bill asked earnestly "What is up?"

"No one knows." Hall said looking guilty.

"Yeah, but what do you THINK?" Bill asked stridently.

We all learned in like conspirators. "All the money comes from Kansas City, rumor is Kansas City has been nuked." A chill went through me, as if to say it out loud was to make it tre. "A lot of other places to."

"Why would the lights be out, here?" Bill almost whispered.

"If it was true they would have popped a nuke in the upper atmosphere to fry all the electronics. The shitty power grid here would be tough to fix. "

"How long might it take?" I asked.

"We are setting up some generators at the Company Office today, I do not think we are expecting the power back on anytime soon."

Of course Hall was right, that night I stood on the catwalk, the only lights in the world where the flood lights around the battalion building, and the moon. They stopped making us run, PT on the 16th as the water stopped flowing in the barracks.

It was oddly like being in the field, but our weapons went into the arms room every night, and we slept in our rooms. It was our turn to guard the command post on the night of the 18th. I spent three hours walking around the battalion build with a 30 round magazine in my weapon, at the end of my shift, Bill and Pedro came to relieve me, Bill was the Corporal of the Guard. He cleared my weapon, gave the Ammunition to Pedro, and I went to bed.

That is how it went every three days we had guard duty. I relieved Billy, Pedro relieved me. The second night we had the Arms room instead of the CP to guard. Nothing changed, the MREs and water diet quickly started to seem routine.

The rumors where maddening, millions dead, billions dead, a radioactive cloud headed our way what would kill us all. Cuban invasion force had landed on the Eastern shore and where headed our way. America had surrendered and the war was over. The Soviets had surrendered and the war was over, and on and on and on.

It was the night of the 24th when I was walking around the battalion command post when I noticed the grass. It had not been mowed, and was looking like nature reclaiming the fort. I got to really wondering about home, and the rest of the world. Where my parents alive? What about all my Friends from High School? I remember the guys that had headed to Italy after jump school. They were on the front line of the Third World War. Weren't they?

I wondered if the Fort Bragg boys had ever made it to Europe. I had the sick realization, Bragg almost certainly been nuked. If they were there, they were all dead. If they made it to Europe they were probably dead. Those long Company formation runs at Jump school, with their seemingly endless line of troops, of all those running young men, I might be the only one still alive.

Hall came out of the building and lit a cigarette. He offered me one, I declined. "You are here late." I observed trying to get my mind back into the here and now.

"Yeah we finally got an HF comms link with South Comm at Fort Clayton." He took a drag and looked dejected. "They don't know any more than we do."

For Thanksgiving they set up the chow hall, and served us 'tray rats' that where like big MRE meals than only needed to be boiled in a field kitchen. A meal of turkey breasts, rice, and green beans was meant to buoy moral that was creeping dangerously low. It seemed to have the opposite effect, I saw to fist fights break out in my short time wolfing down the lukewarm meal.

It was a few days later the first of December came, the night before I could not sleep. I do not think any of use slept much, Pedro who was along in the room when his night terror hit, we were all on the catwalk. The guys where smoking, I was sipping water from my canteen.

"Do you really think it is the end of the world?" Billy asked seriously.

"I guess we will find out tomorrow." Bill said, "How many paydays can they not pay us?"

"How long till we run out of food?" I asked.

Pedro's screaming and wailing continued, in disgust Billy threw the door open, it slammed against the back wall slammed shut again almost hitting him in the face. We laughed at him, and Pedro was silent. We would find out later he has pissed the bed.

It was a dead quiet payday, without any pay. I had guard that night around the arms room, a line of raccoons infiltrating the grossly overflowing dumpsters where the only excitement that night. When Bill dropped Pedro off to relieve me, he told me that some of

Glasgow's guys had snuck out into town that night, and came back pretty banged up. I guess the Panamanians where throwing rocks and bottles at them.

It was December 4th when we had the 'missing man formation', four men were missing at morning formation. Additional Guard posts where added around the barracks, the chow hall and we laid a single strand of concertina wire around the Company Area.

The morning of the 5th we had another 2 men missing, we spent the entire day reinforcing the wire around the Company area to triple stand, to along the bottom, and a single strand over top of it. We constructed as single gate on the road, and several additional posts where added to the Guard mount. With Guard now going 24/7 we ended up with Guard every day.

That ended the disappearances, graffiti declaring us 'the Fighting Mushrooms, fed shit and kept in the Dark', 'Kobe POW camp', and 'Stalag Kobe' started to crop up everywhere. On the 13th there Aviation unit across post rioted, we went on lockdown,

On the 15th of December, we had another cashless payday. Billy and I had roving patrol that night, we were on the quietest part of the perimeter when we found a board through over the fence, and the wire fence was collapsed. We reported it to the Sergeant of the Guard.

A Company formation was called and five more men were missing. The 'buddy system' was initiated. No one could go anywhere alone. Field showers where set up in the parking lot, so we could get a little cleaner.

When Bill and I were walking back from the shower, Hall cornered us, and looked more sneaky than normal. "Hey fellas."

"Where is your buddy?" Bill asked.

He ignored the question and started following us back to the barracks. "So, how much longer do you think they can hold it together?" He asked.

"Hold what together?" I asked.

"The unit."

"Don't you mean, how much longer WE can hold it together?" Bill snapped.

"Yeah we have had, what ten guys go over the hill?" I asked.

"That is less than ten percent of the Company's strength."

"The leg companies are a lot worse, like twenty or thirty missing." Hall reported grimly. "The Aviation Battalion is down to about one third strength."

"They were useless anyway." Bill said convincing no one with his brave words, least of all himself.

"It is not like they are getting far, I have heard a lot of deserters are getting lynched by the Panamanians." Hall said as we climbed the stairs.

"Serves 'em right." Bill said un-comfortably.

When we got into the room, Hall finally got to the point, "What are you going to do when it falls apart?"

"It is not going to fall apart. For fuck's sake, it is the Army. They will get un-fucked eventually." Bill said annoyed.

"What if they don't?" Hall said intently.

"Well what are you going to do?" I asked, hating that somehow always made people state the obvious.

"I know a guy who was ready for this. A guy with enough guns, and ammo to hold up forever if needs me. I have a feeling he is going to need perimeter guards, and the like. " He said with an evil grin.

"You are going to spend the rest of your life in the Panamanian jungle?" Bill said mockingly. "Fuck they, if the world is ending I am going home. "

"Does the term nuclear holocaust mean anything to you?"

"There is NO WAY to know what happened back in the states, and besides, unless the Soviets where afraid of rust and un-employment they will not have nuked Buffalo."

"How are you going to get there genius?'"

"I am not, eventually the Army will send us home." Bill sounded like a man whistling in the dark.

It was a few days later we had 'Christmas Party' the food was tray rats, and everyone was allowed two beers from the lukewarm cooler. The Officers served up the chow in the army tradition, and the First Sergeant stood guard over the beer cooler.

I was in line behind Billy and Pedro, as waited for our turn to get chow. The Company Commander was trying to make small talk with the troops as they went through the line. He asked Corporal Glasgow how he was doing. Glasgow said, "I am fine, my squad is just dying to get a shower and some laundry done."

"We are doing everything we can to get the facilities fixed." The CO said moving on.

"If we rotate squads down to the beach we could at least was in the ocean, and rinse out our uniforms." Glasgow called after him.

Carlos and several of his buddies blocked the CO's path. "What is happening back in the States Sir?" Carlos asked aggressively.

'We DO have a right to know, Sir." Glasgow asked politely, but firmly.

"Look!" The CO went red faced. "We do not know any more than you do right now."

Cries, of 'Bullshit!' and 'Liar' from all around filled the air.

"At Ease!" The First Sergeant shouted only to face a half full coke can flung at him.

"Let us off fucking base!" Someone shouted.

"Free the mushrooms!"

"You Fucking Toad stool!"

"Let my people go!" Someone shouted, it was kind of clever, so I have always believed it was Hall. It became a chant. "Let my people go! Let my people go!"

The First Sergeant grabbed the CO by the collar and dragged him out as he appealed for calm, and everything that was not nailed down became a projectile.

The table with food was overturned, and food when everywhere. Bill shouted "Grab a tray, and didi mau!"

I ran past the overturned table a plucked a tray rat out of the water it scalded my finders, so I kicked it over and used my patrol cap to keep from burning my finger. We beat a hasty retreat back to the room.

When we got there Bill looked around, "OK boys what did we get?"

I looked at the tray I was carrying. "Buttered, Rice."

Pedro help up a bag of paper cups, and looked apologetic. "I just grabbed and ran."

We all looked to Billy who had a large red fire extinguisher. "What the fuck?" Bill asked, "Is that in case we burst into flames?"

"It is better than paper cups!"

"How is that better?" I asked. We all started laughing.

"Now how the fuck are we going to get this thing open?" Bill said examining the tray. In the end we took a survival knife and where able to pry the top open. We all eat or fill of buttered rice using paper cups to shovel it in.

The sickly sweet smell of CS gas drifted in from the court yard. CS is military grade tear gas. Troops where staggering down the catwalk eyes bloodshot and watering, with long tendrils of snot hanging from their noses. We laughed, it was clear they had gassed the chow hall. We had all experienced GS gas in basic training, it was very un-pleasant, but not really harmful. The worst things you could so is touch the effected skin, or attempt to wash it off with water. The gas is made up of tiny crystals that will grind into your skin, or dissolve in water only to reform in your eyes, or open pours.

Glasgow came in stinking of CS and smiling, "You guys missed all the fun."

"Who threw the Gas?" Bill asked offering some rice.

"I think it was Hall, First Sergeant knocked Meeks the fuck out!"

This got as all exited. We begged him to tell the story. "Some of the brother decided we were going to get to the beer, and Meeks was supposed to run interference. I do not think he got a word out before First Sergeant clocked him. He was out cold! "

"Where is he now?"

"The Docs has him over at the aid station."

"What about First Sergeant?"

"He is holed up in the Company Office with the Officers, Hall and a few clerks. There is a lot of talk about wanting to get some pay back for the CS. I don't think you are going to see them in the barracks any time soon."

That proved to be true. Hall started sleeping in the Company Office, and the Officers started carrying their side arms at all times. On the day after Christmas. A very bruised Sergeant Meeks Explained that the buddy system was now replaced with the 'Buddy Team', meaning that no one could do anywhere unless it was with their entire Fire Team.

The next morning, there was no morning formation, we stood on the catwalk and saw troops in civilian clothes walking strait through the makeshift gate towards town. "I wonder if the MPs at the front gate will be so lacks." I wondered out loud.

"I wonder if they are even still there." Bill said sounding crest falling.

"I heard they are hanging deserters." Pedro said.

"What do we do?" I asked stupidly.

"We hang in here." Bill said watching the exodus. "We are thousands of miles from home. We have very little money that people might not take anyway. I mean look!" He pointed at the one of the deserters who was wearing his liberty attire, gold chains and all. "Where the fuck do they think they are going? "

"What about what Hall said?" Billy asked. "First Sergeant Hoef seems like he has his shit together more than anyone."

"Yeah." Pedro agreed.

"I imagine he does." Bill said thoughtfully. "If we end up out of here, I have to find out what happened. I have to go home."

The next day we had tray rats for breakfast and dinner, the lunch MREs seemed to have disappeared. I could not sleep that night. What had happened to home, I wondered. It did not seem possible that it was gone. I just laid there in the dark and listened to the sounds of the encroaching jungle. How long, I wondered until it reclaimed this base? How long until all of the world was a jungle. I drifted off to sleep with visions of massive herd of buffalo grazing among the rusting hulks of cars on the inter-state.

Skeletal remains of human beings slumped in their cars, the sun bleached bones of entire families, and my mind's eye saw them all. Father skeleton at the wheel empty eye sockets blankly watching the eternal traffic jam of death. Skeleton Mother slumped forward, forehead on the dash. Black crow perched on the car seat in the back, infant skeleton, screaming! Screaming I awoke. The screams still filled the ink black air.

"Shut the fuck up Pedro!" Bill shouted throwing his pillow. I sat shaking in my bed. Bill was able to calm Pedro down, I slipped off the rack, and stepped out onto the catwalk. I vomited over the hand rail.

I stood alone looking into the inky blackness of the approaching jungle. I did not want to go in there, I did not want to live here, I wanted the light to come one. Payday was a few days away. They would pay us, and we would go down into the 'ville and drink, mess with the whores, and everything would be the way it was supposed to be. When our time was up and they'd fixed everything. We would go home and go to college. Maybe we could go to the same school, and talk about our crazy days in the Army.

We just had to wait it out I told myself.

That day we had that we had the Guard from 1300-1500. I had the CP, Pedro had the arms room, Bill and Billy where rovers. We were supposed to be relieved by Glasgow's squad. Bill and Glasgow relieved me, just fine. I gave all of my ammo to one of his guys, and went with them to post Carlos to relive Pedro.

None of us where prepared for what we saw when the door swung open to the Command Post. Pedro sitting on a box of ammunition had his rifle to his eye and was sighted in on the Company Commander's Head. The CO was screaming at Pedro. "You are going to fucking jail you little rat! You thieving bastard! You are not going to get away with it this time!"

"What the fuck?" Bill asked.

"Corporal, arrest this piece of shit!" The CO shouted.

"I didn't do nothing!" Pedro almost whispered.

"You have been stealing! " The CO raged. "You are going to

fucking jail!"

"Pedro, "Bill said slowly "Lower your weapon."

"No. I am not going to go to jail." He said quietly.

"No one is going to jail." Bill said calmly "It is the end of your shift, time to give up our ammo."

"No, he is going to arrest me." Pedro said sounding afraid.

The door on the far side of the room opened up a Hall walked in wearing just PT short and a t-shit. "What is all the god-damned noise?"

'Hall, get some flex cuff and arrest this piece of shit!"

Hall looked sleepily around at the situation. Our rifles where still slung over our shoulders, and the Captain's side arm was still in his holster. Only Pedro was ready to shoot. "I don't think so."

The Captain clawed his 45 from the holster, and cocked it at Hall. In a flash Bill un-slung his rifle and aimed at the CO. Pedro put his weapon of full auto. No one moved for a moment.

"You have lost every crew served weapon in your Company Patton! If anyone is going to jail it is you!" Hall sneered.

"You know damned well where those weapons went!" The CO

screeched cocking his pistol.

Bill stepped forward placing the muzzle of his rifle at the base of the CO's skull. "Sir, put the weapon down."

"Hold on." Hall said stepping to his right, so that anything going through the CO's skull would not hit him directly. "OK." He smiled.

The CO slowly leaned down and put the pistol on the floor.

Hall picked it up, and gently rode the hammer forward. He turned the pistol over in his hand a few times them with a downward chopping motion brought the butt of the gun down across the bridge of the Commander's nose. There was a sickening crushing down, and the Captain collapsed dark blood flowed onto the concrete floor. He cocked the pistol and aimed at the CO's head. "Get the fuck out of here."

The CO bolted from the room trailing blood.

We all looked dumb struck at one another. "Well, that's the end of me. I am out of here. You coming with? "

Bill grabbed a can of 5.56mm Ammo, "No thanks, I am going home. "

"I am with you." I blurted out, as he Pedro and I started toward the door.

Bill stopped for a moment and looked at Glasgow. "You going with him?"

"Yeah." He said shaking Bill's hand. "Take it easy bro."

"Yeah, you to. We better get the fuck out of here before Napoleon gets back."

It was an exhilarating and terrifying run back to the barracks. I felt dizzy. We charged up the stairs giddy with fear. Billy was sitting shirtless sharpening a knife as be burst in.

"Grab your packs, we have to go NOW!" Bill shouted, loud with fear.

"What the fuck happened?" Billy asked as we threw on our packs.

"Pedro and the CO got into it. Hall clocked him, now if we do not hall ass you are in deep shit!" Bill tried to explain.

Billy looked perplexed at Pedro. "No he decked the CO!" I shouted shouldering my pack.

"Get your shirt on, we are leaving!" Bill practically pleaded.

We all still had weapons, except Billy. His eyes darted to our rifles, he grabbed a chair and slid it to the sink.

"Come on Billy!" Pedro said.

Billy climbed on the chair and started unscrewing the grate to the air conditioner. "I ain't going empty handed." He climbed up into the duct until only his legs hung out.

"For Christ's sake!" Bill cursed. "Hurry the fuck up!"

Billy struggled to wriggle out. When he finally did, he was holding a black grenade canister.

"Son-of-a-bitch!" I said dumbfounded. "All this time."

"Fuck, I thought we was going to war, and no one would give a shit."

"We can argue about this later! " Bill said stepping out the door.

We sling our weapons and marched in a loose gaggle towards the gate. My stomach was doing back flips. I wanted to run. Billy was getting panicky. "I ain't got a weapon, it don't look right."

"Maybe you should clasp your hands, like you are handcuffed." Pedro suggested.

"Good job Luke Skywalker, we are taking him out, not in." Bill said lightly.

No one cased as we left the wire, we jogged up the hill and past the E club. Once we were on the same rocks we had used for our escape from the riot we flopped down on our packs. At first there was a wave of euphoria. We had got away!

A cold feeling crept into my gut, we were on our own. Bill was passing out ammunition, it was then I realized that like me, he did not have a magazine in his weapon. Pedro was the only one who was locked and loaded.

As we filled our magazines Billy became more nervous, I cannot believe "I am un-armed. Shit a home, I've got a shot gun and two rifles!"

"You've got Pedro's Grenade." I said mocking him a little.

"Yeah, fucker." Pedro added.

"Just keep it in the canister." Bill warned.

Billy became twitchier. "Are you fucking kidding me?"

"You've got that Rambo knife of yours." I added.

I looked into the gathering shadows, "How are we going to get out of here, we cannot walk out the gate with weapons and in uniform."

"Shit!" Bill spat. "Does anyone have any civvies?" No one did. "We are going to have to go through the fence."

"If we follow the creek down and we can probably go under it." I contemplated out loud, "Damn site better than going over and risking a busted leg." The last thing we needed was to carry someone.

"Let's get to it, before it gets dark." Bill said hefting his rifle. "I will take point. Bill you are my shadow. Billy with the holey hand grenade in the middle."

"Not funny." Billy pouted.

"And Pedro you are trail end Charlie. Make sure you look back every third step."

"Got it." Pedro said grimly. He would later admit to me that he felt the weight of this was entirely on his shoulder that we were deserting to protect him. It was not entirely un-true, but I do not think we could have stayed much longer. Billy probably would have joined the First Sergeant's crew, and there was no way Bill was not going to try to see home. Pedro and I were the floaters, I would have stuck will Bill because he was my best friend, though being hired guns for the First Sergeant sounded pretty good to me, I would not have let him strike out for home alone.

When we got to the fence, the gap eroded only about six inches below the fence. Billy and I started pulling rock out from underneath it. While Bill and Pedro pulled security. Before long we were out of rocks and it was still a tight fit.

Billy took the entrenching tool off of his pack and unfolded it. We took turns digging until we had almost a foot deep gap under the chain link. Billy wriggled under and I passed him his pack, the nylon snagged on the fence for a moment, and made way to much noise. I was having images of getting shot for desertion. When Pedro whispered 'Hurry up, someone is coming!"

My heart pounded as I passed my pack through. I could hear footsteps crushing branches, the bushes swayed as someone approached down the stream bed. Pedro was behind a green fallen tree. The soldier that limbered into view did not see him only three feet away, his round face was quickly matched by his eyes rounding as he spotted me. Rather than raise his rifle he waved the back of his hand in front of his eyes in the 'cease fire signal.'

"Praise Jesus its Carlos!" I said so relieved I had to piss.

Carlos smiled dumbly and waved for the guys behind him to catch up. Glasgow and Hall picked their way through the rocks carefully. Their packs where stuffed, and they had multiple bandoliers of ammunition draped off of them.

The five of us made it through the fence as the last light faded. To make it the last quarter mile to the road we had to tighten our column up so much that my hand was on Bill's pack, and Billy's was on mine. When we reached the narrow strip of road that wound down the hill toward the ville we paused and huddled just out of sight in case anyone came down the road.

Bill, Glasgow, and Hall where in a heated argument, in hushed tones. "Ok we will out it to a vote. " Bill announced. "Can everyone hear me? We can either head down to the beach or up towards the First Sergeant's mountain place. "

"How far is it?" Billy asked.

"Three Days." Glasgow answered.

"A day and half!" Hall shot back.

"How far is the beach?" I asked.

"We can get there tonight!" Glasgow answered eagerly.

"It is in the wrong direction!" Hall answered.

"Let's all go to the beach tonight, and get cleaned up. We can decided what to do from there!" Bill said trying to make peace.

"Yeah." I said.

"Fuckin' A' Billy chimed in.

"Sounds good." Carlos added.

"Fine!" Hall said sounding almost comical in his annoyance.

The pack straps dug into my shoulders as we slogged through the jungle. My fears were numbed by exhaustion and pain. Blisters formed on my feel, my rifle seemed to snag on every vine and branch. I was just an animal. Animals do not worry about their homes, or others, or even their own future. They just want rest, food, they are all ID.

The jungle seemed to retreat a little, and sand under my boots felt good. The brightness from the sand underfoot made it possible to see a little. I do not remember it we saw or heard the ocean first, but once we found it we spread out and collapsed. I leaned my pack against a palm tree and finished off a cool canteen of plastic tasting water.

I drifted off to sleep leaning on that tree, and hours later I woke shivering. I took my poncho liner, pulled off my boots, and went back to sleep. The sound of the waves seemed to whisper to us that it had all been a bad dream and everything was 'ok'.

When I woke again the sun was peeking over the trees, others guys where frolicking in the waves like kids. The weapons where piled on packs and uniforms. "Come on in ya stinky bastard!" Billy yelled.

"Not until someone else is done. Someone has to watch the gear!" I responded. "Didn't you ever see Planet of the Apes, I am not going through this naked!"

Eventually I was relieved as Pedro came out of the surf and I took a little swim. I am not sure I got much cleaner but it felt good. Still there was something unsettling about the morning haze and the cool dark ocean. I was happy to gather with the rest of the guys around a small driftwood fire.

"We had better get going." Hall said coolly. Looking at the

lush hills above us.

"Yeah," Glasgow agreed this pack is a bitch, but is not getting any lighter."

Hall looked at us, "Many hands make light work."

"We are going home." Bill said matter of factly.

Glasgow looked worried. "I am not saying anything, but you might want to think about it."

"There is nothing to think about, I am going home." He said slinging his rifle over his shoulder.

Glasgow sighed. "Bro, you will never make it."

"The fuck I won't!" Bill turned suddenly scarlet. "I am NOT going to hideout in some damn jungle for the rest of my fucking life, I do not give a fuck! I am going to find out what happened."

"Bro, you will never make it!"

"How long do you think you are going to last in the First Sergeant's honeycomb hide-out? I will tell you how long! Until the Gechees figure out where you are!"

Carlos hefted his rifle. "We can handle them."

"Yeah Carlos? How many of them? A thousand? Ten

Thousand? A hundred thousand?" They all looked away. "There are millions of them! Millions!" He took a breath. "Who is with me?"

"You know it." I said nervously.

"I don't think I can kill more 'n ten thousand people with my grenade." Billy joked without smiling.

"It's my grenade." Pedro said.

"I am only going as far as Georgia." Billy announced.

"Fair enough." Bill agreed.

"Hey Hall." Billy called with a sudden burst of energy. "Say hi to the First Sergeant's old lady for me!" He gave us a wink we were all slack jawed, believing for moment to be the ballsiest paratrooper in history.

Hall laughed at us, "Don't listen to him Geniuses, that fat bitch never left North Carolina." He turned toward the tree line and started walking. "Good luck!" He called and started whistling.

Glasgow and Carlos shook everyone's hands and wished us luck as they followed him away. We stood there until they were out of sight. Then we headed north towards the canal. The hills where steep, and we cut into the jungle to avoid human contact. It was around noon, and Bill was on point when he stopped with a gasp. We all froze, then to our horror he took of running.

We sprinted to catch up with him, he stopped in a clearing of waste high grass overhanging the water, before us spread out the most wonderful sight I may ever see. The ocean was teeming with ships!. Container ships, oil tankers, car carriers, all sizes milling around like an ant hill. Off to our right they filed into the Chagres river, and then into the canal.

We crept down to the river bridge, we figured when the tide came in, and the ships where high up we could jump onto the roof un-detected. We waited until the evening tide, and the gathering darkness.

We crouched as we ran out on to the bridge as a massive container ship passed underneath. My stomach knotted as I climbed over the guard rail. The ship looked really far down, and moving fast. It was probably a thirty foot drop. I knew if I kept my feet and knees together I would be fine, just like Airborne School.

We all hesitated, and suddenly found ourselves looking down

into churning brown water. "Fuck next one!" Bill hissed.

"Wait!" I said, not recognizing the lettering on the ship. It had a red flag with a green star, and I was not sure whose side it might be on.

"This next one's American!" Billy shouted.

It was small, 105 feet, stem to stern. A small bulk carrier with its super structure towards the back. Being small it seemed much further down. The bins where full of grain, but there cranes seemed dangerously in the way.

"Aim for the life boats!" Bill said, I saw what he meant, there were a pair of 14 foot lifeboats with canvas covers on the upper deck behind the ship's bridge. Bill jumped his feet tore into the canvas and he disappeared from sight. I jumped my feet and knees locked together, legs slightly bent, I seemed to fall forever. I looked down, I was there! My feet, ass, and then head hit the steel deck, my eyes filled with stars, my pack and rifle flew from my hands. The sky turned into the underside of the bridge. My head throbbed, I struggled to look around.

Billy kneeled over me. "Are you ok?"

"No." I said thinking I was going to be sick.

"Pedro didn't make it." He said.

I sat up in a panic, the three of is looked stupidly at one another. Bill pointed to the bow of the ship, as it passed out from under the bridge, a pair of green blurs that could only have been Pedro and his pack fell from the bridge and disappeared into the grain compartment.

We collected ourselves, and our gear. I started to wonder why no one had reacted to Pedro's jump, we slowly crept forward. A young man in his late twenties with greasy black hair, and needing a shave came out of a hatch carrying a tray of sandwiches and some tea onto the bridge, he was mumbling to himself there was a sharp exchange of words in a language I did not understand. I suddenly felt sick again.

Billy slipped forward, his big pig sticker knife in hand. Bill tried to stop him, but it was too late he slid down into the passageway. We sat breathless until he popped back up, his eyes like saucers. "It's a Russian ship!" He whispered.

"We have to find Pedro, before they do!" Bill said sliding his pack into a lifeboat. "Billy stay with the packs.

With knees bent we shuffled silently onto the passage. Bill mouthed 'Cover me.' I realized that though my magazine was inserted, I had not chambered a round. To do so would have caused a hell of a noise now. I slowly raised myself until I could peer into the bridge. The Captain looked like an ancient mariner with a salt and pepper beard, hand clutching the wheel, and eyes peering unblinkingly forward.

I snuck down and caught up with Bill, we were at the door the sandwich guy had come out. Bill wrapped his hand around the door handle, and gestured to be to go in. I gulped, when he jerked it open, I leaped forward. It was a wardroom with a dining table in the center, on the left a large 3 foot by 5 foot picture of a man with a gaudy medal, I thought he looked like Dracula. There where large red flags on either side of him.

We slipped into the room and where half way across the room when the door behind us opened. The sandwich guy came in we both aimed in on him, I chambered a round with that distinct double click.

He dropped his tray with an awful clatter, and started rambling in gibberish.

"Shut up!" Bill hissed.

"Pease don't kill me bro! " He almost cried.

"You speak English?" Bill asked as my heart felt like it was going to burst.

"Sure thing chief! No worries, just chill." He said shakily.

"What kind of ship is this?"

"Cargo, grain my man, no big thing."

"What Nationality!"

"Turkish man! Second Largest NATO Army, after you bro. We are on the same team!"

"Why are you flying an American flag?" Bill said relaxing a little.

"Not American, Liberian. Cheap to register. Everybody does it. No big deal bro!" I looked closer at the red flags, they what a white crescent moon, and a white star.

"Those are Turkish flags. " I said feeling stupid.

"Put your hands down man, we thought you were Russian or

something. " Bill said apologetically.

"No worries my man", he said "I thought you were pirates."

"No shit! There are ships getting pinched all over the place bro!" He said excitedly. "Look I need to get back topside, you want some grub? The mice didn't eat their sandwiches." He said gesturing towards the floor.

"Get Billy, and find Pedro!" Bill said, slinging his rifle. He shook the man's hand. "Bill."

"Ahmed." The grateful to be alive sandwich guy answered shaking his hand profusely.

The sandwiches where roast beef, with cheese, mustard and mayo, and they were the best meal of my life floor grit and all. The three of us sat at the table stuffing our faces when a pulpy raced fat man walked in. He walked past us to the corner, and poured himself some tea.   He talked back out without a word.

We looked at each other perplexed.   Bill followed him out. We all followed Bill.

The man walked up to the bridge where Ahmed was bickering with the Captain, and talking on the radio. The Captain adjusted the helm, put it in park, whatever the Navy calls it. We had just pulled into a lock. Giant iron wheels, and cogs pulled impossibly huge components. To lift the ship to the next lock, there was nothing electronic in them I supposed, or if there was they would have fixed them before the rest of the power grid.

The man with the tea sat with a similar bearded man in the back of the bridge, they took no notice of us. Ahmed smiled, and gestured for us to go away, making the 'shush' gesture, and waved us away.

We climbed back up by the life boats and watched as the sky filled with thousands of bats they came out of the jungle to feed on bugs attracted to the lights of the passing ships. The breeze was cool, Ahmed joined us. "We got a bout ten minutes until the lock fills up. Then I gotta get down their or the Captain won't do anything."

"Why didn't they say anything?" I asked.

"Oh those are my three blind mice." He smiled. "They were on the bridge in Long Beach."

"You saw the bomb go off?" Pedro asked.

"No just the mice, and the deck apes."

"Where are they?" Bill asked looking around.

"Dead, they were on the weather decks. " Ahmed leaned in closer. "It cooked them like microwave. Took them days to die."

"So it is just you and the three blind mice?" I asked suspiciously.

"No there are the three snipes."

"What?" Bill looked suspiciously.

"Snipes. You know, bro. Engine room guys."

"Where are you headed? " Bill asked.

"Well where supposed to take this grain to Asia, but after the war started we set from home. Adana Turkey."

"Any chance you can to drop us off in the states?" Bill asked hopefully,

"Sure bro, we can work it out." He looked down at the water, "I gotta go, you stay here. When we get through the canal I will get you. Introduce you to the Skipper. Tell him you are ant-pirate security dudes, or whatever, and everything is cool, ok?"

Several locks later we passed Fort Clayton, it was a smoking ruin. Fires still burned in some of the barracks windows. I wondered if they were occupied. We stood in silent awe as Panama slipped past us like an all-around drive in movie. I thought, my God, we could be home in days.

To what home, I wondered. Like a child looking at the top of a mountain, or perhaps more aptly the moon. I thought it was as simple as, to go.

We sat in the wardroom facing the giant portrait. It seemed an eternity before Ahmed came in looking Chastened.

"Well?" Bill asked impatiently.

"No worries, bro. "He said apologetically "The Skipper say he cannot leave the bridge, but you can stay no worries. The compass is dead, so we are going to follow up the coast, and across, we can drop you off anywhere, no problem. "

Billy gestured to the picture, "Who IS that guy?"

"Mustafa Kamal Ataturk, Father of modern Turkey, "Ahmed answered with more dignity than We had seen before. "It is a felony in Turkey to disrespect him, so not jokes!"

"No problem." Bill said calmly.

"I will show you the ship." Ahmed announced, opened one of

the lockers, "This is arms locker we have several rifles, and some ammunition to protect the ship. "

Billy seized one of the rifles immediately, followed by Bill. "Turkish Mauser "Billy said opening the bolt. It was an old bolt action, with a long thing barrel, he hefted the weapon and aimed it out the porthole.

"Sights are graduated out to two thousand meters." Bill observed. "A little optimistic."

"You can store your guns in there." Ahmed offered. We wordlessly declined.

The ship was a rusty, rat infested mess. The bunks where were offered were in steel frames with canvas mesh, in a stinking little compartment. There where shower, and a toilet. We agreed we would sleep on deck or in the wardroom.

That evening I was standing with Bill and Ahmed watching the sun do down, the sky was blood red. It was the night of December 29th, "Red skies at night?" I thought out loud.

"A lot of shit in the air, from the war." Ahmed said lighting a cigarette. For days after Long Beach we could not see the sun, or the stars."

"How are we fixed for food?" Bill asked looking for the stars to appear.

"Not good, I try to tell Skipper we need to go hunting. The rats into the last of the bread today, got everything that was not in cans or jars. We have some more beef in cans, but we need to stock up before we try to cross Atlantic."

"What is for chow?" I asked hungrily.

He sighed, "I don't know, bro. I will do dig something up." He headed below decks.

Bill sat down and pulled a roll of parachute cord from his cargo pocket. Measuring 6 feet he cut off a piece, then pulled all of the individual strands out. "I wonder how fast we are going." He mused.

"Ten miles an hour?" I guessed.

He began knotting the induvial strings together. "That is what, like 240 miles a day?"

"Shit, we will be there in no time." I opined as Pedro came up stairs, "That shower is cold!"

"Is Billy in now?" Bill asked without looking away from his knots.

"Yeah he is talking about killing rats." Pedro said looking concerned.

"Those thing are fucking everywhere on this tub." Bill agreed.

"He is not thinking of shooting them?" I asked, not confident he was not.

"No, grain dust." We both looked stupidly at him. "Grain dust can explode if you shoot in it." He said matte of factly.

Pedro looked as though he a touched a hot stove. "What!"

"Are you kidding?" I asked knowing he wasn't.

"Nope."

Billy came up carrying the ridiculously long Mauser rifle. "What are you, as Tusken raider?" I teased.

"I ain't going unarmed, nowhere." He said sitting Indian style on the deck.

"He looks more like a minuteman." Bill grunted.

"You gonna shoot some rats?" Pedro asked.

"Hell no! That damn grain dust would blow the damned ship

up!"

Pedro and I looked at each other dumbfounded. "Really?"

"Yeah, ain't you ever heard of grain silos explodin'?" Billy said aiming in on the horizon with his rifle.

Ahmed up looking upset.

"Chow ready?" Bill asked.

Ahmed just shook his head. "Hey, um…" We all looked at him suddenly concerned. "I need a hand."

I was closest, I flowed him down into the bridge. The Captain stood unmoving at the wheel, he was bathed in red light. The red lights where used at night to ensure the bridge crew's night vision did not get washed out. The tea drinking 'mouse' was slumped over the chart, as we approached he seemed to be making a weird clicking sound.

A cluster of rats was gathered around his face. Billy jabbed at them with the butt of his Mauser. They retreated only a little, and attempted to get back to the man. We pulled at his collar, his nose and lips where gone.

We dragged him out of the bridge, and laid him out on the deck.

We gather around him, not knowing what to do say. Ahmed finally said, "I will ask the skipper what to do. Don't let the rats get him."

The skipper wanted him buried at sea, but would not let us do it until morning, we took turns on guard over the body. The rats where not a problem, but in the pre-dawn light the birds start to gather, and being the tropic, the stench was already bad.

We placed him on a stretcher, under the Turkish flag, and they played the Turkish National Anthem before we dumped him into the sea. As the ships wake indelicately threw him around in white foam the sea gulls descended.

We stared in a long silence, it occurred to me that, this was the first Corpse I had seen outside of a casket, and what's worse I knew it was not going to be the last.

Ahmed tried to convince the Captain to stop so we could hunt, but he refused, at what was worse we were drifting east. The Coastline was fading off our port side. That evening we dined on stew in the wardroom, and spent house fiddling with a cheap television that sat in the corner. We were unable to pick up anything but static.

When we finally settled in to sleep on the floor the skittering of the rats in the wall kept me away. I looked out into the pouring rain, wishing it would stop so I could get out of there. Pedro had climbed up on the table to sleep, Billy say up and stared out the window with me.

"Wonder how they boys back in Panama are doing." Billy mused.

"I don't know, fewer fucking racks." I gripped.

"More bugs thought."

"Did they have chiggers in Panama?" I asked.

"Sometimes, but man! They had centipedes a foot long and as wide as you wrist. I got bit one time crossing a creek, right in my back, they had to medivac me."

I remembered reading a similar story in a book about Vietnam, and I wondered if he was lying, he was at least exaggerating, but I did not want to call him on it. "You missed quite a scene with Pedro and the CO. It was like the movies, everybody pointing guns."

"Hall busted up the CO, did not think he had it him."

"Busted his nose with the butt of his own gun. The old man dropped like a ton of bricks." In the Army Commanders are invariably called the old man, no matter how young they are.

We chuckled a little bit, over that a little, and listened to the rain. "You think we did the right thing?" Billy asked. "I ain't no coward."

"Hell if there is still a war going on, we sure as hell weren't going to get into it there. "

"That is for damn sure."

"I will bet if there is an Army left anywhere, we could just join right up with them." I said hopefully.

"Hell yeah, " Billy smiled, "They'd be all, where hell did you fella's come from?"

"I wonder if they'd ship us off to fight in Europe." I said secretly wondering if they would hang us as deserters.

"Shit, the Russians might have invaded us for all we know." Billy said less enthusiastically.

Somewhere out their beyond that veil of darkness and rain, was a mysterious world. We sailed blindly towards it, thinking ourselves brave, imagining that we had seen hardship, horrors, and privation. We did not know it, but the protective sheen of the civilized world had only warn the slightest bit thin. As I heard the rats scurry, deep in my heart I knew this, and as it in agreement Pedro shrieked.

On the 31th we buried the second of the blind mice at sea. It was midafternoon when Ahmed told us he had passed, thankfully he found him before the rats. As the last notes of the Turkish national anthem played we all around to the area by the lifeboats and cleaned our rifles. Billy seemed so happy to clean his 1938 rifle, it seemed comical to me. As did Pedro's 40mm grenade launcher attached to his rifle, for which we still had no grenades.

Bill went back to his parachute cord project, ignoring all questions as to what the hell he was doing, so we dubbed it his 'knitting'.

An argument in Turkish erupted on the bridge, I am not sure why, but I slipped down the stairs and looked. The Skipper has not moved but Ahmed was clearing pleading with him, it seemed pleading with him to come away from the helm.

I looked closely at the red faced skipper, his white knuckled grasp on the wheel, his feet planted as if in concrete. His boots where tattered, the toes split open. Gnawed open I realized, the tips of his toes where gnawed away, bones exposed. He stood trembling, Ahmed pulled him away, and I took the wheel.

His arm over the old man's shoulders Ahmed gently led him away to the wardroom. I stood there suddenly terrified. I was driving the ship and did not know what I was doing! I know a blind man had been doing it for a month, but that was cold comfort. "Bill!" I called out in a panic.

The whole team came running. Pedro carrying my rifle as well as his own. "Cool, can I drive?" Billy asked. Before any of us could say anything a thunderous shot rang out from the wardroom.

The Captain lay sprawled on the floor, the top of his head gone, a Mauser rifle next to him. Clearly he had put it in his mouth and pulled the trigger. A welter of gore covered the ceiling, and Ataturk was speckled with blood and brains. Ahmed came rushing up from the Galley and fell to his knees by the body sobbing and tearing at his shirt, we backed away.

As the sun went down, so did the last of the blind mice, and we turned our bow Westward towards land and food. Ahmed was sullen and silent, the snipes never emerged to bid farewell to their Captain.

New Year's Day 1984, we came to a halt at a quiet day near the mouth of an un-named stream. The ship did not come to close for fear of reefs, but the team and I rowed ashore in one of the life boats. We dragged it up the beach as far as we could, and Bill started giving instructions. "OK, we need one person to stay with the boat, and build a fire. The other three of us, will head into the jungle and see about scaring up some food." He looked around at us. "Who wants fire duty?"

We all looked at one another for a moment too long. "Fine! " Billy Said. "You Yankees probably couldn't get no fire going anyhow."

"I will stay to." Pedro said, sound scared. Bill did not argue, it was a bad idea for anyone to be alone.

Bill and I headed into the jungle, the bush got thick almost immediately. The brambles cut us, and I kept looking back, afraid we would get lost. After a hour we stopped and drank from our canteens.

Making a ninety degree turn we paralleled the now distant beach. After another hour of seeing nothing, we turned another 90 degrees and headed towards the sea. I felt a rising fear that we were lost. I kept it to myself. We had not seen a single living thing, and had heard nothing but bugs.

One we burst out onto the beach, I breathed a sigh of relief. Trudged all the way to the edge of the surf and sat in the sand.

"Fuck!" Bill said annoyed. "Another few snipe hunts like that and we are in deep shit."

"I don't know what we could do differently." I said pulling my boots off.

We let our feet soak in the ocean for a minute. It cooled my blistered feet. Bill pushed is trouser legs over his knees, tied is boots together and threw them over his shoulder. I did the same and we both took our BDU jackets off and stuffed them into the butt packs on our H harnesses.

We strolled leisurely on the beach back towards the landing site. I kept my eyes on the jungle, hoping beyond hope for some tasty animal to leap into my M16's rifle sight.

After about forty-five minutes I smelled wood smoke. Bill was lagging behind me slightly when I heard a shot fired up ahead the sound of a bullet tore the air over my head. I froze, then dropped to one knee. Bill ran over to me and took a knee "You ok?"

"It was really high, I do not think they were shooting at us." I whispered.

He stuffed his bare feet into his boots, I did the same. "Ok, follow me." He said. We crept along the wood line bent double rifles at the ready. The beach seemed to curve out to sea, creating a finger of land at has a few hundred meters at hit's base. We had to either blunder through the jungle for a few hundred meters or head out towards the ocean, and run the risk of getting cut off with our backs to the sea. Bill clearly thought stealth was more important than position so he headed towards the sea. Another shot ran out and we dove for cover.

"Was that at us?" I asked.

"I think so!" Bill said excitedly.

We crawled on knees and elbows that last two hundred meters out to the point. My knees and elbows felt sandblasted. As we peered nervously around the corner I expected a bulleted smash into my face at any moment.

I could see the other side of the peninsula, at the beach was clear for a few hundred meters, and there I could see the boat, and a small fire. I could not see Billy or Pedro anywhere. The ship sat rusting the better part of a mile off shore, pointing away from us, I was concerned it might be leaving, but my biggest concern was Billy and Pedro. Perhaps they were hiding, or been captured, were those two shots them being executed.

At a pace just short of a run, we closed the distance to the boat. The sand in my boots rubbed by feet raw. When we got came within a few meters Pedro stood up, and damn near got shot for his troubles.

"Jesus Christ!" Bill curses.

"Hey!" Pedro's eye got wide. "What's wrong?"

"We heard, "I panted "Shots."

Bill come shirtless out of the tree line Mauser rifle in hand, "Hey fellas!" In his hand was a small black monkey, not more than ten pounds with most of its head gone. "I hope you like Monkey meat!"

We laughed with great relief. He carried it over to the fire, and threw it on top of two other monkey carcasses. "We need to get these cleaned before they go bad." He said matter of factly. "But if you look at that big grove of trees yonder, they seem to keep coming back. "

I went over to help Billy. Bill took is knitting out of his pocket, and sat down by the fire. "Ya ever clean a deer?" Billy asked.

"No." I admitted embarrassed. "You ever clean a monkey?"

"No but I choked a chicken once." He joked. He pulled out his pocket knife, "You do not want a big blade. The last thing you wanna do is split the guts, that'll spoil yer meat."

I swallowed a little uncomfortably, but tried to hide it. He put the tip of the blade in the animal's rectum, "Now remember you want to cut just skin, but the butt has a lot of muscular so you need to pop that little ring, and them, " he opened its belly like a zip lock bag full of guts. "Wa'la!"

Without a moment's hesitation he scooped out the animal's innards, "Intestines, heart, lungs, and liver, all in the same place in damn near every critter on God's green earth." He said with a smile, dumping the innards on the sand. He thoughtlessly drew cuts of to each of the animal's extremities, "Make sure your cut the skin along the in-seam of the arms and legs, then around the hooves, or whatever the critter has, and around the neck " He took out his big knife, "Start pulling the skin from the neck like yer taking off a shirt." I hesitated a little, "Don't be a pussy!"

I chuckled and started to pull, it kept getting stuck, and Billy kept cutting the connection between the monkey and its skin. Like that the creature was naked.

"Pedro, get this son-bitch hung up!" Billy said with a smile, and handed me the pocket "Next one's yours." I gulped and took the bloody knife, set about my grim task.

After the monkeys were gutted, skinned, and handing from a tree Bill cast his knitting into the stream, throwing a few bits of monkey guts in the make shift net, hoping to attract fish. I sat there washing my hands in the stream. "Careful." Bill said without looking. "There might be gators in this creek."

"Shit!" Billy exclaimed, "You are damned right there is. Pedro, watch nothing eats the monkeys!"

Bill and I both got a laugh out of those instruction, but grabbing his rifle Billy set out along the creek. Small fish did start to gather in Bills net. We waited until they became more numerous, and then he attempted to pull the net up. The school of fish easily escaped.

We re-set the trap and tried it with both of us pulling up a side, the fish seemed only slightly less calm as they evaded us. There was a shot from upstream, we rushed to it. We found Billy sitting in the tall grass staring intently at the creek. "He went under, we have to wait." He whispered.

We sat beside him, and waited. The temperature seemed less brutal than before, and I realized that the afternoon was already spent. "Bill, we need to get back to the ship. "

"Yeah." He said getting up, "Let's go."

"But I got him!" Billy insisted.

"We have to go!" Bill commanded, "Now."

I had already started back, when I saw a flash of white in the creek, about twenty meters towards the beach. "Holy shit, Billy. " I said pointing, "You did get him!" It was clearly the white under belly of a dead gator.

We stood looking down at it. "Well how the fuck do we get it out?" Bill asked.

Billy looked nervous, "I am got getting in there!"

"Yeah, I heard it has Gators in it." I agreed.

Bill handed me his M16 in disgust. "Cover me." He tried to look cool as he splashed into the stream. We stared nervously at him. 'Don't look at me! Look around!"

It seemed an eternity when he dunked his head under the water and grabbed the gator's tail. Be slowly drug it drug it backwards to the shore. Billy and I grabbed his H harness and helped him up. As dragged the beast by the tail, it was very dead and probably six feet long. One of its eyes was gone, and a large chunk was taken out of its' skull.

"Jesus Billy, you are balls on with that Turk rifle!" Bill marveled.

Billy looked embarrassed, "How are we going to get this thing back?" In the end we just dragged it by the tail, it was exhausting work.

When we reached the beach the sun was setting. Pedro was wide eyed. "Where the fuck have you been?" He almost yelled, his eyes never paused on the gator. "Those fucking apes!" He said.

"What?" Bill almost laughed.

"They are coming for us!" Pedro said seriously.

"Look as soon as we get that gator gutted we will be shoving off. " Bill said calmly.

I felt there where thousands of eyes in the shadows watching us. The trees where full of movement. Deep guttural grunts where exchanged tree to tree. They were closing in on us, I kept my back to the fire as Bill and Billy gutted the Gator. Pedro stood beside me nervously clutching his rifle.

I was happy to help drag the boat back to the water, and to load our grisly cargo. I kept glancing back expecting some kind of a last minute rush of the beach, but the sand remained clear and we rowed into the surf. It was choppy and I was afraid we might not get the boat back on board. It took forever to get the lines attached to the boat, there was a winch but, it was really not designed for 'launch and recover' operations.

In the end we got aboard, and Ahmed seemed as relieved as Pedro had been to see us. It seems the snipes and not come out of their hole in days, and he was starting to feel like we were never coming back. When the ship pulled away from the coast I wondered how many more times we would have to venture into the horrifying un-known before we could go home.

That night we made our first attempt at roasting monkey, it was awful, and he decided it must have gone bad already. I recommended we throw it overboard, but thankfully that gave Bill the idea to use it for bait. So we stuffed it into an air tight caulking bucket. The Gator meat we packed in salt, but it took most of the ship's salt supply.

Billy located some surgical tubing and made a slingshot, with the hope of cutting down the rat population. Bill and I took to attempting to sharpen wing nuts into blades in order to make fish hooks out of them small bolts. Pedro was on the Bridge with Ahmed.

Pedro came running into the Ward room. "There is a ship!"

We bolted outside, several miles distance, we saw a square sail. "Ahmed, what do you say?" Bill asked.

"Gotta give help, Bro. Law of these sea and all that jazz." He said calmly. "I will pull up alongside, you guys go on board and see what is shaking'."

"Do we use the boats?" I asked.

"I do not know dudes, lets get a little closer!"

As we drew nearer came into focus, Ahmed said "It looks like a tiny thing, if you can clear off one of the boat davits we can, you know? Bring her on board."

We shuffled up to the boat davit like keystone cops. We wrestled one of the life boats out of the way, "I wish we had a rope ladder." Bill said thoughtfully.

"We can not one of these bigger ropes." Billy offered.

"Easier to climb up, but what about down?" I asked.

"Yer not going to fast rope down." Bill mocked.

"No, Billy and I will cover you from up here. Pedro will follow you down." Bill said eyeing the craft.

"Damn if that thing is barely getting any closer." I gripped hiding the fear that gripped my guts. I was going down there?

We watched nervously as the sail got closer. It hung limply in the breeze, it was not a boat at all, but a raft. It bobbed helplessly in the sea, even though we slowed a great deal, I could tell it was going to be tough to get a line on it.

I bandit slung my rifle across my back and started nervously down the rope. The breeze was cool and I 'locked the rope between the heel of one boot and the top of the other. I could see there was someone on the raft.

I lowered myself further, and looked into the foaming sea beneath me. The raft loomed as I slid to the bottom of the rope, I hesitated to let my feet off the rope, and I missed my chance. The raft darted by the ship turned and the rope sung us away from the side, I hung on for my life. As we turned I glanced over to the raft. Its passenger was lying face down and shirtless. A dead man I thought to myself. The turn was far too wide to get us close, as the ship turned the other way, I was slammed into the side of the ship, and I nearly lost my grip.

The ship continued to slow, the raft came back into my line of sight. We approached closer, it was at least a 6 foot drop I was concerned that I might overturn the raft, I considered dropping into ocean next to it. "Jump!" Bill shouted.

Hesitated, and missed my chance to land on the raft, so I dropped into the water. It was cold, and I had to kick like a mad to get back to the surface. It was east to get to the edge of the raft, but I found it was too high in the water to reach the deck. It was a low rent craft of 55 gallon drums from lashed together with ropes, and deck of driftwood.

The darkness bellow me filled me with fear, I was sure I was being eyes by hungry sharks, I eventually found a rope loose enough I could force my finder underneath it. When I attempted to pull myself up, the weight of my body and legs pivoted up the raft instead of up.

My second attempt had the same results, I tried bushing off the bottom of the raft, but it was slick with algae. I heaved with all my might and managed to rise I a few inches out of the water, and then drop back down, my muscles shook with the effort. I know I did not have many attempts in my before I became weaker with fatigue.

I tried to get a foot up onto one of the roped, but it was just too far, I could not stretch far enough. The ship seemed far away, and I started to wonder if they would ever get me back, or if I was going to die clinging pathetically to the side of this raft.

I pushed myself down, until I was almost inverted under water, and managed to get the heel of my boot hooked on the raft. I paddled desperately to get a hold of the raft, eventually I did. Still only able to get four fingers under the rope, I have to grasp that wrist with my second hand and pull myself up. Once I could push off with my leg, I popped up, and landed on the deck like a fish.

The 'dead man' recoiled in fear, covering his eyes and babbling in a language I did not recognize. "It is ok." I said calmly. The guy smelled like a dead man to. I averted my watering eyes. "How long have you been out here?" He just shivered and mumbled.

I turned my attention to Bill who threw me a line, and we dragged the raft alongside the ship. It was quite a task to get it tied up, I know it could not handle our weight, and this guy was in no condition to climb a rope.

We tied a rope around him, and he was hauled up to the deck. I climbed up after, on the knotted roped. By the time I got to the deck the survivor has been taken below decks, hopefully for a shower.

The raft was brought on board, and we took to inspecting it. It had a bucket in the middle of the deck with some basic fishing gear, an empty canteen, a notebook and some pens. The driftwood of the craft was completely covered in writing, and sketches. There was a well-drawn nude women. A flag I did not recognize, that was divided into three horizontal fields, with a star in the middle. The lettering looked Russian to us.

We discovered the place where he had been ticking off his days at sea. "One hundred and twenty six" I said in amazement.

However he had come to be lost, he had already been lost for months when the War had started. "Boy is in for a surprise." Billy said with a smile.

"Should we hold him as POW?" Bill asked.

"I am not sure he is Russian." I said, thumbing through the notebook, "The writing does look Russian." There where sketches of dolphins, and the moon. All the sorts of thing I suppose one see when lost at sea.

"If we has been out there that long, how the hell did he get here?" Billy asked.

"Maybe he fell off his ship." Pedro said.

"Or he is a deserter." Billy supposed.

"I don't know." Bill said thoughtfully. "How many Russian ships are in the Caribbean?"

"Some, from Cuba. " I supposed.

"I thought they had mostly submarines." Billy said lifting up the sail.

"If he was from a sub he would have had to desert when they were in port." Bill ponder. "I guess Pedro might be right, he might have fallen off a ship."

Ahmed joined us, Billy asked him, "Is that guy a Russian, or what?"

Ahmed shook his head, "No my man, he is from Yugoslavia."

"Are they bad guys?" Pedro asked.

"Fuckin' commies, my man." Ahmed affirmed. "Bill bro, you want me to tie him up?"

"That fuckin' guy could barely move." I pointed out.

"What'd you give him to eat?" Bill asked.

"Water, and some broth." Ahmed said.

"Good, any more than that he'd just puke up. We can try to give him some meat once he gets re-hydrated. "Bill instructed.

"If you want to we can dump his Commie ass over the side." Ahmed offered.

"What about the law of the sea?" I asked somewhat amused, and a little off put.

"Fucking Commies, only think worse than a Yugo is a Greek." Ahmed spat.

"Fuckin' A." Billy Agreed, "We aint got enough food fer ourselves."

"No one is getting dumped over the fucking side." Bill said with finality, though the image in my head where of the three men we had already dumped. As if reading my thought Bill added, "Least not while they are alive."

"If we recovers we might need to keep an eye on him." I observed.

"Fuck that, we will spit the watch now, one person on the bridge, one watching Hugo the Yugo." Bill said coolly. I noticed that everyone had grown accustomed to following his orders, God knows I did not want to be in charge, nor did anyone else. Even Ahmed did not seem to mind, though he could have made a claim that this was his ship. I doubt any of us would have disagreed.

The next day I was on the bridge keeping the shore off to out left, while Ahmed was boiling water to get the salt to pack our next gator. Bill was with me looking along the shore for any sign of a good spot to stop and hunt.

"What is it you are looking for?" I asked making conversation.

"Another fresh water creek, Billy says Gator's like them. "

"He ought to know." I said actually enjoying steering the ship. "Thank God we have Davey Crocket." After I said it, I kind of cringed hoping Bill did not take it as an affront to his leadership.

He shot me a look. "How do you mean?"

"He seems a good hunter is all."

"Damn good shot with that Turkish rifle too." Bill smiled

"That thing has got to be eighty years old!" I said feeling

relieved.

"Look there!" Bill pointed. There was a small boy standing on the beach. Throwing a casting net into a stream flowed into the ocean. The stream was only about two yards wide. "Slow us down." Bill said as more of the stream came into view.

I brought us to ¼ speed, but initially nothing happened. The engine kept humming at near full power. I brought both engines to full power and back to ¼, still nothing happened. We looked at one another nervously.

"Try it again." Bill said.

I did, and the engines slowed. We breathed a sigh of relief. Ahmed came into the bridge. "Hey I think the throttle is sticking." I said.

He looked concerned, "I don't know, man."

"Can you keep an eye on the ship and Hugo while we go ashore?" Bill asked, probably thinking it was a rhetorical question.

"I don't know bro." Ahmed ran his fingers through his hair and looked away.

"Shit it is the same last time!" Bill snapped.

"It is a lot later in the day, how you gonna get back before dark?" Ahmed whined, "And I can't watch that fuckin' Slav!"

"Fine, Pedro will stay with you and babysit Hugo!" Bill slammed down the binoculars. "Come'on Bill, we are burning daylight!"

We threw our packs into the life boat, we had to drag Hugo's raft out of the way to get the boat back in the davit. Everything seemed to take forever.

We eventually got the boat in the water and headed for shore. As we rowed towards the beach the surf sped us along.

"Shit!" Billy yelled at me, "Careful we almost went over!" He and I each and an oar and where attempting to row in unison.

"Damn it!" Bill cursed. "Keep us steady, the rifles are not tied down!" He worked quickly to try and tie the rifles and packs to the side of the boat.

As we struggled several children in bright colored rags gather on the beach, pointing and waving.

"Into the mouth of creek!" Bill instructed, but once we got close the current flipped us around.

"Shit!" Billy said as we desperately struggled to right the boat. It was then we saw that the crowd on the beach had swelled to dozens of kids, a few in their teens. The little ones swam out to us.

Their little brown hands grabbed at everything in the boat. My pack went over the side, I reached for it, and a kid snatched the patrol cap off of my head. "Hey!"

One had Billy's big knife by the hilt. He leaned back to pull it away, the kid was dragged into the boat, one behind him had Billy's Mauser half out of the boat, when Billy kicked the first one in the chest sending him splashing back into the surf.

I grabbed my M16 out of the hands of two of them, as one tried to gouge my eye. Another hall pulled out my canteen as several tried to open my magazine pouch. Bill grabbed the eye gouger by one arm and one leg, flinging him. He threw punches into the masse that threatened to capsizes us.

There was a loud bang as the first rock struck the side of the boat. I did not see the rock that hit me, I fell into the bottom of the boat, my oar falling into the surf. A hundred little brown hands tore it away, as a treasure, I covered my head, as blood ran down my face, and Bill wrestled with the parachute cord he had lashed his M16 down with.

Billy tried to push is away with his oar. When Bill finally cut his rifle free He yanked the charging handle to the rear chambering a round. Snapping it up to his shoulder he fired a shot at one of the rock thrower, I could tell he was meaning to kill the little son of a bitch.

The rock throwers disappeared from sight, and we looked desperately for our gear. Everything that was not tied down was gone, as were all of our canteens and caps, one of our oars.

It was a struggle to row back out to the ship, the method we settled on was for Billy to his at the very tip of the bow and row like a canoe. I was feeling nauseous from the blow to the head, and the growing pool of blood and sea water I was sitting in.

"Hurry up, Pocahontas!" I said making fun of Billy's desperate attempt to get us moving.

"You just keep it up, shark bait!" He answered nervously.

Bill was in the back of the boat watching the beach nervously. "Seriously hurry up!"

"The damn tide is coming in!" Billy griped. "We are barely moving!"

It was true, if we did nothing we would wash ashore, and if we did not get to the ship soon it would be dark.

I looking longingly at the ship, it seemed to hover just beyond out reach. Even once we got clear of the breakers, the oceans swells grew ominous. They were well over six feet, when the first rain began to spatter.

By the time we were within a few hundred meters of the ship the waves where the size of houses, we rode up one side and down the other, the salt water burned the wound in my head and I began throwing up.

Bill bandit sling his rifle, and tried to give some kind of assistance to Billy who just kept repeating. "Hang on fellas!"

The icy rain picked up, and the boat seemed to be riding low in the water.

When we finally reached the side of the ship, I was worried we would be dashed against it. When Ahmed lowered the lines he seemed to plunge they much too far into the water. We were cursing his name as he fished the first one out attached it to the bow.

Bill lunged at the other line as a wave struck us and we were dumped into the sea, the boat rolling over completely. Billy and I righted the boat, but its gunnels where still six inches beneath the surface. The ship was a drifting further from us, and the lines started to be winched in.

"Attach the line!" I shouted to Bill who managed to attach the stern just before the lines went taut. Like a sea anchor the boat shuddered, I thought it might completely buckle, but as it rose from the water, where freed to swing to the side of ship like a hammer. Water exploded from the boat was the gunnel was smashed to splinters.

"Hold on, if you fall we'll never find you!" Bill warned.

The keel of the boat cracked, like a green tree and the middle sagged. I scrambled forward by Billy who was clinging to the forward line.

Water was still pouring out as we were hauled about the ship. With great joy we collapsed on the deck, which I unceremoniously decorated with blood and vomit.

Once the salt, and blood where washed off, we all sat in PT shorts, in the wardroom. It had not occurred to me that the loss of my pack meant I Was down to one set of BDUs. I still had 2 extra pair of socks and a T-shirt in my butt pack.

I sat uncomfortably in a chair as Bill, and Billy inspected the gash in my head. "I do not think it'll need stitches." Bill announced.

"I'd leave it to air out. Sooner it dries the better." Billy concerned.

Pedro same up from bellow looking scared.

"Damn it Pedro!" Bill barked, "What the fuck are you doing? You are supposed to be watching Hugo!"

"That's the problem." Pedro said nervously. "I need help."

We followed Pedro down into the ship leaving weapons, gear and uniforms strewn everywhere.

We got to the crew quarters door, and the sound of Hugo babbling filled the hallway. It was like one long run on sentence without tone or inflection. Bill slowly opened the door we peered in, the rack Hugo had been lying on was empty.

We found in naked, in the fetal position rocking back and forth. His eyes where as empty as a doll's eyes. He just rocked and babbled.

"What is the problem?" Bill asked annoyed.

"He is crazy." Pedro objected.

"So he is fucking crazy that is no reason to leave your post." Bill said angrily.

"What if…" Pedro struggled to explain his fear.

"Just shoot his ass." Billy answered annoyed.

"Yeah, you have an assault rifle, he is a naked starving Yugoslavian. Don't be a pussy." Bill said turning to go back up to the wardroom.

"When is my relief?" Pedro asked urgently.

"For Christ sake!" Bill turned crimson, "You get relieved when you get fucking relieved!"

"I have been in the dark with this crazy person all day!" Pedro said looking pathetic.

"And we nearly got eaten by your country fucking cousins!" Bill said storming off. "Double shift! You will get relieved at 2100!"

As we left, I was torn between being annoyed with Pedro and feeling sorry for him. We had nearly died a few times on that little jaunt, he stayed on the ship, and still had the stones to complain. On the other hand that crews quarters was like a tomb.

In a still damp uniform, I descended the stairs into the crew's quarters. It was silent, I opened the door slowly. Pedro sat in a strait backed chair with his rifle clutched. Hugo was crouched in the corner staring intently at Pedro.

"He wants to kill me." Pedro whispered.

"That is crazy." I said reassuringly.

"HE is crazy!" Pedro said. "Look at the way he looks at us!"

Hugo's eyes looked black as he peered at us, I had to give it to Pedro, and he did look menacing.

"You are relieved, man get some sleep." I said wishing he would stay.

He headed towards the door, I started to settle into the chair when Hugo sprang on him like a cat. I clumsily un-slung my rifle. I grabbed the charging handle, a yanked. It did not moved. I kicked Hugo in the ribs, he rolled off Pedro and bolted out the door.

Pedro and I tore after him shouting. He ran though the passageway, and up the stairs. "Look out!' We screamed.

He ran past the ward room to the open fly bridge aside where Bill was at the helm, without hesitating Hugo vaulted the rail, his spindly legs bicycling the air. He disappeared from our sight, until we reached the rail.

He landed with a thud on the steel deck 3 stories below. "What the fuck happen?" Bill said joining us.

"He jumped Pedro when we were doing shift change." I said.

"Why didn't you shoot him?" Bill asked annoyed.

"I could not chamber round." I said lamely.

"Let me see." Bill said taking my rifle. He tugged on the charging handle, it would not budge. He put the butt of the rifle on the deck and kicked the charging handle to the rear, it scraped back.

He inspected the weapon, bolt locked to the rear. "This weapons is fucking filthy!" He snapped throwing it back at me. "Now go check on your prisoner!"

Hugo was whimpering on the deck, his right leg bent at a horrible angle, his right arm clutched tightly to his chest. Ahmed and Bill joined us gathered around him.

"This guy is fucking done." Ahmed said coldly. "Throw his ass overboard."

"His leg is broken, maybe his arm to." I said feeling horribly guilty.

"Splint the arm, and the leg, and get him back in his hole." Bill ordered angrily.

"Fuck that, throw him out!" Ahmed protected.

Bill looked angrily at Ahmed, I tried to defuse the situation. "Pedro you watch him. I will get the back board from the bridge, we can splint him up on the table in the wardroom."

Getting Hugo put back together and put back into the crew quarters took until around midnight. I lay on the floor of the wardroom, Hugo screams from when I straitened his broken leg seemed to still echo.

The dark constellations on the ceiling and the walls where a mute reminder of the Captain's passing in the same room. The hum of the engine was comforting, the damp poncho linger smelled slightly moldy, I was just happy I had kept it in my butt pack and not my

ALICE pack. Otherwise those little savages that took my pack would have it. In my mind's eye I imagined them all gathered around a fire in a Lord of Flies post civilization, though realistically the entire village was probably right around the corner.

In my dreams distant screams echoed, with angry voices and soft heavy garbage rained onto the roof of my boyhood home. I awoke in the dark, half expecting to be in my bed at home, like a 'scenes from a previous episode' on a TV show it all came rushing back to me, the Army, Panama, the bars, the war, the teaming masses of children, broken boned Hugo. Those sounds continued.

The sun was coming up through a haze that painted the sky blood red. Sweat soaked, Billy came up from below. He was about to make an excuse for leaving his post, Bill silenced him with a wave as he stepped outside.

We followed awestruck.

Beneath the blood red sky was a writhing sea black sea. Our wake cut through an endless field of debris. Trees ripped up by the root, charred black. Bits of furniture, park benches, a mail box, all bobbed hopelessly in the black water. The black sea between the refuse seemed to boil ghostly apparitions of bloated white corpses fed an armada of prowling sharks.

Several birds perched on a floating couch eyed us as we passed. It seemed endless, finally, I managed to say, "What in the name of God?"

"Ships wreak?" Pedro asked.

"No, a city." Bill said. "Nuked"

"Can we just go through it?" I asked.

"God no!" Bill said, snapped out of his shock, "Ahmed, turn us around!"

Are the ship came about our bow cut through all manner of horrors. Men, women, children, even animals intermingled with everything from tires to plastic bags. Everywhere the sharks feasted.

"I never imagined there were so damn many sharks in the Caribbean." I observed.

"Unlimited food supply." Billy said.

"Yeah, when the Iran and Iraq war started the Sharks in the Persian Gulf started multiplying like rabbits, feeding on the dead and dying." Bill agreed.

"It looks like the whole city of Miami is in there." Pedro said.

We headed back South for an hour before the water turned blue again. Bill ordered us into the Wardroom.

"Look guys." He said dejectedly. "I have let you down. We have been letting our discipline slip. That could have gotten some us killed yesterday. We need to keep our weapons clean, and close at hand at all times." We all nodded in agreement.

The engines stopped, we all looked at one another wide eyed. I ran to the Bridge, with the others right behind me. Ahmed kept cycling the helm to full speed, but nothing happened. He jammed a button on the intercom and shouted in Turkish. Back and forth he did this, panic in his eyes.

"Ahmed?" Bill said calmingly. "What is up?"

He just looked terrified. "They won't answer, they won't say anything!"

"Calm down. " Bill said. "I will do down there with you. He gestured for me to follow.

We descended into the bowels of the ship. It suddenly seemed cavernous. The lights were out, but the red back up lights showed the way giving the place a surreal look. In absence of the engine noise, the sound of the rats seemed everywhere.

At length we reached the stern of the ship. An unremarkable watertight door stood before us. Taking a deep breath, Ahmed screwed up his courage, and attempted to lift the handle. It did not move.

We tried all three of us at once lifting it and it did not budge.

Ahmed took a wrench from a nearby locket and pounded on the hatch.

Only silence answered. He beat the door paint chip flew, but no impact on the structure was made. "Wait!" Bill said finally taking the wrench. "Listen!" He struck the top of the hatch, then again at the bottom. "Hear that?"

He did it again, at the bottom it sounded like he was hitting something solid. "It's flooded." He observed. Tapping his way up the hatch to find the level of the flooding.

It was about chest deep, high enough to flood the engines. We knew the snipes must be dead, though God only knew how long they had been.

We all say stone faced around the table in the wardroom, Ataturk glared down at us from his blood spattered frame. Ahmed came in late, carrying a bottle of clear booze. I slammed it down on the table.

"What!" He said charging over to the cabinet and coming back with 5 glasses.

"We need a plan." Bill said ominously.

Ahmed was pouring a small about of the clear booze into each glass. "First, we must drink a toast. "

Billy smiled, "Hell yeah!"

"To Mustafa Kemal Ataturk and the great Turkish State he built!" Ahmed said raising his glass to the portrait.

We all politely followed suit, I almost puked. It was awful stuff.

"What they hell is this?" I asked.

"Raaki." Ahmed said pouring everyone another drink. "Official Turkish drink!"

"I thought Mohamadens where not supposed to drink." Billy said looking green.

"Ah non-sense!" Ahmed said joyfully. "The lousy Greeks try to copy us, with Uzo, but Raaki is the real deal, my man!" He took a drink, "And it is not Mohamaden's it is Moslems. Turkey was the Center of Moslem world for hundreds of years from right after the death of the Prophet Mohamed to the First World War." He took a drink, "We used to follow all that religious mumbo-jumbo, and we went from the world leaders to backwards shit holes." I gestured to Ataturk, "Then General Mustafa Kemal, beat the British Army in the Dardanelles, and overthrew those old fucking witch doctors. He said he would drag Turkey into the twentieth century if he had to drag it by the beard!"

Billy laughed, "Is it true you can have a bunch of wives?"

Ahmed laughed, "Turkey is a modern country! We do not do all that shit. That is what the fucking Arabs do, and only the most backwards ones of them!"

"But, it is allowed?" Bill asked, sipping his Raaki, and obviously regretting it immediately.

"No! That was allowed under the Empire, but under the Republic. It was one of the old Islamic teachings. The Prophet

Mohammed had over four hundred wives. "

"That's Crazy!" Billy said lightly.

"Ha! You think that is crazy? Christians believe in how many Gods?"

"Well, just one." Billy said looking a little nervous.

'Jesus?" Ahmed asked.

"Yeah!" Billy said taking a sip, and shuddering.

"You tell me, the Father, the Son, and the Holy Ghost, are just one dude! Sounds like three to me. Now that my bro, is crazy" Ahmed said downing his glass.

"Alright, guys this is interesting stuff, but we need to get to the fucking point." Bill intervened. "What are going to do now?"

"Don't you know bro?" Ahmed said with a smile. "We are all gonna fucking die."

Pedro looked dejected and downed his Raaki, without a shudder, he clearly believed Ahmed was right. In my gut I thought he might be.

"No we are not." Bill said sternly.

"We are drifting, without a compass, or engines, we do not know where we are, other that South of a radioactive fuckin' thing!" Ahmed said almost angrily.

"How for North did we get?" Bill asked.

"I dunno maybe north of Yucatan, maybe not, what difference does it make?"

"We could rig a sail." Billy said hopefully.

"What if we did?" Ahmed asked. "If not and we turn East and we are not far enough North bam! Cuba! Besides if we lose sight of the shore, we could go in fucking circles."

"Can't you navigate by the stars?" I asked.

"What the fuck am I Vasco De Gamma, I am the fucking cook!"

"Jesus Christ!" Bill slammed the table, "I can find the North fucking star!"

Ahmed looked hurt. "Hey my man…" He started, and then just looked distant. "What if I am the last one left?"

"The last what?" I asked.

"The last…" He got kind of misty eyed and looked up at Ataturk.

"You're not." I reassured him, with no basis in fact.

"Ahmed," Bill leaned toward him. "I do not know what is left of

Turkey, or America for that matter, and you know what? You might

be right, maybe we are all gonna die. But we have a responsibility

try. What He want you to do?" He pointed towards the Ataturk.

A rat scurried across the passageway. "Man, those little fuckers

are getting' Ballsy!" Billy observed.

Bill and I made eye contact with the same thought, "Hugo!"

I ran down the stairs nightmare visions of what I would find

flashing through my mind. I stumbled down the stairs, my feet

nearly slide out from underneath me. I grabbed the door handle,

when the light fell on Hugo he was still strapped to the backboard as

we had left him, set on a rack. He looked up at me and smiled.

I breathed a sigh of relief, as my feet grew cold, water was

soaking through my boots. I looked in horror as I realized there

lower passageway was flooded, my stomach knotted. Like a neon

sign the word flashed in my head, 'sinking'.

Soon that monstrous sea would swallow us all! I ran up the

stairs almost too panicked to speak. Ahmed and Billy worked to get

the lifeboat ready to sail, they fashioned a mast from the surviving

ore or the other life boat, and a boom from her keel. They had Pedro tearing apart one of the motors from the portside davit, Bill figured we could use the long copper wires as lines to sew the sail, and to fish with. I did not realize there was that much copper wire spooled up in an electric motor, but I was never that mechanical.

I grabbed what food and water we had and brought it up to the lifeboat. The aft end of the ship had begun to ride lower than the front. I brought up our improvised fishing gear, and the mercifully sealed buckets of monkey bait.

"Get the flags and sheets for sails." Bill said, then looked to Ahmed, "No Offense."

Ahmed laughed, "Ataturk would approve!"

As I ran back and forth I kept an eye on the rising water, it was not flooding in, but it was not stopping either. An hour after I had noticed it the water reached the second step on the stairs.

When I ran back to the aft end of the ship to secure the Liberian flag, my eyes searched the sea around us of those darting shadows. Those man eaters that would forever haunt return to my thought anytime I saw black water.

I shook myself and took down the Liberian Colors, as I climbed back to the lifeboat. The mast seemed steady enough, the broad portion of the ore providing amble area to nail it to the addition wood nailed to the middle row of seats. Getting the boom to attach and still be able to rotate 360 degrees was proving an engineering problem.

"We need is steel ring!" Billy insisted.

"We don't have one!" Bill answered angrily. "Work with what we have!"

I looked at the parts of the motor, I picked up a quarter of a circle of heavy metal, there were number of them strewn around. "Can we use these, they are about a quarter of a circle each?"

Bill looked at me amazed, "Holy shit!"

Ahmed laughed and rushed over. "Shit man! Do you know what that is?"

I felt stupid, "No."

"That is the fucking magneto from the engine!"

Bill clapped a hand on my shoulder, "Bill if we make it out of this it is going to be because you found us a damned compass!"

The compass ended up being a plastic mixing bowl, a quarter of the way filled with water. Floating in it was a smaller bowl with two magnetos in it, and a wooden ruler with 'N' written in marker in it. Bill insisted we seal both bowls, though the Tupperware top made it a little hard to read.

We nailed a few sealable buckets to the side of the boat to store food and gear in, Ahmed insisted we had to expect the boat to capsize from time to time, as we did not have a running board, so we had better make sure everything was secured accordingly.

We place the compass by the rudder, Billy fashioned out or parts of a chair. The boom   ended up being held on with ropes, it was able to go a little short of 45 degrees in each direction, less than ideal.

It had been several hours and our sails where not made, yet. When I went to check on the water it was half way up the stairs, and rising faster. The ship was leaning a lot heavier to the rear. I worried we were going to do down ass first. I was about to tell the others when it hit me, yet again. "Hugo!"

I headed, back down into the ship, "Pedro, give me a hand!"

Based on the urgency in my voice Pedro came running.

"What's up?"

"Hugo we have got to go get him." I said wading into the water it was cold, and the red light made it black, and horrible. I has to remind myself that there was nothing in this water, but my heart pounded anyway.

The door was slow to open, as the water slowed it was I opened the door. Hugo lay on the back board, water inches below him, it appeared sleeping. "Come on Pedro, get his feet."

We struggled to get him up to the top deck where the life boat was still being prepared. I thought Bill and Ahmed where off their heads when they started using some kind of epoxy glue to stick the compass to the deck by the rudder, and then started gluing everything they had nailed.

"Billy, get the rest of the Mausers and the Ammo, plus whatever tools you can find. " Bill ordered, then he looked at Pedro and I confused. "What the hell did you bring him for?" Gesturing to Hugo.

"That guy is gonna die." Ahmed observed without looking away from his work.

I looked at Hugo, is leg was swollen and purple, it was probably infected, and his arm was not much better. Ahmed was right. "Still we cannot just leave him."

"Put him back in his own fuckin' raft bro!" Ahmed suggested.

Billy came up, his arms loaded with rifles and ammunition, "Seven rifles, and damn near 300 rounds of ammo!"

"We are running out of room." Bill said concerned.

"Well, we are going to need the ammo, if that last stop is anything like what we are going to see for hospitality!" Billy insisted.

"We can't take food out!" Pedro objected.

"The Water is the most important thing, man." Ahmed pointed out.

"You know what do not need?" Bill pointed to Hugo, "A dying man."

I walked away, I was angry, and I wished I could come up with a good reason. He WAS dying, but so where we all. He was worse than useless, but something about this whole thing made me sick.

I walked over to Hugo's raft, we had emptied the cargo bucket, I had his journal in my butt pack, and I thought perhaps I should give it back to him. I looked over at him. His eyes where rolled back in his head, I knew he would never use it.

I unstrapped him from the backboard, if only to get the vision of the damn thing floating upside in the water that my imagination had conjured up to go away. The angle of the deck was starting to get uncomfortable.

"We need to lower the boat, before the ship sinks." Bill announced.

"No power to the davit, my man." Ahmed said rubbing his stubbly chin.

"If we just let 'er drop she will tip over." Billy observed.

"Can we just lower it to the deck?" I asked.

"We are going to have to." Bill said.

We tried to get it free of the Davit, but as the bottom of the boat was not flat it rested at an awkward angle. Pedro and Ahmed got the sails attached. The Liberian flag was folded into a triangle shape, and 'sewn' with wire. It attached to bow of the boat and the top of the mast.

The main sail, consisting of two Turkish flags and some sheeting, was also triangular but it had the boom running through the bottom edge of it. Ahmed and Billy worked out a few places in the gunnels to drive ten penny nails, to route the lines through. I could not picture what they were doing at the time, but I would learn soon enough.

The ship started to shudder, as the bow got higher, and the aft end sank lower. A horrible hiss filled the air, it was the grain shifting rearward. I had always thought the upper deck where on was flush with the back of the ship, but no that it mattered I realized there was at least ten feet difference.   To my horror we realized that when the ship was vertical we would still be ten or twenty feet above the water!

"Brace the boat!' Bill shouted, and we all grabbed the boat, all except Hugo who was lounging on the deck, his good elbow underneath him watching us amused. "The longer we hold it on here the less it is going to fall. Pedro, make sure everything is tied down!"

It started to slide, Hugo's raft stayed in place, out heels slid along the steel deck, by dropping to our knees we stopped it briefly.

"Don't be in front of it when it goes!" Billy warned.

As the boat slid after first over the side, my stomach dropped to. There was just enough space for it to land mast down. I jumped, it seemed a long fall before I hit the water, Bill and Billy where already trying to right the boat. Hugo stood on his one good leg, grasping the railing laughing hysterically at us.

We got the boat on its side, but it would not budge. The sails where holding way too much water. Ahmed and Pedro swam to the other side and lowered the sails. Once that was done we were able to right it, but was full of water. Clinging desperately to the side we decided Pedro, being smallest would go in first.

We pulled on the gunnel until it looked like she might capsize again.

"Bail damn it!" Bill shouted.

"What do I bail with?"

"I don't fucking know!" Bill shot back.

"Use you patrol cap!" I suggested, as chills ran down my spine.

Pedro was the only one who still had his patrol cap, since he was not with us on the failed hunting party, where we lost everything not nailed down.

One by one we all climbed on board. Bailing with our hands, it was no longer before the water was just below our knees.

"We need to get the hell away from that!" Bill said as the ship towered over us.

Billy and I padded backwards, Hugo came back into view, still clinging to the rail, his raft slid off the back of the ship, and landed right side up. He squinted at use, as if trying to comprehend what he was seeing.

The water reached Hugo's feet and he stared down at it. He casually started to breast stroke towards his rafter. Though one are, and one leg where splinted, he sank quickly. His forward momentum continued as he disappeared beneath the waves. We all looked over to the raft expecting him to climb out onto it. It was about a twenty meter swim.

Hugo never re-appeared. The ship slid quietly into the deep leaving a slick of oil, trash and desperately swimming rats.

I looked around nervously, in every direction there was nothing but a hazy blue sky, and the endless blue sea.

There was barely room for all five of use on the boat, it was a delicate maneuver to hoist the sails without capsizing again.

Once they were up, we stare and those handing there soaking wet. Nothing happened.

Ahmed pulled the Liberian flag in the front taut, then tried moving the boom, back and forth. We simply bobbed there, helpless.

"Well." Bill said finally "I guess we row."

Billy centered himself on the ores and watered rowing. Bill centered us dead East. It was at that moment, I was sure we would all be joining Hugo in the dark depths.

After about half an hour, I took my turn rowing. I blistered my hands and my back ached. My neck and head where already burned. I removed my t-shirt and but it around my head, everyone but Pedro and Ahmed followed suite. Pedro still had his patrol cap, and Ahmed just opted to go bare headed.

It was at the end of my second shift when the heat finally abated,

I was enjoying the breeze mindlessly when Ahmed suddenly grabbed the line for the Liberian sail. He routed it one of the nails in the gunnel and it bowed with the wind.

We pushed the boom off to the left and the wind caught the Turkish sail, the boat tipped precariously Ahmed let the sail go. The boom flew out, and snapped back cracking Billy in the head. He cursed, as Ahmed got control of the line.

"Let me see that." Bill said taking the line. We turned us with the wind, and then backed it off until the sail failed. Though we leaned towards it, he was able to keep us upright as everyone threw their body weight away from the dipping gunnel.

I pulled in the oars. We were moving forward under wind power! We cheered with joy just before the boat overturned again.

It was amid angry curses we set the boat right, and though we were able to catch the wind. Most of us where grumbling as we bailed out the boat again. I discovered that though my canteens has been stolen, I still hand my canteen cup jammed it my canteen pouch. It made for much easier bailing. But the time we got down to ankle the sky was blood red again, as the sun seemed to sink into the sea.

I looked into the darkening waters, and I thought of poor Hugo, the blind mice, and all those nameless bodies. Like the sailors hundreds of years ago, the sea was no longer the fantastic undersea world of Jacques Cousteau, instead it was a dark and nightmarish alien world where unseen terrors waited to tear our flesh and feast on us.

Creature erupted from the sea startling me from my thoughts. My heart pounded as a pair of dorsal fins passed within feet of the boat.

"Shark!" Pedro said.

"Two of 'em." Billy said calmly.

They cut across out bow as it plowed through that water. I wondered if they intended to ram us. My eyes darted around for my rifle. It was tied to the gunnel a few from my knees.

Ahmed, laughed, as the dolphins darted past us, and playfully leapt from the water, landing with a splash on it's back, disappearing again. I felt as if the boat suddenly rode higher in the water, as though our lifting spirits made us weigh less.

When the dolphins disappeared, they were missed. We all watched silently for their return. The darkness enveloped us, the clouds churned in the sky, with only occasional stars peeking through.

The wake and the waves, sparked in the dark. My neck and shoulder burned, with the after effects of sunburn. I began to shiver. I had, not been dry for hours. I pulled the poncho liner from my butt packed and wrapped myself up in it.

The damn cool of the evening settled in on us. Soon we were all shivering. Bill sat clutching the tiller, eyes fixed on the sails, it brought the now deceased skipper of the Turkish ship disturbingly to mind. It occurred to me that I did not know the name of our former vessel. I resolved to ask Ahmed in the morning.

Looking at the ash heavy clouds, my mind wandered to that sunken wreck that had been our home. It had liberated us from the Panamanian jungle, and brought us here. Somewhere beneath the waves Ataturk looked over that wardroom table. Where his Captain had blown out his brains after a whispered apology to the Father of all Turks for failing to bring the ship home. What did he see now, darkness, did the man eaters now glide through that ship, or did the lesser denizens of the deep shelter there as we had?

What of our buddies back on shore? Had they found the First Sergeant's jungle fortress? Had the mass of Panamanians found them? What had been the outcome? A steaming jungle Alamo? Or had the survivors of the assault staggered back to town spreading tales of the white devils on the mountain, where rained death on all who dared tread on their territory? Somehow I knew it was the latter, or would be if they were ever challenged.

What, I pondered lay ahead? My lips where dry, I had not eaten or drank all day, but I did not want to move from the relative warms of my position. We were moving forward, but God only knew how fast. There horrors of the black water to the North, if we drifted too far South an entire armed Nation of Cuban with whom we were presumptively at War. The middle path, if taken to precisely could have use blindly sailing between Florida and Cuba strait into the endless Atlantic. That thought to disappear into the endless blue, ever seeing land again until our sun bleached bones ran aground on the African coast, that frightened me most of all.

These where the thoughts that carried me to sleep, that first night on the boat. When I awoke, Billy was relieving Bill at the tiller. The sun was just peering over the horizon. I drank some water from a jug we had tied near me. Hunger pangs stabbed at me. I took some salted gator and chewed in for a while. It was like eating salted rubber.

The heat came quickly, and we damp clothes where almost painful against my skin. The morning wore slowly on. Around noon, Billy pulled out a fishing hook and some line that we had salvaged from Hugo's raft when he cracked open the bucket on monkey meat the stench was awful. Ahmed vomited over the side of the boat. Pedro looked green, and I felt ill.

Billy's eyes watered "Jesus! That is ripe!" He gathered some sea water in the bucket to try to keep the smell down. After that he baited his hook and threw it over the side. He slowly let the line out as it drifted away. Eventually he tied the line to the bucket and watched it intently.

The smell slowly dissipated, but Ahmed still looked haggard. "Take it easy on the water." Bill instructed as I took another sip.

I just nodded. I pulled out the notebook that I had requisitioned from Hugo's raft, and started making notes about what had happened to date. The Polaroid photo of Bill and I with the pissing monkey was my book mark.

As I thumbed through Hugo's un-intelligible notes, I paused on the drawings. The dolphins, the birds, the stars, I was envious of the starts. He had drawn the sky full of glimmering stars, and a massive moon. Free of the death shroud we can become accustomed to. It occurred to be that the black water, and the blood sky where the same. Millions of human beings, and centuries of progress reduced to dust and ash.

Hugo never knew. Or did he? Had he seen the war from his little raft? What had he thought was going on? What did he think of us? Where we angels, or demons?

That, I guessed, I would never know.

The sun slowly crawled across the sky. It was maddeningly slow, as I felt my skin burning. I had the sleeves rolled down on my unbuttoned BDU jacket, and a t-shirt over my head, Arab style, but still I burned.

When the sky turned red and the evening breeze picked up, so did out speed. I lay on my back, with my feet up on the bench. My back ached from sitting all day and night. I knees hurt, as I looked up into the darkening sky. How many day of this could we endure?

It was that night, the monkey bucket got dumped and turned into the mobile latrine. We had to pass it up to Ahmed, who was sick. We tried not to notice him precariously perched over the bucket.

That night I could not sleep as I listened to Ahmed, curled up in the fetal position, moaning. I say up, looking around at the endless horizon. Bill was back at the tiller. Billy was snoring beside him.

Pedro's night terror came at about the normal time, but did not last long.

I watched with dread as the torturous sun climbed above the horizon to beat on us.

By noon my head was pounding and I was dizzy. I felt nauseous. I knew I had to try to drink water, and to keep it down.

Based on the smell Ahmed, was not making it to the bucket anymore. He just lay there mumbling and moaning. Around noon he vomited blood inside the boat.   We all looked at each other too exhausted, to even think of what to do.

No one looked at Ahmed, except Pedro who was right next to him.

"You are not going to die." Pedro re-assured him. "You cannot let the last Turk die."

"I am not a Turk." Ahmed said pathetically. "My Mother was a Turk."

"So, what?" Pedro asked sympathetically.

"My Father was an Arab." He cough seeming to choke on that last word.

"What about your ship?" Pedro tried to encourage him.

"My Uncle let me be the cook. It was a disgrace that is why I am still a cook. No one wanted…" He faded off. "Hated me. All of them." His eyes rolled back in his head, I thought he had died, but I was wrong.

We reached the bottom of the jug of water that afternoon. We passed it around, and everyone got a last swing, Pedro tried to give Ahmed some, but he just choked on it.

"How many more gallons of water do we have?" Bill asked not taking his eyes off the sails.

We were down to five.

"Not more than half a gallon a day." Bill said un-emotionally. "We all take a drink when the sun comes up, at noon, and when it goes down."

No one argued, though I thought to myself, that is not nearly enough. It would get us 10 day, if all things where equal.

The next few says maddeningly the same. Blisters formed on my nose and the back of my hands. We barely moved, the few gulps of water we had where all we had to look forward to. We still had food, but as dehydrated as we where no one eat for than a handful. The notes I took in my book where not more than a line.

It is only because of that notebook that I know it was late night on the eight day when we saw the flickering light off the starboard bow. We turned towards it.

Over the hour it took for us to close we could see it was a fire. A shoreline rose up out of the sea. The sun rose through lush trees. The sound of surf on the beach was music to our ears. A thatch hut with plastic furniture came into view. A beach fire was still smoking beside it.

"Break out the rifles." Bill ordered as we approached the beach. It was clumsy work but we unlashed our weapons. "If anyone asks we are ship wreaked from a freighter, got it?" We all agreed excitedly. "This surf could get tricky, Bill and Pedro, you just out when it is shallow enough and walk us in, let's not dump this bitch again."

I gingerly stepped out of the boat into chest deep water, holding my rifle over my head with one hand and holding the boat with the other. The water was refreshing, and we were all thrilled for a change to our seemingly endless voyage.

"OK Pedro, it your turn to shine!" Bill said happily. Billy was hefting is Turkish Mauser, peering onto the beach for trouble.

As the water got shallower, the surf got rougher. We were still able to beach the boat without tipping over. "Billy you stay with Ahmed." Bill said checking to ensure there was a round in the chamber of his M16.

I did the same, and splashed ashore. There where plastic chairs and tables, but no one seemed to be around. As we headed up the beach, I started to get nervous. I stepped into the area under the thatched awning. The floor was just sand. The whole thing seemed just sitting on the sand with no foundation.

I peered into the hut, there was more furniture, and a bamboo bar, behind which there were two young women, and a monkey. The girls where roughly 13 and 15 years old, they smiled at me, exposing many missing teeth. The monkey stood on a perch made of an old coat rack, and paid us not attention. One of the girls reached under the bar and came up with a liter sided beer covered in sand.

"Cervesa?" She asked.

I lowered by rifle and smiled. Within moments we were drinking cool beer in the shade like it was the old day. I ran out to the boat with two beers under my arm. One for Billy and one for Ahmed.

Pedro was chattering back and forth with the girls in Spanish. For five US dollars they sold us a case of beer, all being cooled by being buried in the sand floor. They did not have any water, or food, but offered to get some. I was ready to send them running, but Bill wisely thought better of it.

They giggled at our antics as we lounged like conquering heroes. Ahmed sat in the shade of the boat sipping his beer. We told ourselves it was liquid bread, though our heads where swimming.

Bill and I started exploring the beach, about a half a mile from the hut we found a town. It was really only obscured from the hut by a grove of trees. The buildings where stout, and pained a sickly green. There were a lot of cars parked along the sides of the street, but none where moving.

"Look at these cars!" Bill wondered, "They are all worth a fortune!"

He was right, they were all classics, and some with tail fins other that looked like John Dillinger had just parked it there to run into the store for a pack of smokes. "There is not one of them from after,

"Then the chill set into my bones. "Nineteen Sixty."

"Holy shit," Bill whispered, "We are in Cuba!"

We looked around, at the ghost town. "Where the hell is

everyone?" I asked.

I do not know, but let's get the hell out of here!" Bill said, our still legged walk turned into a run.

The guys on the beach seemed unperturbed by out sprint except for Billy how grabbed his rifle and sighted in on the tree line behind us.

"Let's Go!" Bill gasped. "We're in, Cuba!"

Pedro ran to the hut.

"Get back here Pedro!" Bill shouted.

Billy and I started pushing the boat into the surf. Bill boosted Ahmed into the boat. Pedro came running out of the hut hugging a number of the giant beer bottles.

We wrestled the boat until it was floating again. The two girls where on the beach waving goodbye. When we had everyone on board, with the bottles of beers rolling around on the deck, and the teenagers waving goodbye we call started to laugh at our own panic.

"I guess it is time to turn North East." Bill said smiling. Our sails where full, and we were suddenly feeling very alive, even Ahmed was sitting up.

The first Patrol Boat charged into view, and our good mood evaporated. It was barreling in on us from South West, a second appeared in its' wake. Suddenly it seemed like we were standing still.

I saw the muzzle flash from the lead boat before I realized what it was. A half a dozen jets of water erupted in front of our boat. Moments later the sound of a heavy machinegun fire caught up with us.

"Shit!" Bill looked back for the next burst. "How far away are they?"

"That was a click at least!" Billy answered fiddling with the sights on his Mauser. "When they get to within five hundred meters, open up on full auto."

Billy fire a single shot with his rifle and worked the bolt. Pedro opened up and emptied 30 rounds at the boat. "Not yet!" Billy shouted. The boat turn away and fired another burst churning the water to our left side. "Shit, he is staying out of the range!"

The second boat ducked in too close, Bill and I opened fire, and it turned directly away. Billy drew careful aim. As the boat was headed directly away he was able to hit it directly in the ass from about 800 meters. Black smoke poured from the Patrol Boat and it cruised to a glide.

The second boat fired another burst the rounds cracked overhead. The impacts where close enough to soak us with the splash. We reloaded as the boat prepared to close in for the kill.

Billy drew a bead on the boat as it turned away, but held his fire. The boat pulled alongside the second patrol boat, to render air. He kept aimed in, and Bill got us sailing again.

It seemed like an eternity, as no one shot. "Why don't you shoot?" Pedro asked.

"So he won't." Billy said sensibly, and with that the Cuban boats slowly faded from sight.

That night we were feeling ten feet tall. The night was darker than before, and I grew worried we would head back into the black water, as easy as this boat was to capsize I had images in my head of being torn apart my sharks, or less rationally pulled to the depth of the sea by bloated dead hands. These things kept me from sleep that night, even as I glanced backwards for Cuban Navy pursuers.

As the sky seemed to catch fire and turn blood red with the morning light looming before as was a dark could, a wall of soot and ash, it had to be the black water, we held our breath as we gingerly turned eastward, and trimmed our sails.

When we did not capsize, we all breathed a sigh of relief. Ahmed seemed better, he was sitting up, and though he looked haggard, we all did.

It was before mid-day when we spotted another boat. A fishing boat between us and the cloud. Its engines where not running but it did not appear to be in any kind of distress. An hour later we spotted buildings off to our left. We edged closer to the dark in order to head towards them.

The water became shallow, and turquoise we cruised outside of the surf zone, and along the beach. We came to a harbor with a beach to the right, and another river to the right of that, not knowing channel markers, or any of that other sailing stuff, we opted to beach between the two.

The beach was only about 500 feet across, we pulled the boat ashore, the same as we did in last time. Ahmed and Billy found some shade by the boat and cracked a beer. It was strange behind us was the turquoises sea and the white beach, ominously close ahead was the towering wall of black.

Bill and I edged to the right, weapons at the ready, and Pedro trailing behind us. We came through a thin grove of trees and found ourselves on a two lane paved road. We turned right and headed in land through and abandoned industrial area, after several hundred yards we came to some a hand full of small boats docked to our right and a place called the Shrimp Shack.

We walked around the Shrimp Shack and found a number of people selling fish laid out on tables and newspapers between their and the next building called the Hogfish Bar and Grill. We stumbled into this open air fish market looking like anything but American soldiers, our uniforms hung off us. Bill and I had T-shirts on our heads. I was the only one with a BDU jacket, and that was not buttoned. Pedro had the only patrol cap, but he and Bill where stripped down to their T-shirt, None, of our boots where bloused, every last bit of polish was worn off our boots, and we all straggly beards.

"Sling arms." Bill said quietly as the fish mongers eyed us nervously. We put our weapons on our back and walked between the fish sellers, though it smelled awful, I was suddenly starved.

Bill spoke to the nearest fish monger who was a nearly naked black kid, of maybe twelve years old. "Hey buddy, where can a guy get something to eat around here?"

He smiled, and pointed Hogfih Bar and Grill, with a look that said I was probably the dumbest person he had ever met.

We walked into the bar, it was dark, but looked like a standard beach bar, with plastic fish, next, and nautical junk on the wall. In the corner a black man in a pair of brightly colored jams shorts was playing a steel drum, I recognized the song as being by the Kinks. He was singing;

I don't feel safe in this world

No more don't want to die

in a nuclear war.

I want to sail away to

a distant shore

And make like an APEMAN.

A round faced man with an unlighted cigar in his mouth, and a crew cut gave us a cross eyed look. "Holy Shit, Robinson Crusoe if that you?" He limped up to us, eyes us spuriously but remaining very gregarious. "Where is Friday?" His eyes fell on me, "Holy Shit! Troops?" I realized I was the only one with any insignia identified us as Army troops "Where did you guys come from?"

"Panama." I answered coolly. We whistled and rolled his eyes thoughtfully.

I'm an APEMAN

I'm an APE

APE MAN

I'm an APE MAN.

I'm a king-kong man

I'm a voodoo man

Oh , I'm a APE MAN.

"Shit boys! Grab a seat!" He gestured to a table. "Jean get these boys some beer!"

"Water." Bill added quietly.

"And water!" He shouted, turning a chair around and shook each of our hands in turn Scott Thompson, I a P3 driver, or was anyway."

We all settled into chairs.

"So you are in the Air Force?" Bill asked.

"Navy." He said. "Jean get these guys some steaks, but it on my tab."

My stomach did a back flip.

"I have two more guys guarding our boat." Bill said humbly.

"No worries!" Scott smiled, "And two to go!" We all looked at each other awkwardly as the waiter brought a pitcher of beer and a pitcher of beer. The singer continued.

But give me half a chance

and I'd be taking of my clothes

and living in the jungle.

But the only time that

I feel at ease

Swinging up and down in a coconut tree.

Oh, what a life of luxury to be like an APE MAN.

I'm an APE MAN

I'm an APE

APE MAN

Oh I'm an APE MAN.

I'm a king-kong man

I'm a voodoo man

Oh I'm a Ape MAN.

"So boys, how did you come to get here?" Scott asked, sounding for the first time like an Officer.

"Well sir," Bill began, but Scot interrupted him with a wave."

"My name is Scott, or my call sign is Chunk." He said pouring a beer.

"We hitched a ride on a Turkish freighter, but the bitch sank on us, so we have been sailing in lifeboat for about a week. " Bill said matter of factly.   It sounded so simply, and easy when you laid it out like that.

"Sir," I asked "What the fuck HAPPENED?" I asked suddenly

realizing that he might know a lot more than we did.

"All we knew was the light went out and the rest of the world seemed to disappear." Bill said quietly. Almost apologetically, perhaps worried we might be in trouble for leaving Panama.

"Well you know we got nuked?" He said calmly.

We nodded dumbly. "How did it start?" Pedro asked.

Scott sighed. "No one will ever know for sure. They went on alert when we started an Exercise called Able Archer in Germany. A couple days later 3 Mig-25s penetrated West German Airspace and where shot down."

"Why the fuck would they DO that?" Bill said angrily.

"Well." Scott leaned back. "They were on the third day of their alert, my guess is they lead pilot fell asleep. His wingmen probably were told not to break radio silence." He saw we could not believe it. "Seriously, when I was in flight school , I fell asleep at the controls of a T-28 over Alabama, and woke up over Texas, and my flight instructor was in the plane with me, and he had fallen asleep too! The Foxbat is the fasted fighter in the world, if the guy drifted off he probably did not know what the fuck was going on until he was getting shot down. "

Scott looked around to see how Jean was coming with the food.
"Then they rolled their ground forces out, and that damned
Lufthansa jet got shot down.   They called up their Reserves, we
tried to de-escalate by NOT calling out our Guard and Reserves, but
they just assumed that meant we were going to go for a nuclear
knockout. "

Scott paused sadly and downed his beer. "We do not know why.
I think they had some kind of a system failure and one of their
regional commands lost contact with everyone else, assuming he was
the only one left, he launched. They pulled Reagan out of the UN in
mid-speech because we detected the launch.   The first Soviet Salvo
hit 27 targets in the US. That was November 13th 18:47 hours.
Within a few minutes, the short range stuff was flying all over
Europe.   When we lost contact with NATO we launched a massive
counterstrike on the Soviet homeland, around 21:00 that night."

"Did they hit us back?" Bill asked.

"I think so." Scott signed.

"So is it over?" I asked.

Scott shrugged. "It is for me." The waiter came with food. "Sorry the only steaks we have a shark steaks." He smiled.

We were too hungry to care. The steak was good, but I could not get my mind off what the shark had been eating. Shark eats man, man eats shark, is the man a cannibal? Like marrying one's first cousin I supposed, I was dodging the cannibal label by a technicality. What is worse was that it did not bother me.

We wolfed down our meals, and picked up the 'to go' meals for Billy and Ahmed. Scott joined us on the walk back. When we got to the beach the Billy was a stripped down to his BDU trousers with the legs pushed up over his knees looking relaxed, Ahmed was sitting in the shad of the boat.

"You came in that?" Scott asked shocked.

"We're braver than you think." I said and we all cracked up, as it was a Star Wars joke.

While Billy and Ahmed tore into their meals we sat in shade at the edge of the beach. "Are the causeway's intact to the mainland?" Bill asked.

"Yeah, but you can't use them." Scott said pointing north, "All the fallout from Homestead and Miami. Even the North Side of the Island is un-safe. We only use it to dump the dead. Stay south of the Highway whatever you do."

"So we can't go North OR East?" Bill said dejectedly.

"Where are you trying to go?" Scott asked.

"New York." Pedro answered.

Scott shook his head, "It's gone."

"Bullshit!" Bill shot back, "We need a map!"

Bill, Scott and I huddled around a placemat with a map of the United States on it. Scott crew a circle around Miami with a magic marker and colored it black. The then extended lines to the West and crossed it out. "This is the downwind blast area, you need to stay the hell out of there."

He did the same to Jacksonville Florida, and Charleston, it was like watching the end of the world in cartoon format as he blacked out Atlanta, Memphis, Washington, Baltimore, New York City, Chicago, Detroit, Kansas City, Long Beach, Denver, Huston, Wichita, Seattle, and on and on.

We figured we could come ashore somewhere near Savannah

GA. Stay North of the Atlanta dead zone, and pick up the Appalachian Trail in the Blue Ridge Mountains, but through central Pennsylvania, to home. It was just that simple.

That night, we slept peacefully on the beach. What the little strip on sand to ourselves. I was dead asleep when Pedro woke me, for once he gently shook me away instead of his normal blood curling screams.

"What?" I said annoyed at the first decent night's sleep I'd had in what seemed like forever being interrupted.

"Ahmed is gone."

I looked over expecting to see a corpse, but instead I say only beach where Ahmed had been sleeping. "Bill!"

"What?" Bill snapped. "Ahmed has wandered off."

"Good! Fuck his lazy ass." Billy said rolling over to go back to sleep.

"Shit!" Bill said. "Alright Billy and Pedro stay here, we will go find his ass!"

We grabbed our rifles and threw our boots on. As I threw on my H harness, I said "I think he was feverish, he might be nuts."

"I am half tempted to leave him." Bill said as we started down Front Street. The town was dark, save for an eerie orange glow to the North.

We headed towards the light. It cast weird jumping shadows on the ground. The smell from the fire was atrocious. As we got further inland we could see the fire, it was raging from house to house. We watched as several blocks of tightly backed housed disappeared. From hundreds of feet away, I felt it was going burn my face.

We wandered back to the beach, Pedro was so relieved to see us, I thought he was going to cry. Billy was asleep.

The next morning the smoke hung low over the Island, we refilled our water jugs, and got ready to push off, with our navigational placemat. Scott came still chomping on an unlighted cigar.

"What the hell happened last night? " Bill asked.

"I don't know, but we lost a lot of houses. Most of the folks here are just squatters, Everyone that could got out. All the decent boats are gone, or I would recommend you get one." Scot said watching us lash everything down.

"If Ahmed does not find his way back here, we have room for one more." Bill said.

"If my squadron ever comes back from their dispersed sites, I need to be here. Meantime the fuel they left behind makes me a rich man." He smiled a little sadly.

"The tide is starting to go out, we best get goin'" Billy said grabbing the side of the boat. "What about Ahmed?" Pedro asked pleadingly. "We can't just leave him!"

"If he turns up, I will see that is he is ok." Scott offered.

"I think it is bad luck!" Pedro said crossing his arms. Bill and I joined Billy and started to get the boat moving.

"You can wait for him if you want." Bill said.

Pedro looked panicked and grabbed hold of the boat. "I am just saying!"

Scot waved goodbye, and turned back towards the smoldering city, I had this awful feeling that Pedro was right, we would never see any of them again. Scot, Ahmed, Hugo, Hoef, Glasgow, Hall, Carlos, Ajjima,,,, The world was shrinking, being un-peopled. Like the husks of corn everything was being peeled away, everything and everyone. Down to what?

Houses burned, Ships sank, people dies, and things were destroyed. What was being MADE?

The wind filled our meager sails, and the four of us, headed east. I heard Billy mumbling 'Weren't one of us anyhow." I knew he was worried about Ahmed, and what his loss meant to us. We all feared Pedro was being prophetic.

The sun was starting to beat down on us. "Back to this shit." Billy said giving voice to our thoughts. The Florida Keys Causeway was visible off to our left. My mid-day we were South of Big Pine Key.

We silently passed the water around, I noticed no one sat in Ahmed's spot, the sea started to get choppy around 1500, "We are headed north east." Bill said to no one in particular.

The highway and the islands remained, just visible on the horizon, with the black cloud backdrop. As the sun slowly set, the twisted steel skeletons of wrecked sky scrapers filled the horizon. The red sunset have it a hellish appearance. How many lives, I wondered had ended here. It seemed even the sea was silent as we passed.

The light faded and we sailed into the inky black. After a while Bill asked. "Who has a flashlight handy?" No one moved. "Seriously I cannot see a fucking thing."

I started digging through my butt pack, and found my Army D cell flash light. I turned it on, the red lenses was still on it. Bill checked the Compass and adjusted the sails slightly. It seemed the light could barely penetrate the black.

I fell asleep in the gloom, and awoke the shriek of seagulls. The sky was clear, and as the dawn broke over the Atlantic hulking condos rose from the sea to our West. Their windows reflected the sun.

"Do you see that?" I said exited. "They still have windows!"

We chattered excitedly. Everything seemed fine, Bill turned us slightly westward, we should interest the coast somewhere north of those condos.

"Are we going ashore?" Pedro asked.

"No." Bill said calmly.

"Shit don't you want to see?" Billy asked.

"We have a long way to go." Bill said firmly.

"Where do you figure we are?" I asked hoping to defuse the tension that seemed building over Billy's desire to land and Bills desire to keep going.

"Well, "Bill sighed, "according to our precision chart here. We should be coming up on a 5 mile tall building that says "NASA" on it. We should not go ashore as there is a Giant Mouse lurking by a mono-rail a few inches inland from there."

Billy looked over at the placemat, "Better watch out of that whale, he is about the side of Cuba."

"I never been to Disney." Pedro said.

"You didn't miss much." I said. "Long lines, and the food is expensive.

"I bet the lines have never been shorter." Bill said ironically.

"Fuck Disney, let's stop a NASA take a Space Shuttle!" Billy joked.

"At that point we had better put some distance between us and the shore. "He handed be the placemat to me, the bottom edge of black circle drawn around Jacksonville extended half way to Titusville. "What do you think Billy, how far out do we do, to get around Jacksonville without going to wide?"

"Ten, or fifteen degrees." I estimated, "Much more and we will risk overshooting, and hitting that dead zone around Charleston."

Billy laughed. "Hey fellas! That is a fucking cartoon placemat, from a bar! Your compass is fucking Tupperware! "He said bitterly. "What the fuck are you talking about? If we lose sight of the shore we are likely never going to see it again!"

"But, "I started pointing towards the black circles Scot had drawn around the nuke sight.

"Those are hand drawn estimated something or others from a drunk pilot! We have been IN that black shit before, we sailed right by Miami! Why the fuck risk it?"

"Yeah, why risk going next to another nuclear impact site if we don't have to?" I asked back.

"Because it will work!" Bill said angrily.

"Hey!" Interject, sure they were about to go to blows and overturn the boat. "We have gotten this far, let's keep focus. "

"Holey shit!" Pedro said, "Look!"

The distinct giant building of Cape Canaveral where visible in the distance.

That night, I am sure Bill intentionally kept us away from the shore, it was out there with some stars finally peeking through the clouds, I allowed myself a moment of hope. I sat up in the cool breeze, and looked back a Bill clutching the Tiller.

"Thing we are clear of Jacksonville by now?" I asked.

"I imagine." He said.

"I do not like the look of those clouds." Billy said.

They seemed to be pilling up on top of one another off to the East. A flash of lightning in the cloud seemed to answer him.

The sea began to swell, and the clouds moved in. Bill turned us toward the North West, we were traveling faster than we ever had.

In spite of our increased speed, the clouds were closing in rapidly. My stomach knotted as the bow rose a good twenty degrees as we climbed a wave greater than the length of the boat.

We crested the wave, and dropped like a flume ride. We struggled to keep the boat upright. Rain began to spatter us, and the bow rose again. There was no way, I thought, we would survive this night.

The wind whipped our sails, and the mast creaked. "We need to get the sails down!" Billy shouted.

Bill let the boom out as far as he could but the wind tore the line from the gunnel. Boom catapulted around, it struck Pedro mid-chest and launched him into the foamy sea.

The boat capsized, mast down dumping us all. Pedro swam through the driving rain. He and bill clung to one side of the boat, Bill and I the other.

The waves picked us up and heaved us, then we dropped I lost touch of the hull, I feared I would be washed completely away. I managed to get back to it just as the next have dropped us, and I lost it again.

"Get over to this side!" Bill shouted.

We worked out way over to him, as the next wave pulled us away.

Once we were on one side, we were able to pull on the keel and get the boat to slowly roll towards us. As we slowly righted her we saw the boom was completely gone, a single strand of red cloth, all that was left of our sail.

The Liberian flag up front survived, still attached to the mast and bow, but otherwise flapping meaninglessly in the gale. "Keep the bow facing the waves!" Bill shouted.

We all kicked and shoved desperately, but with the next wave it went back over. This time we stopped it before it completely turtle, and managed to set it right before the next wave.

Billy climbed in and grabbed the tiller, he managed to keep it upright through the next wave. One after another we managed to climb in. The rain stung out faces, and the boat seemed on the verge of sinking. We bailed desperately as Billy kept us faced into the waves.

We bailed desperately, as the rain poured in. We didn't dare stop for a moment. The rain seemed never ending, each wave seemed the verge of disaster. The night lasted and eternity, and the dawn brought no relief.

Eventually, sometime in afternoon the storm slacked, but we were unable to make gains against the flooding, I know exhaustion slowed us down, but I started to think the boat was also sinking.

It was around dawn, the sky was gun metal grey, and the rain stopped. Pedro spotted it first. Rising out of the sea to our South a towering ship, it looked like a moving mountain. It was headed for us!

Bill stoop up, grasping the masts, and waving the t-shirt off his head. We could not tell if it saw us. It was a tanker, with the super structure towards the rear.

It seemed to be passing without noting us, until it was almost abreast of us. A flickering signal light from the bridge let us know they had seen us.

I felt my heart swell in my chest, we were saved!

A geyser of water rose over a hundred feet in the air from the middle of the tanker. The horrible sound reached us several moments later, I felt punched in the stomach.

An enormous steel panel flew skyward carried by a bright plume of fire. The ship cracked wide open releasing a torrent of fire in every direction. We could feel the heat from nearly a mile away when the ship broke in half. A geyser of burning fuel shot horribly skyward. The gasoline smell reached, us as the firestorm spread, flames marched across the sea like hell's own Army.

The heat became uncomfortable as the wall of fire spread, Billy unlashed an oar, "Let's get the hell out of here!"

Our tattered Liberian sail filled with fuel smelling wind, and Billy took the first turn rowing. The column of black smoke that reached into the sky, dwarfed the world. When land appeared we made strait for it. It was all low and swampy.

We found ourselves at the mouth or a river, we headed into it, it started about two miles wide, and after a decent sized gulf we found ourselves in a narrowing swamp. We came to a fork in the river, "North our South?" Bill asked.

"North." Bill said calmly. "If this is the Savannah River it'll take us to Augusta!"

The river narrowed, but there where so many tributaries coming from each side, I feared we would get off of the main river and be lost in the swamp. After about an hour the river narrowed to a few hundred meters and turned west. "This is it!" Bill said triumphantly. As the river meandered North and South and a highway bridge came into view, we started to cheer. Against the red twilight the steel of the bridge seemed hard evidence of our deliverance, though the river banks where still primordial with trees, vines, and Spanish moss.

"Shut the fuck up!" Bill scolded, "Break out the Rifles, and get you H harnesses on!"

Still waterlogged, and knee deep in water we broke out are gear with fingers so shrived that they bled.

"I saw something!" Pedro gasped.

"What?" Billy asked. Checking the chamber of his Mauser.

"Where?" Bill asked looping the sling of his rifle across his shoulder, so that his rifle was across his back.

"The bridge!" He hissed in horror.

The setting sun made it painful to even attempt to see the bridge as it loomed closer. Bill released the surviving sail and we slowed to a crawl.

The shadows lengthened, and the gloom closed in from the all sides. Mosquitoes descended on us, as we tried to see though the bridge. "Maybe we ought to beach, and scout it out on foot." Billy suggested.

I peered into the black between those trees, and wanted nothing to do with it.

"I don't know." Bill said. As we got closer, "I don't see anything."

The river current has started to push as backwards. Bill tried to get the sail working, but the air just hung there, dead. "Pedro, start rowing. " Bill ordered, "You two keep an eye on that bridge."

I thought I saw something move in the dying light, on the bridge, but was not sure. Soon it loomed overhead again. We were about to pass under it when a storm of rocks and bricks suddenly pelted us, accompanies by inhuman shrieks from above.

A cinderblock missed me by inches, as a brick struck me in the thigh. The boat immediately capsized, I clung to my rifle as the water seemed to boil with projectiles. I tried to raise my rifle, but could not get it high enough. A cinderblock hit the bottom of the overturned boat with a crash. An arrow thudded into the boat not far from my head. "Make for shore!" Billy shouted, desperately scissor kicking with his rifle held out of the water like we had been taught in basic. I followed suit, the rocks kept coming and the several hundred feet to the shore seemed to take an eternity.

As my boots found the muddy bottom of the river, Billy was staggering out of the water ahead of me. A shotgun fired from the tree line, its bright muzzle flash the size of a pumpkin in the twilight. Billy sprawled back with a shrill howl. I thumbed the selector lever on my M16 and sent a stream of bullets into the tree line.

"I'm shot! I'm shot! "Billy screamed. "Jesus I'm shot!"

It seemed like running in a nightmare, as I struggled to get out of the putrid water. When I got to him, his t-short was slick with blood, he struggled to sit up, and grabbed his rifle, "Look out!"

I spun around and a swarm of dark figures was pouring down the hill from the bridge screaming towards us. I grabbed Billy's arm, and we stumbled into the trees. I shotgun fired from the bridge peppering the trees, I angrily squeezed of a burst. The bolt locked to the rear after 5 rounds, I was empty. I slouched against a tree and dropped my magazine, fumbling for another. "Are you ok?" I asked.

"I don't know." Billy answered. He brought his rifle to his shoulder, and fired at the bridge. It clattered into the mud and he dropped to his knees, crying in pain. I picked up the rifle, and slung it over my shoulder, half dragging him further into the wood line.

The light from torches, and angry shouts, announced the closing ring of our unseen enemies. That where attempting to corner us against the river. "We have got to move!"

We stagger through the trees into a suburban street, there were no lights, and a line of apartment town houses, a small black boy peered from behind a tree, I had almost shot him when he appeared, I breathed a sigh of relief, and started towards the street when he shouted "Over here! They're over here!"

Billy kicked at him, he ducked out of sight. "Gimme my rifle!" Billy said panting with pain. I slid it off my shoulder, "Here." I said. He took it in his left hand. To more horror the kid re-appeared behind him wielding a long barrel shotgun. He brought it to get shoulder aiming at Billy's back. I snapped my rifle to by shoulder losing a stream bullets, the kid's chest cracked open as he tumbled backwards spraying blood.

"Come on!" I shouted as we rushed across the street. We ducked behind a parked car, its' windows exploded showering us with glass as several pistols where fired from across the street at us. Billy fired left handed without aiming, and clumsily worked the action on his rifle. They had Highway Bridge to our North, now obscured by trees, and they were between us and the river to our East, I was sure the river curved to our South as well. If we did not break contact west, they had us. I pointed to the townhouse building to our West. "When I open up, get back there!"

Billy nodded, I took I knee and fired into the building and tree line across the street. "Set!" Billy said when he got there.

I ran to join him, the hairs standing on the back of my neck as I ran, waiting for an unseen gunshot to hit me in the back. Billy fired his rifle, the shot tore past me, thumping into the building where the pistol shot had come from.

When I joined him, we both bolted town the aside street. I dropped a magazine, and was reloading on the fly, to our right rear I head as woman shrieking. A Mother had found a murdered son, murdered by me.

To our left rear I heard a burst of automatic weapons fire. Billy and I dove behind a tree, we turned to see Pedro in a full sprint

223

coming towards up. "Pedro!" I shouted.

"Over here you can make it!" Billy called. We watched in horror as be ran towards us, both expecting him to be cut down at any moment. He caught up to us panting.

"Have you seen Bill?" I asked.

He shook his head. "I thought he was with you!" He said.

A black teenager wearing nothing but jeans, and rag on his head peaked around the corner from where we had just come. "They over here!" He shouted.

"Fuck!" I said grabbing Pedro, "Let's go!"

We ran down the side street, from shadow's trashcan lids banged to announce our passing. Our pursers tried to stay just out of sight, but like a pack of wolves they were everywhere. We came to a swampy area, and ducked into the trees. Knee deep in water, we managed to slip away from them.

After a few minutes we found ourselves in a more built up area. There was a Catholic Church left side of the, we snuck into the grave yard, which had a low stone wall around it. We sat their panting for a long moment, listening for pursuit.

We crawled over to the church itself, the doors where broken open, we crept into the main part of the church, and up the stairs to be balcony. Most of the windows were broken out, and the pews where gone. Christ remained crucified; the desecration of the church seemed to somehow add to his pain. As I imagined did the blood spatter of that kid, I had killed, the anguished cries of his Mother still echoed in my ears. They still do.

We heard movement outside. Weapons at the ready we peered down into the street. Five young men, walked loosely down the street. One had a shotgun, two carried bats, and two seemed empty handed, I assumed they had pistols.

The steered clear of the graveyard. We relaxed the slightest bit. "How are you doing Billy?" I asked quietly.

"I got a load of birdshot in my chest an' shoulder." He said calmly, "It hurts like a bitch, but I ain't gonna die. How are we on ammo, and water?"

"I have four mags of 30 left." I said

"I have five." Pedro said.

"Alight, no more full auto, or we are gonna run out. " I got about eighty Mauser rounds but they rest of the damned Mausers are in the river." Billy said calmly.

"What about Bill?" I asked feeling like a complete coward for having been so worried about my own ass that I had not even thought about my best friend.

"If they'd have found him we would have hear a ruckus." Billy smiled. "They won't get Bill."

"How are we gonna find him?" I asked feeling a sudden fear I would never see him again.

"We aren't" Billy said looking sad. "We don't know where we are."

"We should wait here for him." Pedro suggested.

"Buddy, where is here?" Billy asked gently.

"In the church."

"We almost did not come in here. There ain't no telling where he will hole up." Billy grimaced in pain as a moved. "Besides we need to get going before morning."

"Why?" Pedro asked innocently. "Because them sons-of-bitches are gonna be a lot braver when the sun is out, and if you're ass falls asleep, you are gonna bring 'em down on us ."

"Why would I do that?" Pedro asked looking confused. It made we wonder if how much he remembered about his night terrors.

We eventually moved out, and found that past the church where four baseball diamonds, we skirted their edges, and soon found ourselves looking across the street at the empty shell of a McDonalds.

We had not seen anyone for a while, and where becoming more bold.

Past the McDonalds there was a grocery store, and across the street was a mall with a sign that read 'The Islands Mall Shopping Center.'

"Where the fuck are we?" I asked.

"We need to get a look around." Billy said. "Bet we can get on the roof of that place."

Pedro and I both looked at him stunned, "Are you crazy?" Pedro asked.

"Don't be a pussy" Billy said stepping off at full speed, not waiting to see if we would follow.

The road we crossed, was wide and empty, as we approached the mall we could see another bridge connecting the land mass we were on to another. We went around the mall and into the bushes on the other side. The elevated highway crossed another small river.

We crawled to the edge of the bush and saw there was a loose barrier of cars, furniture and trash strung across the bridge. Several figures milled around on the bridge.

"We can take 'em." Billy assessed.

"We could sneak past them in the water, they would never know." I suggested.

"I don't think I can swim like this." Billy confessed sheepishly.

"All we need to do is get across that stretch of water, their road block is on this side. I bet we could find something that floats." I encouraged him, "Besides we need to conserve ammo."

We found the water deep, but slow, Pedro and I split up Billy's gear on the swim across. It was shaky, but he had it.

That night we walked on the highway for a few miles until we came to another bridge. The sun was rising in the East, and from the bridge we could see the distant pillar of smoke from the burning tanker.

"Why do think it exploded?" Pedro asked.

"Torpedoed." Billy said confidently. I looked out to the horizon, how many Russian subs were still trawling out there, and why? Was the war over, or wasn't it?

Across that bridge we founded Savannah Georgia, or more accurately the ruins of Savannah.

The store fronts stood empty, the street as motionless as a mural. Every step of our feet seemed to echo. We realized that we had been going all night and stopped at a McDonalds. There was not a crumb of food left, but it was otherwise in decent shape. I took a look at Billy's wounds. We were able to pull most of the pellets out of his chest as they had no gone in very far. There was a bloody half-moon from his right collar bone, to his sternum, and across his right pectoral muscle. We counted 21 pieces of bird shot, of which all but seven came out using a Leatherman tool. Four that where in too deep where in the upper and three in the shoulder.

I took off my boots, my feet had been wet for days. They were shriveled and white, the stench was horrible. The flesh looked grey and dead. Billy looked at is seriously, "Trench foot!" He spat Shit! We are fuckin' stupid." I started to apologize, he cut me off. "Hell Bill, mine ain't no better!" He started taking his boots of "Take off everything that's wet, and let's get it in the sun!"

We all stripped, our flesh was painful and split in places. I fell asleep naked in the shade of a picnic table in down town Savannah, with my raged clothes drying on the table above me, and no one was there to notice or care.

Later I awoke hungry, I put on my now dry trouser, and dug though my butt pack to see if there were any MRE components left. There was nothing, but my last pair of dry socks, and my wet poncho liner I had been using as a pillow.

Pedro was sleeping on a table nearby in the sun, Billy was cleaning his rifle at another table.

"Get yer rifle clean, we might need it." Billy said calmly, "Them dogs have been getting; bolder."

I realized that less than a block away there were several dogs of various breeds watching us intently. "Shouldn't one of us have his rifle together?" I asked.

"Yup." He said slapping his together, "And I am done!"

Pedro say up, looking concerned at the sound of the rifle bolt closing. "What's up?"

'Nothin' clean yer rifle." Billy instructed.

The dogs eyed us wearily, and kept edging a little closer. "Suppose we need some chow, and a map." Billy mused.

"We could have dog." I said somehow feeling I was hearing someone else speak.

"Yeah, but how we gonna cook it?" Billy said. "How about we find the river, we follow it inland we will be a lot better off."

In the end it was only two miles due North to the Savannah river, had we waited just a little bit longer to turn inland in the boat, we could have all been together, my stomach hurt from more than hunger when I looked at that slow moving, wide river. I wondered if Bill was alive, or dead.

The first person we saw was a clean shaven elderly black man, with wild white hair. He eyed us nervously. "Hello there." He said calmly.

"Hey there old timer." Billy said joyfully. "Don't mind us, we ain't pirates or nothing."

The man laughed heartily. "Well praises Jesus! Son, you about gave me a heart attack!"

"We did run into some pretty rough costumers back in them island though!"

"Sweet Jesus, you can though Wilmington Island!" The man said shaking his head. "You are blessed to be alive! "

"Yer tellin me! They sank our boat, shot me an' our friend went missin'." Billy said with some swagger. "Do you know where we could find something to eat around here?"

The old man laughed, "Sonny there ain't naught to eat around here but what they scrounge up for the river, or the rats and dogs!" He turned serious and in almost a whisper he said, "If someone tries to sell you pork, don't you touch it! No Sir!"

"Why not?" Pedro asked.

The man laughed again, then suddenly his mood darkened. "There are not pigs anymore son. Those who say they are selling pork or pig, are out to make a cannibal of you. Don't you let them son!"

"We won't" Pedro promised earnestly.

"Well follow the river down to the old historic district, but be careful, it is a wicked, sinful place, and though they barter for everything there, the hidden cost might just be your immortal soul!" He then laughed, realizing how serious he was sounding.

"Thanks." Billy said as we headed further into the city.

The streets where lined with haggard looking people, though more so than us I am sure. We got many a sidelong glances. It seemed like a vast yard sale, every manner of thing from antique lamps to engine distributer caps was laid out for trade, on tables or blankets, sometimes on newspaper.

People shouted, offered, and begged. The only thing that seemed in short supply was food. The first food vendor we came to have any had line of rat kabobs on what looked like pieces of coat hanger. "Rat kabobs, get you rat kabobs!" He shouted, "Fresh free range rat, organically fed, fresh never frozen rat kabob!"

We pushed past him, to a fish monger who has cat fish in a red child's wagon, the stench made my gorge rise.

A painfully thin woman, grabbed the suspenders of my H

harness and shouted in my face, "Help me!" She was on the verge of crying. "Help me!" I did not know what to say, her eyes where wild, and empty. "Why won't anyone help me?" She screamed, I shoved her away. She fell to her knees, "Please! I'll suck you cock!"

I brushed past her blushing in spite of myself. She grabbed Pedro's hand "I'll suck your cock!" She screamed, several of the men hawking their wares laughed. She grabbed Billy's arm he screamed in pain and collapse, she feel on him clawing at his gear attempting dislodge anything of value. I spun around and drop kicked her in the face. She sprawled on her back sputtering blood and teeth.

Pedro and I helped Billy to his feel, he looked shaken. The bloodied woman ran off, and we continued on our way. I was amazed at how no one cared about what had transpired.

In the end we managed to get a few liters of clean water in plastic coke bottles that we were able to jam into our canteen pouches and some rat kabobs that we wolfed down on our walk out of the city.

As soon as we were clear of the bazaar, we found ourselves surround by old antebellum Savannah, tree lines, streets and iron gates. There were some candles in some windows.   The lawns where overgrown, and no one was on the street noticed us.

After a few miles, the quality of the architecture went down, and the number of people seemed to go up. No one approached as, probably a rough appearance, and our rifles carried at the ready, served to encourage caution.

It was around sun up when we reached the a bridge across the river that lead in South Carolina, we back tracked a few hundred meters and turn onto another road that took us to Highway 30, the Augusta Road.

The shoulders of highway was overgrown with weeds, but the concrete was smooth walking. Before long the sun was beating down on us.

There where the occasional broken down car, some of which had been burned to the frame but the biggest feeling was of a vast emptiness. The sound of cicadas filled the air.

The I-95 Interstate toward over the road, we spread out, eyes peering desperately for movement on the bridge. The Augusta road narrowly ducked under the interstate, he paused, to drink water and consider what to do.

"We gotta go over the top." Billy said looking sweaty and pale.

"Yeah," I agreed. "We get hit down there, there's no place to go."

Pedro just looked exhausted, with dark circles up his eyes, seemed beyond caring. Our tactics devolved into a trudge up one side of the highway, and down the other. There was no cars to be seen in either direction. What had once been a major artery connecting vibrant cities, was now a strip of concrete between smoldering holes in the poisoned earth.

A few abandoned motels and we were back in the wild, it occurred to me as flies descended upon us that I had never seen a highway so clean of road kill.

I brushed the flies away from my eyes, as we marched along, it was maddening. After an hour we started seeing houses again. My feet felt like they were on fire.

We found the highway running between a Food Lion and a Walmart, from out vantage point we could see down into both parking lots. The pavement was obscured by a rainbow patchwork of tents and tarps. Small cooking fires added a haze to the glaring day. Wordlessly we staggered down into the teeming mass.

People sprawled in the shade, lazily brushing away flies. We wandered the narrow pathways and found ourselves in the Walmart entrance. An obese women with a clip board looked wearily at us. "Where you coming from?"

"Panama." I answered.

"Florida?" She said, she pointed to her left. "Over there, does anyone have any contagious illnesses?"

"No, but my friend has been shot." I answered.

She looked contemptuously at our weapons, as if thinking we had brought the shooting on ourselves. "You cannot come in here armed.' Two shotgun wielding men, noticed us, and walked slowly towards us.

"We don't wanna come in, damn it!" Billy said annoyed.

"Well, we do not have a Doctor!" The woman sneered. "Do you

want to get on the list or not?"

"What fuckin' list?" Billy asked.

"I do not appreciate your language!" She spat back.

"Hey!" I said putting a hand on Billy's good shoulder. "My friend is a little cranky on account of being shot, and all. Do you know where we could find something to eat?"

She snorted unpleasantly. "There ain't no food."

"Yeah yer wastin' away!" Bill said as we turned back towards the parking lot.

There was a pack of kids playing soccer in spite of the heat. An ancient old woman sat beneath a lawn chair watching them. She eyed us wearily. "Where ya comin' from boys?"

"Panama." Pedro answered.

"Did you get on the list?" She asked exposing a cluster of missing teeth.

"No," I Said, "What is the list for?"

"To find folks!" She smiled. "You tell them where you're from, and where you're staying and if anyone comes lookin' fer ya, they can find ya."

"Does it work?" I asked.

"Oh yes!" She gestured to the tent city. "We have reunions every day here!" Then she looked sad. "Funerals to."

I handed Pedro my rifle. "I will be right back. I am going to see if Bill has been here."

The unpleasant fat women, took my name, and directed me to the New York isle. I went until I found Buffalo. There where notes, scribbled on every manner of paper stuck to the shelving. I tore a page out of Hugo's book, and scrawled a note. 'Bill Collins! Bill we are made it this far. Billy is shot, but ok. Heading up the Augusta road. Catch up or wait up damn it! Airborne! Bill'

I looked for a note from Bill, after I hung the note up. The Buffalo section was sparse, there was no section of Ithaca, and so I checked Rochester. There were notes, all people who had lost someone or and were lost. It was painful to read.

I headed back into the parking lot, the kids still playing soccer, but Billy and Pedro where nowhere to be seen. Panic gripped me, my stomach knotted. I suddenly felt dizzy.

I saw Pedro step out from under a tarp waving me over, I

breather a sign or relief but still felt ill. The tent was crowded with odd bits of furniture. Billy was lying shirtless on a couch, a middle aged women was giving him water.

"What hell happened?" I asked.

"He passed out." Pedro said.

A grey haired man, helped the women, pull off Billy's t-shirt. His wound was a dark bruise peppered with scabs where we had pulled the shot out. The deeper wounds, where the shot remained inside, the wounds were still open. Dark blood flowed slowly from the wound, the arm was swollen and red. "It looks like he is fighting an infection." The woman said.

"Are you Doctors?" Pedro asked hopefully.

"No." The man said looking at Billy's wound. "I install carpets."

The women shook her head slowly. "You need to keep him out of the sun, I think."

"You can let him rest here for a while." The man said, "This place is packed at night, but you will be ok in the meantime."

"I am sorry we don't have any food to share." The woman said sadly.

"Kick yer boots off fellas." Billy said weakly. "Let's give 'er a rest."

I slouched into a large padded chair and took off my boots. "Thank you very much!" I said leaning back. I was asleep before I heard an answer.

"Wake up, ya damn buzzsaw." Billy said shaking me awake with his good arm.

"How are you doing?" I asked pulling my socks and boot back on.

"Shitty, but I'll be doin' better when we can get some huntin' done." He said with a smile.

Streams of kids where coming into little home as we left.

The cool of the evening made for a much more pleasant walk, though we still sweated horribly. The humidity seemed near 100%.

The town of Rincon was dead to our eyes, and the darkness beyond seemed as endless as the sea. For hours we walked into the darkness. An abandoned truck stop loomed out of the dark. We spread out and walked across the parking lot like it where a rice paddy in Vietnam.

The windows were smashed, and the shelves bare. We picked through the wreckage for anything worth salvaging, but it was pointless.

Just as we turned to go, a reflection on the wall caught my eye. I squinted and I could not make out exactly what it was. Billy lighter, and in the flickering light I saw the map, with the red star announcing

"You are here."

We pried the Plexiglas from out of the frame, and Billy took map out, we were just South of Springfield, Billy folding it joyfully into his pocket. He seemed recharged with energy, we told us we were going to take 119 to Clyo that night.

Around three in the morning we were all exhausted, and when we came to a fire break South of Cylo, we decided to stop for the day. We found a small grove of pines off of both the highway and fire break. I collapsed onto the soft pine needles. I looked up into the pines, and fell fast asleep.

We spend the day by that fire break napping and eventually

scouting out a nearby stream to fill out canteens, which course by that were now plastic bottles and have a less than hearty meal on cat tail roots. I did not know it previously but the roots of the cattail are a white tasteless part of the plant that you can eat. We pulled up enough of them to get our bellies more or less full, and we getting ready to head out in with dusk. When I noticed the itching around my waste.

It was a tick, "Shit!" I cursed.

Billy smiled weakly, "Alright fallas, tick check!"

This was a standard, though humiliating process that was standard at the Infantry school. I took my jacket and t shirt off. Billy used the same Leatherman plyers that I had used to pull the bird shot out of him to pull four ticks from my under arms, ten from around my waist.

"OK Pedro, you're turn!" I said relieved. I was annoyed that he had only one, and it was not even embedded yet. We turned to Billy. The wound in his shoulder was turning blue, and had puss running out of it. The skin around it, around it was scarlet and burning hot to the touch. "Jesus Billy!" I said looking at it.

"Fuck it." He said annoyed, "Let's get goin'"

With that we stepped off, into the twilight. We skirted the edge of town, and headed up a narrow country road skirting the border between Georgia and South Carolina. We stopped when we hit the highway again North of Slyvania.

There was not any shelter worth speaking of so we stumbled North towards Hiltonia one we reached a fork in the road, the sun was up and we were out of water. He headed west, mumbling about the salt in our eyes, and the pain in our feet.

There was an abandoned bus by the side of the road, it was over grown with weeds, but we opted to use it as shelter from the brutal Georgia sun.

I slumped on the rusting floor of the bus, and took my jacket off. My boots where steaming how while I removed them. I leaned back with my sweat soaked jacket under my headed and tell asleep. My midafternoon, Pedro and I where beating the bushes for food. We left Billy in the bus, as we did not want him to waste his energy, he was looking worse all the time.

A four foot long rat snake killed by a terrified Pedro stomping it to death was our only prize but, when Billy skinned it was actually pretty good.

Billy laid the snake skin out on the roof of the bus to dry. "What the hell are you going to do with that?" I asked.

"Shit we are gonna need somethin' to trade sometime. " He answered sensibly. That got Pedro to thinking, and he was trying to tear pieces if the bus off for trade.

"How about the alternator?" Pedro asked.

"Good idea!" We attacked the engine only to find that without tools we could get nothing off of it.

Discouraged but with a little food in our bellies we headed out.

That night we made it to the outskirts of Augusta. The city was dark except for the small fires at in some of the yards. Watch fires, we would later decide. The sound of banging trash can lids Filled the night was we approached an impromptu road black made of furniture and old cars .

We tried to skirt around it to the West, but ran into another. Block after block we bounced of the hard scrabble shell of Augusta, until we were directly west of the city.

We climbed up onto highway 20 to try and peer into the city, it was from there we spotted the torches coming our way from the West. Clamoring and screaming, a horde of figures came towards us. Billy tried slung his rifle and attempted to wave, in order to show that we meant no harm.

A rifle shot tore the air over head, "Jesus! Let's get out of here!" Had they held their fire until they were closer they would have had us, but we had several hundred meters on them, and we soon bolting ahead of them.

Our tiredness left us, as we ran through the night.

Like game animals we were driven, when we went too far right we hear the clanging and shouting of from the city, if we slacked off or wandered to far left we saw the torches of our pursuers.

After a half an hour we collapsed into a grove of tree. We sat there panting and listening. Our torch carriers had fallen behind, but they were still following. They had lost sight of us.

We started walking quickly through the tree line, like on patrol.

"Damn it, these guys just won't quit!" I bitched after over an hour.

"We get a good bit of ground, we'll lay an ambush." Billy said panting.

It was just a few minutes later, we ran into a lake. We turned our back to the lake and took up positions behind pine trees, preparing our last stand.

Billy awkwardly withdrew black canister containing Pedro's grenade from his gear and cracked it open. He hefted the green egg like weapon in his left hand. He could neither throw nor shoot well in his current state. This knotted my stomach thinking until he had been wounded, I had never seen him miss.

We wait for hours, the sun rose, and through the mist on lake, we could see a bridge across it. We edge over to the bridge in as the morning fog burned off. It was a highway bridge.

As we got closer we could see people moving on the highway and the bridge. As we get closer I noticed they were milling around, and did not seem armed or aggressive. "What do think fellas?" Billy asked.

"I think we need to just walk though like we own the place." I said being more tired than brave.

"Sounds risky." Pedro cautioned.

"We can take 'em if we have to." I responded.

"Damn right." Billy said striding forward.

They looked like skeletons on their feet, staggering around on the bridge. We walked silently past them. Some were obviously blind. May where losing hair, and teeth to radiation sickness.

We crossed the lake and cut effortlessly though the masses of the living dead. Somewhere lying dead by the side of the road, fodder for the enormous turkey vultures. The vultures paid us no more mind that their next meals did as we passed.

All day we walked though this horror show, I felt the blood and sweat soaking my socks, but I dared not speak. No one spoke on the skeleton road.

As the sun started to set, Billy sat briefly on the guard rail and dug out some water. We joined him. No sooner had the water reached my lips than the skeleton like survivor began crowding around begging, and pleading. I reminded me of a zombie movie.

We gruffly pushed past them, I was angry I had not had a chance to adjust my socks, but they could not keep pace with us, though we were getting slower with every step.

As the sky darkened the moans and cries seemed more pronounced. We call developed different pains, a knot in the small of my back felt like I was being stabbed. Billy began to shiver. I gave him my BDU jacket, he buttoned it up tight.

We passed under I85 without a thought to scouting above, or around, as the sun rose on the second day I was carrying Billy's rifle sling over my shoulder, and Pedro has his H hardness over his own.

We tried to stop but they swarmed up again, Billy was deathly pale and I knew we had to get off this road. There was no sign, or exit ramp, but a road passed underneath, and the pine covered hills of the Chattahoochee National Forest looked like a heaven with this hell was passing through.

We Billy leaned on him with his good arm, right entire right arm was swollen and red. We passed over the first hill with only a few of the skeletons following, so we headed up another, higher one, when we were half way up it I caught a whiff of a fire.

When we made it to the top of the second hill, there was a dirt road, to our right, it curved downhill and interested with the paved road that had passed under the highway. To our left it wound uphill, and out of sight.

We followed it up, when the roof of a red barn came into view. This brought out hopes back to life.

A stockade of pine logs fenced in the barn and the a few other houses around it that we could see.

We approached cautiously, there was a gate, that was locked, and a small door to the right of it. We went up to the door.

A grey bearded old man in a flannel shirt sat asleep and snoring by it. We walked gingerly passed him. He has a lever action rifle on the table next to him.

Once we were through we could see there were about ten houses inside the stockade, a plump young women came around the corner of one of the houses, when she saw us, she screamed.

"No wait!" I shouted nearly dropping Billy. "It's ok!" The old man stepped out of the guard shack with his rifle at the ready. Pedro and I had our rifles across our back and were defenseless.

The young woman's face was beat red, "You old bastard! What

the hell are you doing letting everyone in!"

"Our friend has been shot." I said, her hard blue eyes fell on Billy. She pointed to the nearest barn, "Get him in there, you're probably all lousy!"

A middle aged man with a goatee came out of the house carrying a shotgun. He took one look at Billy, and said "Get him in the house!"

"But, Dad they are probably all lousy!" The fat girl objected.

"Well get over to Clayton's and get some water boiling. I will handle them, and get you Mother!" He commanded. He turned to us. "What happened to him?"

"He got shot." Pedro answered.

"Are you boys really in the Army?" He asked suspiciously.

"Yes Sir," I answered "Alpha Company, 87th Infantry, and Fort Kobe Panama. We have been trying to get home."

It turned out Clayton was a veterinarian who had a hot tub on his back porch facing the mountains. There was no power but they dumped enough hear boiling water in it make it tolerable, and enough chlorine to kill anything that was living on us. The man

introduced himself as Pat Miller, the girl was his Daughter Tammy.
"Just put you clothes in this trash bag, " He instructed "my wife
Carol will boil them, and you will get them back. " He looked at
Billy, "It does not look like he can wait. Do not let the water get into
his wound, I will be right back."

The water stung our bloodied feet, but I figured the chlorine
would kill any growing infection. The Miller's carried Billy and our
clothes away. Pedro and I say there exhausted until the water turned
cold. Then we dried off with come towels from a nearby shelf, and
walked around Clayton's house warped in towels.

There was nothing to indicate anything was different in the
outside world, there was a huge tv, nice furniture. The electricity
being out was the only clue to the horrors that had ravaged the world
beyond our sight.

We found Pat examining Billy's arm with a flashlight maggot
where squirming in an out of the wound. I thought Pedro was going
to faint. "Jesus! Get them off!" He gasped.

"No," Pat said firmly. "They might just save his life."

Pedro looked at me in disbelief when I said. "I have heard of that, in World War One, they'd say 'the worm are your friends.' "

"Yeah, they only eat dead stuff." Billy said weakly.

"I am worried about that infection." Pat said gently probing the swollen arm. "We need to keep blood flowing through the arm. The only blood thinner we have is aspirin but it will have to do."

"Do you install carpets?" I asked, making Billy chuckle in spite of his pain.

"No," Pat said looking confused "my wife and I raise horses."

We went with Pat over to the main house after Tammy came by with our uniforms. They were pretty raged, and faded now they were clean. He induced us to Mr. Cooper, who was the old gentlemen who had been asleep at the front gate when we arrived. He explained to us, that there where ten families, thirty people in all inside the compound, and that each family volunteered one man for town watch. They had been having real problems with people coming in and stealing.

Most of the horses, dogs and cats had disappeared. They had some orchards that they patrolled, but with only ten men, most over the age of fifty five, it was hard enough to keep the stockade guarded, and they were afraid once the peaches started coming in they would be picked clean before they had a chance to grow or ripen.

Pedro and I quickly agreed to help, while we were waiting for Billy to recover. Much to our amazement we sealed the deal with rabbit pie, and supper with at the Miller's Dinner table. Tammy did not join us, as she was bringing a portion for Billy.

We told our sea stories of all we had seen in the six months since the world ended, Pat helped us understand a little more of what we had seen. Just as the Augusta had been nearly overwhelmed by the flood of refugees from Atlanta being destroyed. For every one killed there where dozens, dying on their feet, and hundreds hungry and homeless. They had descended on the outlying towns. Scavenging turned to begging, begging turned to looting. So the city sealed itself up tight, just like the Millers has done with their little community.

They told us we could stay at Clayton's place. Apparently Clayton had been skiing on Colorado when the war came, and no one knew what had become of him. Though he was a 'Jackass' we were asked to treat his home with respect.

I slept that night on the mysterious Dr. Clayton's couch, and I slept like a Stone. Pedro got the bed in the spare bedroom, and Billy was set up in the Master Bedroom. I awoke in the morning to the smell of food, as Tammy brought breakfast to Billy, she told me there was food at the main house.

I got dressed and was about out the door when the thought occurred to me that my weapon and H harness where still by the couch, I could just picture the look Bill would have given me. I could hear Hall saying in my conscious saying "How about your gear genius?" I wondered if Hall was still alive. I wondered where Bill was, if he was alive or dead. Was there more we could have done? I felt a lump in my throat, with a thought I could not get rid of: He wouldn't have left me.

I walked down to the front gate, a heavyset white haired man was on guard duty. He smiled when I came up, "Good morning, there young fella."

"Good Morning!" Answered amazed at the beauty all around. Bird songs filled the cool morning air, the morning fog had yet to burn off so the ashen grey of the sky was still hidden.

"Jim Roberts" he said shaking my hand.

"Bill McGill." I said happily. "How does your shift?"

He chuckled, "Quiet. Saw a family of possum come by around midnight."

"Quiet is good."

"Got that right." He said. "How's your friend?"

"Still pretty rough."

"If Damn Clayton weren't off bein 'a damn playboy he'd have a better chance." Jim said bitterly. "He was a Veterinarian." Jim smiled, "And a pretty good one too, when we wasn't chasing women around."

"He has a nice house." I commented.

"Oh yeah! " Jim laughed. "Pat Miller hated that damn hot tube! I thought he was going to put one in just to show him up!"

"So do you guys to a guard mount?" I asked innocently.

"What is that?" He asked.

"We'll how do you know when you have watch?"

"Ah, Miller puts up a list here." He pointed to the wall in the little shack.

I looked at the list, I assumed 'new guy' was me and 'Spanish new guy' was Pedro. "I see we are on already. "

"Yeah," He gestured to the big barn "We get together every night around six, you get yer rations then, and they let you know if we are going to send out a patrol and the like."

I smiled, "That is a guard mount."

"Where'd you boys come from?" He asked looking off into the trees.

"Panama."

"Jesus you came all the way from Florida?" He whistled.

"No, like Central America Panama."

"Is that where yer buddy got shot?"

"No that was near Savannah." I looked out into the Woodline. "We were ambushed, one of our guys got separated, I am hoping he catches up with us."

That evening around six the ten member of the town watch gathered at the barn, I noticed it left the gate un-attended, but anyone that came though would bump right into us.

I noticed Mr. Cooper had a 30-30 lever action rifle, I wondered if it was the same one that Jim Roberts had at the front gate.

The men where all chatting pleasantly, and eying Pedro and I with fascination. They were most fascinated by our weapons. "What is that there?" One asked about the grenade launcher under Pedro's M16. "It is a forty millimeter grenade launcher." Pedro explained.

This was greeted with great enthusiasm. He was bombarded with questions, how far did it shoot? How big was the blasts? Did it kick much? Ect, ect.

"It is good to four hundred meters, but is supposed to be effect out to one hundred and fifty. "Pedro said proudly. "It has a five meter kill and fifteen meter casualty radius."

"How many rounds do you have for it?" Pat Miller asked seriously.

Pedro averted his eyes. "We don't have any."

There were some disappointed moans.

"We have about a hundred and fifty rifle rounds each." I offered, and that seemed to cheer them up.

"And Billy is a dead eye with that Turkish rifle of his." Pedro added.

"It's true, when we were hunting for food, he was a regular Daniel Boone!" I added enthusiastically.

"How he don't have an M16?" A goatee wearing man, with a bitter look asked.

"He was our Machine gunner." I tried to explain.

The man pulled off his baseball hat. "Where is the machinegun?" He asked angrily. "We sure as shit could 'a used that!"

"Shut the hell up Tom!" Pat Miller shot. "Where the hell do you think you'd find Machinegun ammo around here?"

Tom mumbled something bitter under his breath. Pat ignored him. "Alright listen up!" Pat said, as I noticed for the first time the Colt 357 Magnum he wore on his hip. "I see ya'll already noticed our new friends here. Why don't you introduce yourselves boys?"

"I am Bill McGill from Ithaca New York." I said. Awkwardly.

"Um." Pedro looked even more awkward that I felt. "I am Pedro Torres, from the Bronx, New York."

The Barn was deathly quiet, finally Cooper said, "You boys know, New York is gone?"

"Ithaca is hundreds of miles from the city." I said almost defensively.

Pedro just nodded.

"Alright, let's get down to business." Pat said as his wife Carol handed a small basket to each of us.

"Now please drop your basket off empty outside our kitchen in the morning boys." She addressed us.

"We share everything we have, but some days are better than others." Pat warned.

"We are just grateful for anything." I said feeling ill.

"Ok. Cooper, Tom, Baker, and Stephens have the patrol tonight. Bill and Pedro have the Guard. In the morning Roberts, Williams, Ray and I will take the patrol. Schmidt and Hickey will have the guard. "There was some grumbling.

"We got two more guys, we could go to eight hour shifts instead of twelve." Tom complained.

"You think I don't know you split them up into six hours as is?"

Pat shot back angrily "And still you fall asleep half the damned time!"

"I don't never, it these old bastards!" Tom was in his later thirties or early forties, and had obviously been the youngest man until we showed up.

"Enough!" Pat said. "We are going to four man patrols, and that is the fucking end of it!" The barn was silent. To my amazement, that was the end of it.

I stood the six PM to midnight shift, the only instructions for my post where not to let anyone in, and to ring the bell if I needed help. Jim Roberts offered me the 30-30 rifle, but l assured him I preferred to keep my M16.

The little guard shack, was stuffy, but I had stood worse posts. I stood there in the ink black, peering into the nothingness. The faces of the departed, the burning sea, where the hell was Bill? Would Billy survive?

I heard something move in the bushes. My heart pumped, and I brought my rifle to my shoulder. Shit! What was I supposed to do?

The rustling got worse I could see the bushes move, I moved my selector lever to semi-automatic.

The grey fur of the possum glowed in the gloom as it lumbered by, followed by a half a dozen small possums. I smiled at my stupidity, though my gut still hurt from my fear.

About an hour later, Tom came by, carrying a camouflaged long barrel shotgun, Cooper had a double barrel, and Stephens, a bolt action rifle. "We are headed out don't fucking shoot us!" Tom said un-pleasantly.

"Do you have a far recognition signal?" I asked honestly.

"What the fuck are you talking about?"

"Do you have a flashlight?" I asked.

"Why the fuck would I want a flashlight?" He asked angrily.

"I do!" Cooper offered.

I turned to him, not wanting to deal with Tom. "When you get close enough see the gate, just give it three quick flashes, so I know it's you." I suggested.

"Good idea!" Cooper said happily.

"Yeah." Stephens, who looked close to seventy years old agreed.

"Come on!" Tom snapped heading the door. "Old Bastards."

I watch them disappear into the gloom and I had an uneasy feeling. Feeling a little ill I sat waiting. Pedro came around midnight to relieve me.

"How's Billy?" I asked.

"He is sleeping." Pedro said, then added, "I think he is getting better."

We sat in silence for a long time. "I told the patrol to flash their flashlight three times before coming in."

"So what if someone else comes?" Pedro asked nervously.

"It could be Bill." I said hopefully.

"What if it's not?" He asked anxiously.

"Don't let them in." I answered weakly, knowing full well that was not what he was asking.

"I don't know if I can shoot someone." He almost whispered.

"You shot when we were on that island." I pointed out.

"Yeah but I do not know if I hit anyone. Besides, they were out to kill us."

I understood, the boy I had killed haunted me, and there was no doubt we would have killed Billy. Of course, I mused I could have shot to wound. Or maybe just smacked him with my rifle butt. Then maybe gone back for Bill, my regrets where stacking up, and there was not chance to go back and fix it.

"I am not sure I can shoot someone for wanting food." Pedro said slowly. "If Mr. Cooper had not been asleep, they might have shot us."

"You don't have to shoot anyone. Just squeeze of a round or two, and they will leave." Like I should have done, I thought bitterly.

The next morning I awoke on the couch, and slowly sat up. The shag carpet on my bare feet felt like heaven as I wiggled my toes in it. I walked barefoot into the hallway, Billy was snoring in the Master bedroom.

I went into the kitchen, and opened by basket, it has a jar of jam, some strips of jerky, and an apple. I took the apple out, and started eating.

Pedro came in from the end of his shift. "Empty your basket, and I will take it over to the Miller's kitchen." I offered. He nodded, "How was your shift."

He shrugged, "That Tom is a real asshole."

"Yeah, "Agreed, "I do not know what his problem is."

"I think he hates us." Pedro said emptying his basket on the counter. "We do not belong here."

"Fuck him." I said. "We are not going anywhere until Billy is one hundred percent, besides he is not in charge around here."

"No but I think he was the bad ass before we got here." Pedro observed.

"Yeah, I see that." I said already down to the core of my apple. Slipping my boots on, I took up Pedro's basket, and headed for the door.

The morning was idyllic, I stopped to watch the horses milling around for a while before dropping off our baskets on the pile outside the Miller's place. When I set them down I realized I had not brought my gear or my rifle. A chill went down my back as walked quickly back to Clayton's.

When I got there my gear was in the kitchen, I put the H harness on, and slung my rifle. I stepped back on the deck by the hot tub. I looked up into the mountains and wondered what horrors lay beyond, and where in the world was Bill Collins.

A white haired old lady with arthritic hands and a stooped walk gently treaded up to the edge of the deck. "Good morning." He said in a shaky, but pleasant voice.

"Good morning Ma'am." I said.

"I am Estell Stephens, she said with a weak smile, "My husband Hector and I are your neighbors. "

She looked weak, I gestured to a chair on the deck. "Would you like to sit down?"

"Oh, no. Thank you." She smiled, "but I was wondering what you had gotten in you basket, and if you might want to trade. "

"I got an apple, some jerky, and some jam." I told her honestly.

"Do you think we could trade?" She said nervously. "We, Hector and I that is. We cannot eat this jerky, it is too tough! We will trade you all off ours jerky for your jam."

"Sure," I shrugged, ducking back into the kitchen, and retrieving my jar of jam. The handful of jerky seemed like a poor trade. It seemed less that what I had in my basket.

"Now about that apple." She said cleverly.

"Already eaten Ma'am."

"And, your friends? " I was getting annoyed. "Too tough to eat I'm afraid."

She laughed and thanked me, as she went on her way waving a hook like hand.

Pedro and I had a lunch of jerky and jam on the deck. I gave him half the jerky Estell Stephens had given me, and we shared his jam. We dunked the jerky into the jam, and used it as salty edible spoons. I would not say that it was good, as the tastes were all contradictory, but it was good to eat a meal. The jam would have been great if had bread, but having been so intimate with hunger those previous weeks we were just happy.

I went to check on Billy after we heat, I heard Tammy speaking to him, and hesitated at the door. I knocked, and she said "What?"

"What is it?" She wagged a finger at me. "Come on in but don't you keep him up, he needs rest!"

Billy chuckled as I came in, "I wanted to see if you wanted anything, but it seems like Nurse Ratchet has it covered."

"Yeah, she is a regular Black hat." He said making reference to the instructors at Airborne School.

"How you doing?" I asked.

"Well nothin's eatin' on me anymore, so I guess that's something." His arm was less swollen, but at least as red. "This damn is itches like all get out!"

"You eating alright?"

"Yeah, meat an' jam." He smiled, then looked serious, "Any sign of Bill?" I shook my head. "How about these folks here?" He asked.

"A squad sized town watch, mostly senior citizens and not enough guns to go around." I said honestly.

"Solid folks?"

"They seem it. Pat Miller runs the place, they all seem pretty happy to have us here, except for one asshole."

"Ah hell, there's always one." Billy said leaning back.

That night at the when we gathered in the Barn for our assignments, and food baskets for the next twenty four hours, Pedro and I tried to blend into the back ground, it did not work.

"Fuck that 30-30, we need to keep them M16s on the front gate."
Tom started in, a murmur of agreement made my stomach cramp,
where the fuck where Bill or Billy to have this fight? I had a point,
but there was no way I was giving my weapon.

I saw by the look on Pedro's face, he was afraid. I smiled and
tried to laugh it off, "That bitch nearly drowned me twice on the way
here."

"There is no reason you need it more than anyone else." Tom
said defiantly.

"It's mine." Pedro said quietly.

"Bullshit, I will bet it says property of the US Government on
it!" Tom spat.

Pat stood armed crossed in the corner considering the
proceedings and saying nothing.

"Who's going to use it TOM?" I asked angrily "Your Fat ass?"

"Yeah, why the fuck not?" He raged.

"What do you do if you get a double feed?" I shot back, he
hesitated and I shouted "Torres, double feed!"

"SPORTs! Slap the magazine, pull the charging handle, observe the chamber, tap the forward assist and attempt to fire!" Pedro shouted.

"How do you insert the firing pin retention pin into the bolt carrier group TOM?" I stepped towards him. "If you do it wrong the weapon won't function, how does it do in, TOM?"

Pat waved to shut me up, "Alright, listen up. Night patrol is Tom, Big Hickey, Stephens. And Schmidt. Baker and Little Hickey have the night watch. Williams, and Pedro have the day watch. I will take Cooper, Roberts, and Bill on the day patrol."

Once we had our baskets Pedro and I were headed back to Clayton's in the cool twilight. "That guy hates us." Pedro said coolly.

"I know." Looking into the gathering gloom. "We got lucky on that one, he will keep trying, but why?"

"Why anything? It doesn't matter why, it just matter what he is going to DO."

"I don't think he knows yet." I said wishing we had Bill with us.

We climbed onto the deck and slumped into chairs. I peer into the blackness hoping for stars. I just wondered at all that was in that darkness, the remains of millions of people, and while cities, and here we were, worried about what one fat man thought. Had been on guard that day, I knew in my heart he'd have shot us dead.

"We keep out weapon's with us at all times, from here on out." I said.

"Yeah." He agreed. "Think he will try to take Billy's rifle?"

"I don't know," I mused "It is nothing from a technology standpoint, but he might do it just to prove a point."

"Billy will skin his ass if he tries it." Pedro observed.

"Yeah" I smiled "He loves that damned old rifle." I noticed Tammy walking in towards the master bed room with a basket of food. "What about her?"

"I don't trust none-of these people." Pedro said sadly.

The next day, our patrol went out around nine AM. It was not really a patrol, there was no order, and I did not know what we were doing. It was more like a walk in the woods with guns.

First we went down the dirt road to where it intersected with the paved road. There were several logs and a few strands of barbed wire strung across the dirt road. "We did not have nearly enough wire to build a proper fence." Pat Miller said apologetically.

Our route curved around, away from the road, to a cluster of small peach and apple orchards. We skirted the edges of them, I noticed some deer tracks in the soft earth. I gestured to Pat. "Yeah, there will be plenty of them in the fall, if we can keep the trees intact. "

After meandering around through orchards and fields we came to a valley cutting northeast. "There is a town at the other end of that valley that is where the raiders always come from."

"Not the highway?" I was surprised.

"Sometimes they come stumbling off the highway, but normally they just die." He sighted though the scope on his high powered rifle. He adjusted the zoom, "look there, just North East of the fence."

He gestured for me to take the rifle, I sling my M16 and took it, it was a very nice 30-06 with a top of the line Leupold scope. I could see running towards us, with stringy hair flapping an emaciated woman, she ducked right and left wildly. "Highway person." Pat explain, "Turned away by the town, no doubt."

I was still puzzled by her speed and erratic course. "Why is she running like that?"

"The dogs." Pat said quietly, taking his rifle back.

"They turned dogs lose on her?" I asked horrified.

"Maybe, but more likely they are a pack of feral dogs, once they have started eating corpses they go wild. The wolf comes back out in them." He said coolly. "They start looking at people as food. Once they run out of dead, they look for the dying, or the weak, or the slow."

The women, fell into the road about five hundred meters, the dogs swarmed her, I was grateful she was too far away for us to hear. A thunderous shot rang out from Pat's rifle, and she sprawled, the dogs disappeared. They would not be gone long.

"Only thing to do." Pat said auctioning his rifle, and pocketing the ejected cartage.

"There but by the grace of God." Cooper said sadly.

"Go we all." Roberts finished his thought.

The rest of the patrol was quiet and gave me time to process what I had seen. To be shot, much better than to be mauled to death by dogs. Still, the cold bloodedness of it all stuck with me. The power of life and death over other human being weighed lightly on Pat Miller. No, I thought, not lightly, but naturally. In days gone by this man was might have been a noblemen.

Then again, was he NOT a nobleman now? He had land, and livestock, and he had us. I was grateful to be there. I had food, shelter, and a respite from the nightmare all around us. Seeing the highway women beset by dogs reminded me of small and fragile our sanctuary really was.

That night in the barn Tom sulked silently, Pedro was assigned day patrol, and I had the watch. Mrs. Stephens came by to swap soft food for hard, and we slept in doors.

The following night, patrol with Cooper, Roberts, and Stephens. There was not one of them less than twice my age, yet when we got to the barn they all looked expectantly at me.

"What do you say soldier?" Stephens asked.

I felt sick, "I guess, follow me." I said stepping off uncertainly. We got to the gate, and I asked if any of them had a flashlight no one did.

Tom was on guard, "Just get out there!" He said annoyed.

I headed into the gloom feeling his eyes on my back. I did not like knowing that hateful man was behind me with a loaded shotgun. I was more worried about coming back in.

Once we were out of sight of the gate, I stopped and did a security halt. You are supposed to do one to get accustomed to the sounds of the area, and to let your eyes adjust to the dark. After a few minutes, Cooper asked me "Is everything alright?"

I did not want to try to explain, but I could not see either, but I started down the hill all the same. We came up to the intersection, and a crawled up to where I could see the road, if barely. It was frustrating, I could not see any meaningful distance.

Out patrol was far from stealthy as we stumbled around the orchards. Though they were louder than grunts, I did notice that they cursed a lot less. We paused at the short stone fence overlooking the valley where the highway women had been shot. A stared down into that darkness for a long time, waiting for some sign of life, or death, but it was a still as an oil painting.

I pushed off the fence and headed back down to the blocked dirt road, with a sigh I headed back up the hill, in the gloom I saw the two figures following me. I paused, something was wrong. Two? There should be three! Stephens was gone!

In a panic I charged up the hill the other two struggling to keep up. Stephens may have fallen, a broken a hip or something. We HAD to get to him before those damned dogs did.

"Stephens!" I hissed in a stage whisper. "Stephens!" The other two slowly panted up the hill. Cooper sat down on the stone fence panting too hard to speak. "Stay here!" I instructed, I attempted to retrace our route. My first patrol, and I lost someone! I thought, I am a Private First Class, why am I in charge of anyone!"?

I say a figure slouched on a log, "Mr. Stephens?"

"I am sorry." He whispered. "I must have dozed off." With great relieve we joined back up with the others, and headed up the hill. "I woke up alone, I thought I was a goner."

The next morning I woke to the sound of laughter. It had been so long since I had heard a women laugh it sounded both musical and foreign.

I headed out to the deck with a bruised apple for my breakfast and found Pedro already there.

"How was watch?" I asked attempting to ignore how soft my apple was.

"Fucking boring as shit." Pedro said stretch. "These fucking mosquitoes have never tasted Puerto Rican before, and they like it!"

Billy came out shirtless and joined us, he looked painfully thin, but a lot better. He smiled broadly. "What's shakin' fellas?"

"Look at you!" I said joyfully. "Almost done gold bricking there troop?"

"Damned right!"

I heard the jingle of dog-tags, Tammy gathered up all the baskets from the kitchen, and said cheerily, "See you tonight!" to Billy as though the rest of us where not there.

"Havin' dinner at the big house tonight, seen as I was under the weather when we got here." He said after she left.

"Was she wearin' you dog tags, man? Pedro asked.

Billy blushed like a schoolboy, "Ah didn't have nothin' else to give her, seen as she's…"

We busted out laughing, life and suddenly seemed normal, and good. "So what'd I miss?" He asked stretching his shoulder gingerly, eager to change the subject.

"Not much by the look of it." I said, giving Pedro the giggles.

"Have some damn dignity Pedro!" Billy scolded, jokingly.

Estell Stephens came up the path, with her basket. "Oh boy, here comes the master negotiator." I joked,

"Oh I heard what you did last night!" I waved a knotted finger seriously.

"Me?" I asked nervously.

"Yes and on your first patrol!" She clucked disapprovingly. Oh, shit, I thought here it comes.

She smiled and reached into her basket pulling out a wine bottle, "Thank you for bring that old geezer back! We have been saving this for something special, and we decided having the old fool around longer enough to plant my vegetable garden was it. "

After she left I explained what had happened the night before on patrol. We all agreed to crack the wine open after Billy got back from his dinner at the Miller's.

When we gathered at barn, Tom seemed more incensed than ever, he looked as though my humiliation of him had been just moments before. Miller paid him not mind, "All right listen up!" He began. "I would like to introduce Billy Orson, he is going to be helping us out."

"Great, another mouth to feed!" Tom bitched.

"Billy is coming to us all the way from Panama, and will be on day patrol with me, Stephens, and Roberts tomorrow. Bill and Cooper will have the day watch. Baker, and Schmidt have the night watch. Tom, Pedro, both Hickeys and Williams have night patrol."

Billy, Pedro and I sat on the back porch, staring off into the dark woods. Billy cracked open the wine grinning like a goon. "What the hell you happy about?" I asked.

He just smiled and poured the wine. Old man Stephens came by shuffling towards the barn, he waved at us and shouted something about good evening to the young Prince.

"What was that all about?" I asked, but Billy just grinned looking up into the murky sky. Pedro on the other hand seemed nervous.

"Pedro's gonna go on patrol with Tom." I said "elicit some

kind of response.

"Well if he can manage to stay alive for one night, it will be fine." Billy said cryptically.

"What the hell are you talking about?" I said joining the flushed feeling face from the wine.

"Oh and just that he were to be doing the night patrols, just the three of us from here on out." He said smiling ear to ear.

"Billy that is great!" I said overjoyed, Pedro was obviously relieved, though still apprehensive about that nights' patrol.

The next night was 21 May 1984, we build a basic terrain model in the barn, and Billy put together a better patrol order than one would expect of a Private First Class, even if he had been a Specialist for a few months. We had check points, routes, everything but on call targets, since we had no mortars to call.

The patrol went well, we were feeling our oats when we got back to the trailer. We did an after action review, just like we had done in the Army. What we thought went right, what we thought could be improved. It was all self-congratulation, though we did not see it at the time. By our fifth patrol we had extended our patrol route, and included a number of listening and security halts. We were in lying under some low scrub brush where we first heard it.

It sounded like background noise on an old record, as it got louder it changed, 'Vehicles!' Billy said in a stage whisper. Our eyes desperately strained to pierce the inky blackness.

It kept getting louder, and our hearts left when we realized it was coming from behind us. We scrambled out of the bushes. All tactic went out the window as we ran down the road towards the Sanctuary, "We have got to get between them and the farm!" Billy shouted.

There was no way, by the time we were ascending hill there was a thunderous crash, and the sound of gunfire. I could barely see Billy as he pulled ahead, sprinting up the hill, Pedro was somewhere behind me. The sound of engines, shooting and shouting filled the night. I could see the gate had been crashed, whomever had been on duty was undoubted buried in the rubble.

There where shots being fired from inside the main house, Billy rushed in through the front door. I stopped by the crashed grate and saw the white pickup truck skidding to a halt in front of the

Stephen's place. Two gunmen piled out of the back of the truck, I raised my rifle to my eye and squeezed the trigger. Nothing happened, I cursed myself as I flicked off the safety and ran forward, try to see them again. They were kicking down the front door of the trailer, when I shot the first one between the shoulder blades. His buddy did not even notice, before he caught one in the back of the head. The trucks backup lights came on and it careened backwards towards me. I leapt into the open door of the barn, landing squarely on our terrain model; I thought the barn was coming down on me when the truck hit it.

The tail end of the truck was lodged into the side of the barn, as I ran out and aimed in the driver, I saw his face by the dashboard lights, and he was young, in his twenties, wiry beard, and a backwards ball cap on his head. As I aimed in on his face, he burst into tears. I could not shoot. Pedro caught up a few minutes later, and opened the truck door, "Get on your belly you piece of shit!"

"Please don't kill me!" The man pleaded.

I left Pedro and ran to the main house where Billy was now on the front porch conferring with Pat. "Is everyone ok?" I asked.

"We got two in here." Pat answered.

"I got two by the Stephen's place, and Pedro is holding one by the barn." I reported.

"What do you mean holding?" Pat asked sternly.

"He surrendered." I answered nervously.

"You and Billy search the compound, make sure we do not have any others running around." Pat ordered us in a flat dead voice. The search took over an hour. Every shadow was searched.

When we got to the Stephens' place, Estell was frantic, apparently Mr. Stephens was on duty at the front gate when the attack happened. The two dead men on her front porch had been carrying shotguns. "I'll cover, you search." I said to Billy, who slung his Mauser over his shoulder and picked up a shotgun. I tried to not look at their faces, but I did. They were young, early twenties, I supposed. We would later learn that they had come from the town across the valley.

It was good to know, but it came at a price. When we finally collapsed back in the trailer, Pedro was already there. "Where is your guest?" I asked.

Pedro looked more worried than normal and my guts seemed to squirm. "They have him in the barn. Tom is working him over for information."

"Figures, that sadistic fuck!" I spat.

"Fuck 'em." Billy said taking the bolt out of his rifle to clean it.

"You get one with that?" Pedro asked.

"Naw, Mr. Miller plugged 'em both with his 357."

I her the jingle of Billy's dog tags coming behind us. "Anyone hear how Hector Stephens is doing?" I asked hoping Tammy would answer. I found it nerve wracking that she came and went without knocking or announcing her presence.

"He is alive, but with a nasty head injury." She answered. She leaned over Billy and hugged him. "Daddy wants to see you,"

While we were waiting for Billy to come back, we heard a commotion over that the Stephens' place, Pedro and I grabbed our rifles and ran over, past the dark blood stained walk way, I burst into the living room. When we threw open the door to the master bedroom, Estel Stephens was curled up in the corner, Hector was thrashing on the bed like a man possessed.

"It's a seizure!" Pedro said dropping his rifle. "Get him away from the wall!" We could not get a hold of him. The seemed to have the strength of ten men, a kick to the stomach, knocked the wind out of me. A moment later Pedro landed next to me in a heap.

I looked over at Estell her eyes where wide, and she seemed unable to speak, we rallied "Grab his legs." Pedro Said, I did the best I could. I took a knee to the face and could not see what was happening when I heard Pedro scream. When my vision cleared, I saw blood covering Hector's face and Pedro on the floor cradling his right arm. I let go of Hector and kneeled by Pedro, 'Let me see that."

"He fucking bit me!" Pedro griped looking pale the wound was in a double half-moon shape, with dark blood flowing from it. It looked deep.

"We need to get that thing cleaned and dressed before it gets infected." I said, glancing at Hector who had suddenly ceased moving. I checked to see that he was breathing. His breathing was labored like he had just sprinted a mile, and his heart was pounding.

I was worried he would die right there on the spot.

I policed up my and Pedro's rifles and we headed back to the trailer to dress his wound. Billy came running in, 'What happened?"

"Hector bit Pedro." I answered.

"Why?" Billy looked frightened,

"He was having a seizure and we were trying to prevent him from hurting himself."

"Pedro, you gonna be able to patrol tonight?"

Pedro nodded, "Airborne."

"Good, we are doing on a recon patrol tonight. The raiders last night came from a gang that is holed up in the High School across valley."

"What are we reconing for?" I asked as I bound Pedro's arm.

"Gonna have to find a way to take'em down." He answered excitedly.

We silently gathered our gear and headed to the barn. Pat was overseeing the repairs on the front gate. He turned to us, "Listen boys, we need you to get a handle on how many of those guys are holed up in the High School, and we need to see what their weaknesses are. Stay out of trouble, and get back before sun up."

"Not a problem." Billy answered earnestly.

After a brief talk over the ruins of the terrain model, we headed out. I was on point, peering into the bushes, more worried about the feral dogs than anything. We crossed the orchard where the dogs had run down that highway woman, the sickly sweet smell of death hung in the air.

We hand railed the road for a little ways, but the bush was thick, and I was afraid we would give ourselves away, Billy and Pedro agreed so we used the road, and tried to stay in the shadows. It seemed like the valley went on forever, I found myself wondering if this was necessary. We had killed four of theirs, and captured one. Hector Stephens might still die, but it had cost them dearly, and they had nothing to show for it. Perhaps we could send the captured guy back with a message to stay away. Of course if Tom was beating the hell out of the guy, he might want payback.

The first house we came to looked abandoned, its doors and windows were gone. The yard was overgrown. The church tower was the first thing we could see of the village itself. I would have put a sharp shooter up there, but without a night vision scope it seemed unlikely they could see us.

As we got closer we could smell burning wood. The streets seemed surprisingly normal. The grass between the roads and the sidewalks was long, and several wrecked cars were abandoned, their windows smashed.

We eventually found the High School, there was light at one corner of the first floor, as we crept to the edge of the tree line we could see that there was a fire burning outside the library. A figure stood over the fire. Park benches where scattered around the fire pit.

"What do we do now?" I asked after we watch the guy by the fire for a while.

We are going to need to see inside." Billy said thoughtfully.

Pedro looked terrified. "Are you crazy? There is no telling how many of them are in there!"

"That is what we are here to find out, damn it!" Billy hissed.

"How the hell are we going to get close enough to see?" Pedro almost pleaded.

"Well the grass is pretty tall, if we did a high crawl they would not be able to see." I offered.

"Shit, if they did, from the top floors, we would be dead meat!" Pedro shot back.

"To see us they would need spot lights, if they light up, Billy can take out the light before they can get a shot off."

"So we crawl tree hundred meters on our bellies and he sits here waiting for a light to come on?" Pedro asked incredulously.

"That is about the size of it." I answered.

"What if they have night scopes?" Pedro asked defiantly.

"Aw hell, I will get him from his muzzle flash." Billy smiled in the dark.

"After he shoots one of us!" Pedro said in almost a cry.

"Pedro! What townies from Northern Georgia have fucking night vision scopes?" I asked.

"Besides you are darker they are much more likely to shoot Bill!" Billy encouraged.

A few minutes later, as I was slithering on by belly towards to the school, that joke became a lot less funny. The sky was murky and dark, but the shattered windows of the school stared like the eye sockets of some horrible skull. The high crawl is what the Army called it when you crawled on your knees and elbows, it keep you low, but is exhausting. It seemed an hour before we got to the edge of the building. I was soaked in sweat, my knees and elbows rubbed raw.

Pedro slithered up to me, as I chugged some foul tasting water from my 'canteen'. As my heart rate slowed to a steady pounding, I glanced around we were right next to the building, and had not run into any defenses.

I tried to walk along the edge of the building, but the broken glass made too much noise, but I crouched as low as I could and walked around the end of the building until I could peer into a door. Most of the glass of the door was intact, cracked, but there was no way to get through it. My rifled held by the pistol grip, I reached out with my weak hand, and pulled on the handle, it opened.

Pedro came up behind me, tugging on the back of my H harness, urging me back to the wood line. Bill had been right, we still did not know anything. I shrugged towards the darkness, for him to follow. With a heavy sigh Pedro followed me into the

darkness.

Two step into the inky blackness I took a knee. I closed my

eyes, attempting to will my eyes to dilate faster. Fantastic terrors

with razor sharp teeth filled my mind's eye. I could feel the

darkness closing around me, I opened my eyes to see near total

blackness, and the only thing audible to me was the pounding of my

heart.

The gloom receded a bit as my eyes adjusted. The hallways

was littered with paper trash and broken glass, ever step seemed to

make enough sound to bring the defenders down upon us. As we

crept down the hallway we could here vermin scurrying away. As

we rounded the first corner, the foul smell of the backed up toilets

assaulted our noses.

I peered around the corner, the hallway was a black hole,

Pedro bumped be from behind, we stood there back to back as a little

mobile Alamo for a long moment. There was the unmistakable

sound of movement ahead. I aimed my rifle into the murky

blackness. I gasped as a light cut the darkness, I ducked around the corner, as a flashlight cut towards us down the hall.

The shuffling sound of someone coming our way seemed thunderous, as the sightless eye of the flashlight bobbed on the wall. The sound grew nearer, I stepped back, and preparing to shoot whatever came around the corner.

We were suddenly in darkness again, our night vision washed out we stood there blind. It seemed an eternity as I attempted to will myself to see. The sound coming from the darkness brought some relief, apparently the owner of the flashlight did not think the bathrooms where too overflowing to be used.

Pedro tugged on my H harness, "Come on."

"Wait." I answered annoyed that we had spoken at all. Eventually the flight returned and headed the other way down the hall, I hazarded a glance around the corner. I could clearly see the outline of a man in short and a T shirt shuffling down the hall. He opened the door to the library and went in.

I bumped Pedro and we headed back down the hall from where we came. Over the next several hours we skulked all around the High School, we could find no other signs of life, or the appearance of any defenses.

Exhausted we headed back to the wood line at a low crouch. "Billy." I called in a stage whisper. "Billy." I said slightly louder, the lack of a response got my heart racing. "Billy!" I said in a loud voice just short of a shout.

"Damn it!" Pedro cursed.

"Shut the fuck up!" Billy finally answered, "What the hell is the matter with you?" Billy said appearing from behind a nearby bush,

"Man there is nothing there! Like one guy." Pedro shot back.

"Are you sure?"

"No," I answered, "we only saw one or two guy, but there are absolutely no defenses, the only early warning they seem to have is the guy on fire watch out front."

"We need to move anyhow, it is getting' late." Billy pronounced in a manner that made me wonder if he had been asleep behind that bush.

We withdrew through the valley with the sun rising, Tammy

met us at the gate, I looked away as she and Billy said their hellos. The sound of raised voices from the barn drew our attention, we walked into a bedlam. The prisoner was set in the middle of the floor, tied to a chair. His eyes where bruised and swollen almost shut. His lips split and bloody.

Tom Baker was wagging his bloody finger at the Roberts brothers, it seemed the entire population of compound was in the barn and engaged in a shouting match. "Tom wants to hang the looter." Tammy explained. "The Coopers want to release him."

"What does your Father want to do?" I asked.

"No one knows yet." A wise King, I thought. He provides the food, the security, but he does not want to alienate his minions. To appear too weak is to invite a challenge to his authority, to just string this kid up, might make him a tyrant in the eyes of some. I wondered where his priorities would prove to be.

We filed into the Miller's kitchen, and were seated around the table, Mrs Miller brought us some water that we attacked with gusto. She looked kindly at Pedro "Let me see that arm."
Pedro rolled up his sleeve, revealing an inflamed wound. Mrs.

Miller clucked disapprovingly. "Tammy get in here! " She commanded then looked kindly down a Pedro, "Do not worry son, we will get you right."

"Carol, you see to that," Mr. Miller commanded, then looked sternly to use. "You two come with me. We followed into Mr. Miller's 'study' it seemed half library, half command center, and half throne room, more than the sum of its' parts, you might say.

He sat behind his oak desk and gestured for us to sit. We sat before his desk as he asked, "What are we looking at boys?"

"Well, it looks like they are holed up in the library, but we can't tell how many there are." Billy answered.

"How is their security?" He asked me.

"None existent, they might have an early warning out front, as there seems to be one guy keeping the fire going. We were able to walk right into the building, and get within grenade range of the library from two sides."

"Are they all in the library?" He asked coolly.

"There is no perimeter, and no sign of organization. I doubt they all stay at any given time." I supposed.

"What about weapons?" Miller asked as the furrows in his brow deepened.

"We did not see any." I answered, only deepening the lines on his face, he turned to Billy, "Where you during all this?"

"Billy was in over-watch." I answered, receiving an icy look from Miller.

"Ah needed to cover them on the way in and out." Billy said, drawing nods from Miller.

"The prisoner says there are thirty plus men there." Miller said sternly.

"It is possible, but it does not seem likely." I said noticing that the tension seemed unusually thick. "He could be lying."

"Why would he lie?" Miller asked, almost rhetorically.

"To scare us off," Billy said. "Maybe to keep us from hittin' back."

"Or maybe there were other patrols out." I said thinking it unlikely as I said it.

"You would think they would scout spread out and attack in strength." Miller said pounding the table. "That is it, they hit us with everything they had and failed. We need only to mop it up and be done with it."

We shuffled back to the trailer, the sound of Hector Stephen's screams filled the place. As I tried to sleep his words seemed to echo off the back of my skull. "Devastation comes on the Wings of abomination!" He shrieked over and over again.

I could not sleep, I stumbled into the kitchen, and Pedro sat at the table cleaning his rifle, with a distant look in his eye. "You ok?" I asked sitting across from him. I could see by the look in his eyes, he was not.

"We are not going to make it." Pedro said sadly.

"Sow the wind, and reap the whirlwind!" Hector bellowed, still fevered and deranged from his head wound.

"Why not?" I asked putting my feet up. "We made it this far."

"Did we?" He almost sighed. "Bill, Ahmed, and how many others are gone? We are losing"

"I am becomes death destroyer of world!" Hector screamed.

"I am afraid if we do not get out of here soon, we will never leave. We don't belong here Bill. The Spic and the Yankee, come

on! They are going to lynch that prisoner, and we are going to cross

the valley, for what? "

"We have to route them out so they so not come back, I

supposed," I said weakly.

"Odysseus! Don't do it!" Hector raved.

"They are not coming back" Pedro pleaded "When does it

become just murder?"

"Odysseus, they are your own men!" Hector shrieked

"Cannibal! Cannibal!"

"Shut the fuck up, you crazy old bastard!" Pedro suddenly

shouted. I was taken aback, and after an awkward moment we both

burst out laughing. Hector laughed in a demented hyena laugh.

Billy came in, "What the hell is Hector on about?"

"The Odyssey." I said, and saw the looking more confused.

"Odysseus? Troy?"

"We didn't go to college." Pedro said absent mindedly.

"Jesus man, how about High School?" I said annoyed.

"Greek hero, angered the Gods, ended up eating his friends." "

"Why did he do that?" Pedro asked.

"A witch had him thinking they were sheep?" I answered.

"People eat sheep? And what was that whole, Desolation thing?"

"Book o' Daniel. Billy said off handed, getting a look from us that got him laughing. "Ain't ever heard of Sunday school?"

The unmistakable sound of a gunshot from the barn had us leaping for our gear.

We rushed into the barn and like fell in behind Pat Miller who had his 357 magnum revolver aimed in at Tom Baker's face. Tom was standing over the corpse of the prisoner, till tied to the chair, like a dead roach his legs grotesquely up in the air. A dime sized hole between is eye brows, and the dark blood of his brain leaking intro the dust of the floor.

Tom had 45 caliber pistol aimed at Pat's belly, I drew my rifle to my cheek and aimed at Tom's head, Pedro did the same. Suddenly the king of this little world had three US Army Soldiers behind him like God's own firing squad, of course only Pedro had a hat, and Billy was sporting a Turkish Mauser, but we were the US Army in this locality.

In spite of all that happened later I think this was Pat's crowning achievement. By witch I think cemented his position as King while we drew down on Tom. He dropped his pistol and looked like he might cry.

He walked out of the barn, and we did not try to stop him.

"This ends tonight. " Pat announced. "Billy, get whatever gas is left in that truck, and make some Molotov's. I want to hit them at sun up."

We drained the fuel from wrecked truck and poured it into assorted glass bottles. "How does these work?" Pedro asked.

"We stuff a rag in the bottle, light it on fire and chuck it." I answered.

"Can it explode in your hand?" He asked.

"No they do not explore, you need to make sure it smashes when you throw it." I answered. I saw Billy was giving me a funny look, "I read more than Greek mythology."

"Poor Man's James Bond?" Billy asked.

"Anarchist's cookbook." I answered, he nodded knowingly.

Pedro smiled, "White people are weird. Then he looked serious "What are we going to do with these?"

"I figure chuck them in library." Billy said calmly give them the choice of stayin' and burnin' or running out to mah rifle sights."

"Support by fire position on the far side of the parking lot?" I asked.

"Yeah, I reckon we get a few rifles out there, they ain't got a lot of cover, and they'll be easy pickings'"

"This is wrong." Pedro said glumly.

"Look," I opined, "had Baker not killed that guy, maybe we could have sent him back with a warning. Fact is now we have to polish them off, or they will come back for payback."

"How they know we did not kill him in the attack?" Pedro asked.

"This is what we are doin'." Billy said annoyed.

"But why?" Pedro almost pleased.

"Look Pedro, I see you point, but here is the thing. We are guest here, this is Miller's little kingdom. We have a good deal, and all we need to do is provide security. This what he wants for security? " I said patiently.

"We could have stayed in Panama with the Hoef if we were going to just be hired guns." Pedro said.

Yes, I thought, and Bill Collins would still be alive. "This is not permanent, we will move on, find Bill, and make our way back home."

"What home? Pedro's home got nuked." Billy said screwing the top onto a bottle.

"You can be a real asshole sometimes you know. I am going home to Ithaca, Bill to Buffalo and Pedro is welcome with either of us."

"They got any Puerto Ricans in Ithaca? Pedro asked trying to smile.

"You might be the first." I said.

"Chicks like exotic." Billy encouraged.

"Now let's get theses over to the barn. Keep the tops screwed on tight until we get there, then stuff the rag in and title it upside down for a second or two, just enough so what the rag is wet then light it." I said.

"Anarchists' cook book again?" Billy asked.

"We did a little field testing." I said as we headed to the barn. The muscles ached and realized that we were all exhausted. We should sleep before we stepped off again. It had feeling we would not.

The men where all gathered in the barn, to include a very pale looking Hector Stephens looking much the worse for wear. He smiled at us weakling, his head was bandaged, and he was a patchwork of bruises.

"You alright Mr. Stephens?" I asked.

He smiled weakly, "Above ground, Estell is getting' some sleep, guess I've been keeping her up."

Pat Miller walked in pistol on his hip, and rifle slung over his shoulder. "Alright folks, this is the plan, we are going to move out as soon as the sun goes down, and hit 'em where they live. " He pointed to the terrain model. "Billy's boys will lead up through the valley." I wondered at what point we had become 'Billy's boys'. "Once we get here, McGill and Torres will break off with the

Molotov's. Sneak into the school on the same route they used last time." My stomach tightened a bit. "I will take the rest of the folks around the far side of the parking lot. Once we are in place, you two "Pointing to us. "Through the Molotov's in, and do not let anyone run out your way, if they run out we will get them. If they stay in place, they'll burn."

"How are we supposed to know you are in place?" I asked, surprised at the scowl I received.

"We can use a signal, a flash light." Pat said off handedly.

"We will not be able to see it from inside the building." I said getting annoyed at the half assed manner this thing seemed to be thrown together.

"Why don't we hold off on going into the school until you have the support by fire position set up?" I asked. "Once we get the signal you are in place we will go in."

"We won't be able to see it from the wood line, school will be in the way, we will have to go with them, an' come back. " Billy pointed out looking intently at the terrain model.

"Good." Miller said "Good thinking Billy."

My annoyance grew, I was not sure I liked being 'Billy's boy'.

"Ok everyone back here at sundown." Miller said, turning and walking away. My stomach knotted. This was as well planned as a trip to the grocery store. What is we got hit? What about withdrawal? How would we handle casualties? I wanted to scream, but everyone was just leaving, and I did not want to look afraid. I was after all the Yankee, of the outsider Yankee/Spic faction. Besides, I was exhausted, the lure of the warm dark trailer, and peaceful sleep were the siren song that drew me away. Hector was lucid now and should not disturb our rest, now I was the one thinking of sirens. 'They are your own men Odysseus', what a crazy world.

The smell of the jungle filled my nose, the door was open, and Billy was on the catwalk smoking a cigarette. I walked out onto the catwalk Bill Collins was already there. The orange glow of pre=dawn showed a handful of soldiers dragging luggage across the overgrown Company areas. "Legs! Go AWOL in your own Company area for Fuck sake!" He took a cigarette from Billy, and smiled at me. "Pedro should be at it again soon."

"Time to go." Billy said shaking me awake. The sun was going down over our little sanctuary, and we were about to go one mission to kill more of our fellow Americans, even in my dreams, the happy times I dreamed of where after November 13th, after the end of the world.

As we gathered up our gear, I pulled out Hugo the Yugo's journal, thumbing through the sketches of sea life, and the Serbo-Croatian scribbling, I found the first blank page, I wrote the date 22 May 1984, and stared at the blank page, thumbing back through the book I found the Polaroid picture of Bill and I with the shrieking pissing monkey in Panama, I smiled and I got a lump in my throat. It was a lost world, I swore if I survived the night, I would not let it be forgotten.

I was the point man as we trudged across the valley, the smell of the dead woman's remains, served like a check point in my mind, a chill ran up my spine, the pack of dogs that brought her down was still somewhere. Of course it was Pat Miller's Savage 30-06 that really killed her. As brutal as that act struck me at the time, I would rather take a bullet to the head that be torn apart my wild dogs. I shuddered to think of it, but with the crunching of feet on gravel filling my ears I thought it was not the brutality of the act that had struck me, but the lack of it, or any other emotion. Not only had Pat shot that woman without as much as a shrug, he had not seemed phased by seeing an innocent woman attacked by wild dogs.

Then I supposed that the human race had been pretty severely pared back just six months before without a cross word or a bloody nose. Missiles passing in the upper atmosphere each passing its' opposite number's home country, it brought to mind what the cartoon wolf and sheepdog, 'Good morning Sam' would say one to the other, 'good morning, Ralph. I'm off to slaughter your makers, you?' 'Oh off to kill your makers.' 'Well, have a good one, you too.' I blinked hard, and focused into the inky black, need to focus I thought to myself.

Focus on what? The fact that you are crossing this valley to murder Americans, it was as if Ralph had crashed into our compound and I was Sam. Off to kill his makers in their sleep. Burned to death, I thought was perhaps a worse way to die than the wild dogs.

The empty streets and the rotting car hulks were the same, but the night seemed darker than before. Our little patrol sounded like a herd of buffalos, I could hear my Fort Benning instructors in my conscious, and we are too loud. We are too bunched up, one grenade would take us all out. I almost stopped in m tracks, why the hell were we not throwing Pedro's grenade? Billy still had it, damn it!

Billy hissed 'Bill, keep yer head on a swivel, I have been tryin' stop you for twenty fuckin' yards!'

"You want to walk point?" Pedro asked.

"Shut the fuck up, the guys behind us fell behind! I'm gonna go get 'em! You to stay here, don't shoot me when I get back!"

"We need a challenge and password." I said, frustrated that we did not already have one.

"All the way." Billy responded with, I recognized it as one we had used in Panama. "Blue lightning, for running password?" I asked.

"Yeah, hang tight." He said before disappearing into the gloom.

We sat there in the silent gloom as Billy's footsteps faded. Like had been trained we had the soles of boots touching and each of use covered one hundred and eighty degrees with our rifles.

I wondered how much noise a pack of dogs would make before an attack. I rested my cheek on the stock of my rifle. It found my eyes closing for longer and longer intervals until I faded off to sleep. I awoke with a start, the ghosts of my Fort Benning Infantry instructors shouting in my mind that I just 'got my whole platoon killed.' It was still inky black all around me, I tapped my foot to check that Pedro was still there. The sole of my boot hit nothing.

I rolled over and sat up, "Pedro!"

"Shut up!" Pedro answered. "You scared the shit out of me."

"Where the fuck is Billy?" I whispered.

"Shut up, he will be here." Pedro answered annoyed.

I waited in silence, Pedro was right of course. The last thing we needed to do was get chatty in enemy territory. Of course the term 'enemy territory' stuck in my mind. Who was the enemy? It seemed forever, a chill had entered my bones and it was all I could do to keep my teeth from chattering.

The sound of gravel crunching got my heart racing. It was coming from the wrong way! I struggled to ensure the muzzle of my rifle was pointed in the right direction. It was hard to tell.

I took the safety off my rifle, it made a loud click.

"All the way, damn it!" Billy said in the darkness.

"Where the hell where you?" I asked and he knelt by me.

"Ah missed ya on the way up, the rest of the patrol is in the wood line by the school." Pedro and I stood up with joints creaky from in activity. "Come on!" Billy ordered, Billy's boys I guess we were.

We reached the wood line by the school quickly, but it took a good twenty minutes of flailing around to find the rest of the patrol. Once we did, it took the better part of an hour to get them to a position across the parking lot to where they could see the library. We could see the blackened windows in the gloom, though there was no light coming from the place.

By the time we got to the point we were back behind the school, the night had begun to lighten. "We are running out of time, I think we need to all go at once." I whispered.

"Yeah, I think so." Billy agreed. As we crawled the Molotov's in our satchels seemed to make a rackets as the clinked together. The smell of gasoline surrounded us, clearly they were leaking.

By the time we got to the edge of the school, I was soaked in sweat, and more than a little gasoline. I was worried that once we got in there and went to light the Molotov's I would be engulfed in flame.

Billy kneeled by the door and opened his satchel, removing the caps on the bottles, he stuffed the knotted rags into them. "Pass me your bag", he whispered. He prepped my Molotov's, then Pedro's. "Bolt action rifle ain't much good in there. I will carry the Molotov's."

I entered the building with Billy behind me, the hallway was the same, and I was slightly less frightened. I was trying not to think about what was going to happen when we got to the end of the last turn. It seemed a much shorter trip when, I found myself peering around the corner, of the foul smelling hall.

The light coming down the hall made it clear the sun was

coming up. I took a deep breath, my heart pounding to the point that I swear I could hear it. With my rifle brought to my cheek I crept forward. I was sighted in on the library door, waiting for it to fly open.

When we reached it, Pedro came around me to open the door. I was not ready when Billy light the first Molotov, Pedro jerked the door open, and Billy chucked it in there was a loud 'whoosh' from inside followed by a second. The door slammed shut, there was a commotion inside, and the sound of breaking glass, I grabbed it back open, Billy threw another Molotov, as did Pedro. I could see the holocaust engulf the library, human forms flailed and shrieked a sound that I will carry with me forever. The last satchel Billy through in without lighting it, know it would all to the firestorm, as I slammed the door I caught a glimpse of a familiar shape painted on the wall, US Army parachutist badge, above it was the a banner with the word 'Airborne'.

We ran back down the hall, smoke almost blinding us. We heard the rattle of gunfire behind us. Automatic gunfire, though the Pedro and I carried the only automatic weapons in our patrol. The though burning in my brain was, what have we done?

The wood line was a mad house of shouts and curses. A shot when over our heads, we could not tell who was shooting at who. Pedro look at me wild eyes, I look to Billy. "What do we do? Do we shoot back? "

Billy looked on panicky, "Fuck!"

"It could be our own guys!" I shouted stating the obvious. "I say we break contact!" In a proper break contact drill we would have one of use firing while the other two moved. Then once they stopped, they would fire as he moved, however in this case we just ran like hell.

The three of us sprinted past the town, and nearly collapsed by the fence line where Pat had shot the woman, the sickly smell of her decay still in the air. "We should wait for the rest of the patrol. Set up an ambush for anyone that might be following us?" I suggested through my exhaustion.

"Here?" Pedro asked horrified.

"Yeah, Bill is right." Billy has smeared the sweat on his forehead on his BDU sleeve.

"We need to get them when they try to get across this fence. Any further back and we will be in the orchard an' they could get behind us. "

"We need to do this right, split the sectors of fire, and make sure no one gets past." I said.

Billy pointed to a lone tree clearly visible in the growing light. "Bill you take the right side 'o that tree, Pedro you take the left, I will run interference if any of our folks show up, an' if anyone else follows I'll nail 'em whichever side. "

The Hickey brothers came stumbling across the field first. Billy hollered , "Fellers, over here!"

An exhausted Jim Roberts came next red faced and staggering. "Jim, ya hit?" Bill called out he shook his head and staggered our way.

Pat Miller came in next with the rest of the patrol, they were in staggered line. When Billy stood and waved to him, he stomped up to us brandishing is rifle. "What the fuck is wrong with you morons? Why the fuck did you come out the fucking window?"

"We didn't go out no damned window!" Billy shouted back.

314

"Like hell you didn't, it was you!" He aimed his rifle at me, Billy grabbed the barrel and jerked it skyward.

"He did not!" Billy shouted "We threw the Molotov's and ran out the back, just like in yer dumb ass plan!"

"You shot at us!" Pat Bellowed.

"We never fired!" Billy shot back.

"There were troops in there!" I shouted "You had us killing our own fucking kind!" I shouted my own rage overcoming my fear.

"Everyone let's calm down and get back home, huh?" Jim Roberts suggested.

"Yeah. If there are more troops out there we do not want to get caught with our pants down." Billy said, drawing a nod from Miller.

Back at the compound you could have heard a pin drop, every rustling branch, every moving shadow seemed the vengeance of some rouge Army unit ready to lay waste to our little world. The blow up between Pat and Billy was an unspoken dark thing, as was the half a trigger squeeze away that Tom Baker was from having his guts scattered around the barn.

The men staggered back to their corners of our little world, like zombies in a horror film, Hector Stephens sat groggy at the reconstructed front gate. I collapsed onto the couch and stared at the ceiling, what had we done? What had I done?

Sleep kept into my bones, and I was aboard the ship again, the dead Captain at the helm, eye sockets empty saying nothing, a rotting zombie of Ahmed shuffled in with rotting rat sandwiches, Bill Collins spoke over the ship's loud speaker, "Why Bill?"

"You killed us all Bill, and you'll kill Billy and Pedro to." Hall said as he wandered by in starched BDUs.

I tried to apologize, but only got as far as "I am,,,"

"I am becomes death, destroyer of worlds!" Hector shouted, as I snapped awake. The sound of a woman's scream filled my ears. In terror I scrambled for my gear, they had come!

"No Billy, no!" Tammy screamed, when I bolted into the mid-day glare as saw Billy's booted foot stomping full forced onto Tom Baker's face. I dropped my rifle and ran to tackle him, throwing him off after another boot stomp was narrowly averted by Cooper's bloody forearm.

"I'm gonna kill that son of bitch!" Billy said straining to free himself of my grasp.

"Stop, for God's fucking sake!" I struggled to retrain Billy.

"Lemme go God Damn it!" Billy shouted twisting out of my grip. Tom had struggled to his feet, only to be kicked in the stomach by Billy, doubled over in paid, he caught a kneed to the face and went down again.

A thunderous gunshot rang out "What the hell is going on here?" Pat said from behind me, I turned to see him gesturing with his 357 in a manner that was both casual and menacing.

"This is between me an' fat boy!" Billy said angrily.

"Then what is he doing here?" Pat asked aiming at me.

"I heard the commotion and tried to break it up?" I answered feeling my guys trying to part to dodge any incoming bullets.

"Why would you do that?" Pat asked not wavering.

A chill went down my spine, I could think of only answers that would get me shot, like because I am a decent human being and am not going to let two grown men beat each other to death?

"It is all my fault!" Tammy sobbed.

"Bullshit!" Billy raged, moving as though he might charge at Tom in spite of the revolver in his hand "Son of a bitch tried to have his way with Tammy."

"I didn't do anything that we have not done a thousand times before. " Tom said through split lips "Before you punks came along."

Pat turned scarlet, I feared he might shoot them both, or perhaps all three, he had 5 rounds left, that would be enough for all of us, and one left over for poor Pedro. My rifle lay in the dust were I had dropped it, now twenty feet away. It might as well been back in Panama or on the ship at the bottom of the sea for all the good it was going me now. "I should shoot you both!"

"And have to raise your Grandchild yourself?" Tom panted, still stooped over. I thought to myself, oh shit we are all going to die.

Pat turned that hand cannon towards me, it's muzzle a sightless eye staring me in the face, "This is a family matter, go away."

I stammer for an answer, but slunk away, grabbing my M16

out of the dirt and leaving Billy to his fate.

As soon as I got to the trailer, guilty was chewing on my guts, "Pedro!" I said running to where my pack was stored. "Pedro!"

Pedro staggered into the room still have asleep. "What is going on man?"

"Pack your shit! We have got to get out of here, fast! Pack Billy's shit too. Get everything eatable that is in this trailer. Keep you weapon handy." I ordered.

His dark eyes went wild with fear. "What the fuck happened?"

"We are going to die in the oldest ditch in the world, man." I said dragging a backpack that I have salvaged from basement into the kitchen.

"What?" He said not moving, and rubbing his eyes.

"Tammy!" I said wrapping jars of preserves into hand towels and placing them in my pack. "Shit, I need so duct tape."

"Wait, what?" Pedro asked groggily, "Why?"

"So the jars do not bang together as I move."

"No why is Tammy the oldest bitch in the world?"

I laughed in spite of by fear. "No, the oldest ditch in the world, is jealousy. We are figured her a Billy were getting it on, but apparently she was seeing to Tom Cooper at the same

time, and now one of them has knocked her up. I walked in on them about to kill each other, her Father showed up with that 357 hand cannon of his." I took a breath to hide my shame, I had yet again left a comrade in the lurch. "We have got to get Billy away from them, and get the fuck out of here before Miller starts killing folks."

The door swing open and Billy staggered in, "Jesus, Billy are you ok?" He looked pale. "I am sorry bro I…" I started do apologize, his dismissed it with a wave of his hand and flopped down on the couch.

"Ya walk in on me monkey stompin' some son of a bitch, what was ya' gonna do? Got some water?"

Pedro handed him a warm bottle of water. Billy continued to speak "I'd damned sure o' killed 'im if you didn't stop me. Now I gotta fight 'im at sundown."

"Fuck that Billy, we will be half way to North Carolina by then!" I interjected.

With a wisdom I had never seen before from him he shook his head slowly. "Naw, I ain't running. That just might be my baby in her belly, and he don't need a coward for a Daddy. No matter what else we do, I gotta face that son of bitch. Whatever we gotta do after that, don't matter."

"Yeah?" Pedro stomped "It doesn't matter to you! We can get away now! After you are dead they are not gonna let us leave with our guns!"

"They can't go that." I said not believing it myself.

"Like hell, there are a lot more of them than there are of us." Pedro said as he went back to packing what food we had the cupboard into his pack, which appeared to be a boy scout back, another basement salvage, I am sure.

"We have the only automatic weapons, we have the holy hand grenade, and these guys are all old and fat." Except Pat Miller, I thought to myself, he would be sure to get a shot off and probably take one of us out. "Besides, I do not think any of these guys would shoot at us, except Tom and Pat."

"Tom ain't gonna be in a state to do shit when I am done with him," Billy said rubbing a wet cloth on his swollen eye.

"Yeah," I agreed "You got him down last time, you can do it again."

"That is the hard part" Billy said bitterly.

"Sorry about that." I answered embarrassed. "Look he is a big dude, do not go toe to toe with him. Keep your eyes on his hand, make him wear himself out swinging at you, then he is all yours." I advised wondering what movie that advice was from.

Billy looked thoughtful, "Wonder where the hell she is. "

"House arrest, I imagine." I said wondering if she was coaching Tom Baker right now. I thought not. My gut instinct was that if she had a favorite in this it was Billy, or perhaps that was wishful thinking.

By the time the sun started to set, we were packed up, and we meandered over to the barn, it seemed like everyone was there, every except the Millers.

Tom Baker was pacing the floor in a muscle shirt and jeans.

His face was a mess, and his knuckles bare. Though he was fat, there was something of primal rage in him. An angry gorilla came to mind.

No one would look directly at us, I had not felt as much like an outsiders since we had first arrived. Pat Miller walked into the barn with his 357 on his hip, "Listen up!" He shouted and the barn fell silent. "We have survived up until this point through unity and that unity has been violated, by Mr. Cooper and Mr. Orson. We cannot have disunity, this ends here, and now. When one or the other wishes to submit, they need only say the word, and it ends. No one may interfere. "He rested his hand on his pistol. "All weapons are to be staged outside the barn, now"

Billy handed me his Mauser, stripped off his H harness and BDU jacket, and handed them to me. I went outside with Pedro. "Pedro stay here and keep an eye on our gear ok?"

Pedro nodded, and looked relieved. We were both concerned that win or lose, we might all be the unarmed outsiders any moment.

When I came back into the barn I saw Tammy and her Mother where sitting on top of the stables allowing them to look down into the barn. The arena I thought. It has seen the execution of the night rider, and now, gladiatorial combat. Then I thought these where not gladiators, this was not for the entertainment it was a trail. Trial by combat, I guessed this was the post nuclear version of a civil trial, I might have found it funny except I was afraid, for Billy and for all of us.

There was a long moment of the two just staring at one another, it seemed a lifetime. My heart was pounding and my guts churned, I could barely stand, I could not imagine how Billy could fight in such a state. He looked like a skinny kid, with his Army issue glasses, only the scars from his shotgun wound separated his from the young man that had graduated High School, less than 2 years ago.

Tom lunged at Billy with a wild right hook, Billy dodged it, but Tom kept advancing. Billy blocked another, and then took a hit to the right side of the head. There were some gasps and some cheers.

Billy dodged another wide right and caught Tom's elbow, this allowed him to land a punch on Tom's left ear, it did not seem to have much of an effect. Both fighters staggered back and eyed on another.

Tom rushed forward taking an elbow to the eye he tackled Billy, pinning him to the dirt. The two struggled through brute strength Tom managed to slowly, inexorably snaking his arm around Billy's neck. I cursed myself for not letting Billy stomp this fucker's face in when he had him down.

Tom's hands clasped around each other with Billy throat in the crux of his elbow, it would not be long before his arteries would be constricted to the point Billy would be knocked out or dead. I glanced backwards, to see how far the barn door was. I was not about to lose another friend, I will murder every last one of these fucking people, but there was no way. I might have been able to get past the folks behind me, and not get shot in the back by Pat Miller.

Billy's teeth sunk into Tom's knuckles, his grip loosed just enough that Billy was able to grab his pinkie, he twisted it until it snapped. Billy rolled free, and sprung to his feet, I shouted with joy, as did many others. Tom threw a handful of dirt at Billy's eyes, only to get the toe of Billy's jungle boot in the bridge of his nose, blood sprayed out, Tom managed to struggle away on his knees.

Billy pounced on him, and to the sound of cheers he seized the back of Tom's head, slamming his face into one of the pillars of the barn. The cheers died down, and the relentless thumping of Tom's face against the pillar continued. I looked up to Miller, thinking he would call a stop to it. He just watched.

Billy's skinny frame was slick with sweat and dirt, his wire like muscles trembled until his finally dropped to his knees. The dark pool of blood spread around Tom's head as a lay face down in the dirt. Billy panted to the point I thought he might pass out. He looked up to Pat Miller, like a man looking to God for his judgment.

Pat looked down and nodded slowly, leaning back to his wife he gave her a command and stood up. He looked down on the bloody scene before him, or more to the point beneath him. Carol Miller checked Tom Cooper's pulse, and shook her head.

I edged towards the door, this could get ugly fast, I thought. Then it occurred to me that I had just seen a man beaten to death, and I was thinking it would 'get' ugly.

"Mr Orson" Pat said with authority, Billy stood, I worked

my way to the door, Pedro slid my M16 to me, I held it behind me, I could not get a clear shot on Pat. I needed to make sure if he raised that revolver to shoot Billy I would have a split second to drop him. "You have settled you have settled your dispute with Mr. Cooper. Does anyone here have any issue with Mr Orson?"

There was a long moment or thick silence. "Then, I will distribute Mr. Cooper's property will to the community, and we will continue in peace and unity. "I breathed a sigh of relief, and edged back towards the door, catching an evil look from Mrs. Roberts who spotted my weapon. The barn was full of applause and people lined up to shake Billy's hand. I went out to get some fresh air, and dropped to my knees vomiting violently.

Billy soaked in the hot tub, as people brought little gifts by. Tammy was nowhere to be seen, Estel Stephens brought us a bottle of wine which we promptly cracked open.

"Don't get to comfortable in there Rocky, we did not heat this water just for your ass,"

"Yeah, you best throw in another one before you taker yer turn," I said climbing out. "How is the wine?"

"It's Crappy with a kick." He answered honestly. Handing him a cup.

"Dang that was close." Billy said taking a sip.

"Not as close as you think." Pedro smiled, "I slipped Bill his M16."

He looked worried. "Did anyone see?"

"Mrs. Roberts saw afterward." I answered, "But, that was after it was over, we only need to say that we thought it was ok, get bring them back in."

"But that weren't yer intention was it?" Billy smiled.

I blushed a little, "No, we were not going let you die here." There was an awkward moment, made a little more so when Billy stood up, and offered a toast, still wrapped in just a bath towel. "Airborne!"

"Airborne!" We responded and tank.

I stripped down and climbed into the tub. "There was a set of jump wings on the wall of the library." I said matter-of-factly. "Damn this water is getting cold."

"I will get some more." Pedro said stepping over to the fire.

"Do you think that might have been Bill in there?" I asked.

"The whole 82nd was at Fort Bragg, probably one of them tryin' to get home." Bill said getting dressed.

"It is on the general route we had planned." I said, "Watch it!" I shouted at Pedro as he poured boiling water into the tub

"What are the odds?" Pedro said, "It is a big country. "

"Not as big it used to be," Billy said, sipping his wine.

"Not in people, but much bigger in geography. Without phones or mail service, it is like we can only get word from other people. "I took a drink. "We have not received any word from the outside world since we holed up in here. We left a note for Bill back at Walmart, but there was no place or time for a meet up. If he found it would not do any good."

"The only people we have met have been trying to kill us." Pedro objected.

"We are better off stay here." Billy chimed in.

"Safe?" I shot back angrily "How fucking safe are we? You just had to beat a man to death! And what if Bill came our way, wouldn't we shoot him before we knew it? Fuck we might have burned him alive!"

I took a deep breath, I was not prepared for the rage I found spewing from me.

"So what do we do?" Pedro asked nervously.

"We stick to the plan, we get on the road, find the Appalachian Trail, and head towards home." I said defensively.

"Your home!" Billy shot back angrily.

"Bill's home that is the path he will be on!" I almost shouted.

"If we are gonna find Bill we need to head back to Savannah to where we lost him." Billy answered.

"What is suicide?" Pedro objected.

"So is goin' north. " Billy answered, as we all turned to see Hector Stephen coming onto our deck.

"Billy, his majesty wish to speak unto you." Hector said with a cackle. He was no longer fevered, but he had seemed off since his injuries and fever.

I was writing in Hugo the Yugo's book when Billy came back that evening. He came in with a smile and a 45 caliber pistol on his hip.

"Cool!" Pedro said "Where did you get the gun?"

"Pat gave it to me, it was Tom's." He smiled proud. "What reminds me, I told them we would cover day patrol tomorrow so that the others could bury Tom."

It seemed the perfect opportunity to slip away, I thought. As if reading my mind Pedro said, cool, we can beat it then, and by the time they realize we are not coming back we will be long gone."

"We might want to stage our packs tonight so they do not see us leave with them. " I said.

Billy slumped into the easy chair, "I ain't goin'."

"What? Are you crazy?" Pedro shouted.

"I said I was going as far as Georgia, and this IS Georgia." Billy said sadly.

"You are not from here! You met these people when we did this is not HOME!" I agreed.

"Atlanta." Billy said plainly. "I am from Atlanta."

"Your country fried ass is from a city?" Pedro almost laughed.

"I was. " Billy said sadly. "Now I am from here." He took a deep breath. "Fellas you are the only family I got left. Everyone else is ashes and dust." He swallowed hard. "I hope ya'll stay, at least until my weddin', an' then if ya' still want to go, I'll see you sent off in style."

"Billy," I said choosing my words carefully "Are you going to want to do that, even if..."

"Yeah," He said giving me a look that ended all doubt that the topic was open to discussion.

Thing returned to an odd kind of normal after that, Patrols ran into nothing. Not even the dogs returned. On the 25th Pedro and I were sent into Tom Cooper's trailer, to inventory what was left in there. It was a pretty humble compared to Clayton's. It was cleaner than I would have expected, I suppose it was because Cooper had been such an ass, and that he was fat I expected it to be messier.

"Keep an eye out for any kind of maps, or compasses." I said to Pedro.

"I'll tell you Bill, this weird. " Pedro said glancing around,

"Like we should not be here."

"Shit Pedro, Tom is dead. He does not need this stuff anymore." I said dismissively.

"No I mean here,, still." He said as he opened a drawer.

"We will be out of here as soon as Billy gets hitched." I said looking through the closet.

"That is not what I mean. Billy said everyone from his home was ashes and dust, same is true of my people. God knows what happened to the boys back in Panama. How many people are left? Why are we?" Pedro said, with a sadness that I did not even notice anymore.

"Why not us?" I asked back. "It is not like it has been easy to stay alive."

"It is going to be harder with just the two of us." Pedro said before perking up. "Look!" He unfolded a centerfold. "Allow me to introduce, Tracy Voccaro from Glendale California. Her favorite books are Atlas Shrugged, Jonathan Livingston, and the Prophet."

"Let me see that you semi-literate bastard. " I said taking the Playboy magazine gingerly from his hands. "You know that this is?

This as close to a bachelor party as Billy is gonna get." I looked at the perfectly airbrushed body of Miss October 1983, her ambitions were to work with competent people that advanced her career. I scoffed bitterly, good luck with that. Ashes and Dust, most likely the last image of her was burned forever into the retinas of those crew of Ahmed's ship. Her favorite thing make have been watching children grow, but I doubted that she was doing much of that anymore. I dropped the magazine, "Anything useful?"

"Not much, a bunch big and tall clothes, and shit else." Pedro said "This guy dressed like an extra in Hee Haw." That got us both laughing a little.

"He did kind of remind me of that Junior Samples, guy" I joked.

"What one was that?" Pedro asked.

"He was the one in the overalls." I answered.

"They were all in fuckin' overalls. " Pedro answered, getting us both laughing.

Billy came into the trailer and Pedro hid the magazine. "Hey Fellas, how is it goin'?"

"Not too bad, it looks a lot cleaner that I expected." I answered.

"Good, good," Billy said averting his eyes.

"Oh shit, what is wrong?" Pedro asked.

"Well," Billy said averting his eyes.

"You are kicking us out of Clayton's place." I guessed.

"Shit!" Pedro raged. "That is fuckin' bullshit!"

"No it isn't." I soothed, "If Billy is going to stay here, and we are leaving, it is no big deal. He is going to be starting a family." Like Tracy Vaccro never will, I thought. "Besides, who wants to live with their in-laws?"

"Yeah, my cousin Manny lived with his girl's parents, and it sucked." Pedro grinned.

"So what is the word from the big house?" I asked Billy. "Are you setting a date for the spring?"

"Yeah, I guess June." He said blushing.

"Shit that is just a few weeks." I said encouragingly.

Pedro laughed, "Are you registered anywhere?"

"Seriously Billy, when do you need us to move over here?" I

asked.

"I figure around 10 June." He answered, blushing.

"No worries, bro. "Pedro assured him.

The night of 10 June 1984 we had Billy's Bachelors party, it was a subdued get together, all the men where there, except one on duty at the gate. There was very little booze, mostly homemade wine, and the Playboy we gave him was the only gift. At the end of the evening, on Billy, Pedro and I where left.

"Tomorrow is the day huh?" I stated the obvious.

"Yeah," Billy said sadly, "I suppose you are getting edgy to leave."

"Yes, it is a long walk up there, if we are going to get there before fall we are going to need to get started." I said apologetically.

"I am worried about the harvest, without you fellas I do not know how we are gonna keep it secure long enough to ripen." Billy said glumly, and his eyes brightened a bit. "If you had horses you could stay through the harvest, and ride up within a couple weeks."

"That is not going to happen." I said seriously.

"It can!" Billy said. "I talked to Pat about it, if you guys will stick around until September first he will give you each a horse and as many provisions as you can carry!"

"September?" Pedro explained, "That is like forever!"

"It is like seventy days, and it would beat the shit out of walking the entire Appalachian trail." I counseled him.

"You were never too happy humpin' a ruck Pedro!" Billy chided him.

"I suppose not." Pedro though out loud. "That would be a long hump. "

"So we stick around until 1 September, and we ride out of here." I said realizing this is the first time in a long time we had a plan.

The next few days went quickly, Pedro and I got settled into Tom's trailer, it was cramped and the couch was uncomfortable. On the 14th of June Billy came by in the midafternoon, "Hey fellas."

"Billy! Get your butt in here!" I called to him, genuinely glad to see him, we had only seen him on night patrol since his wedding. "How is married life?"

Billy turned around a kitchen table chair, and sat in it

backward, "It is good." He said smiling. "How is the new place?"

"It is a little tight, but we will get by." I said honestly.

Pedro came into the kitchen, smiling. "Hey there redneck."

"Spico" Billy nodded with a smile, stretching his back.

"Is Hector still serenading you at night?" I asked.

"Naw, he has been fine." Billy said, "It is the wife keeping me up."

"Good that stuff was spooky." Pedro said.

"I never understood what the hell he was going on about." I confessed. "I am becomes death?"

"Well," Billy cracked his knuckles, "he was talking about Armageddon. When Jesus left, he left as a lamb, and in the end of day he shall return as lion."

"What about this whole 'I am' thing?" I asked.

"I am, is God, when Moses went to Pharaoh to get the Jew out 'a Egypt he said he was sent by 'I am', at the end of the world when Jesus returns 'I am becomes death." Billy said with a patient smirk.

"You guys are creepy." Pedro said, nervously.

"Why?" Billy asked "This ain't the end of the world dumb ass. It's jus' World War Three."

"What the hell are you talking about Billy?" I asked surprised by my own anger.

"Look lots o' folks died, the damned Government seems ta' be gone, but life goes on. When my kid is born they ain't gonna know what it was to have electricity, or air planes." He answered calmly.

"Millions, maybe tens of millions of people are dead!" I almost shouted.

Billy nodded calmly, "I am sure when Bill Sherman marched from here to the sea, and it looked like the end of the world then too. 'On the wings of abomination he brought desolation', but it all got re-built."

"It has never been like this before." Pedro observed.

"It could take centuries." I supposed, my guts churning. "We need to go back across the valley." I announced, they both looked at me like I was insane.

"Why?" Billy asked.

"What if that was Bill that we chased out there?" Said chilling myself to the bone at the thought of it.

"There ain't no way." Billy scoffed.

"No there IS a way! I am not saying it was him, or even that it is likely, but it IS possible!" I pounded the table.

"Even if it was, what are the odds that he is still there?" Pedro asked.

"Slim, but there is a chance, and if it was him, he could still be there, or at least there could be some clue as to where he went." I said.

"We know where he was going." Pedro said calmly.

"It is worth a shot." I said, "Let's do a daylight patrol and check it out."

"We are on night patrol." Billy answered.

"So we start late, and come back after sun up, you are the Prince, you can make it happen!" I said trying not to sound too angry. "Bill would have come for any of us, and you know that!"

Billy nodded, "We will be there when the sun comes up, if there is a sign o' Bill, we'll find it."

The valley was a nightmare of Impenetrable shadows. The stench of the dead woman seemed more pungent. I wondered of Bill was laying out there rotting somewhere, thanks to us. His own Fire Team, logically I thought not, if it was him that bolted from the school, it seemed unlikely that the guys hit him, whoever it was they had put out a lot of rounds, and broken contact before much fire came back at them. On the other hand, a single bullet could cause all kinds of trouble. We had almost lost Billy to a single blast of bird shot, after all.

The dogs started barking before we got into the town, I could not see them, but everyone in the world had to know something was up. As we passed the overgrown car hulks, I could see movement in the shattered windows. I could feel a thousand eyes on us. The sky was starting to glow with pre-dawn light when we reached the school. We stared across the parking lot from where the rest of the patrol had come under fire.

There was no light coming from the school, and the town was far enough behind us that we could be confident no one could see us anymore. In the growing light my   eyes searched for some evidence of the violence that had been here, bullet pocked trees, empty shell casings, there was nothing. It was as if nothing had happened.

The dawn relieved the first evidence of our attack, as the back scarred brick above the widows of the library came into view. "You want to over watch us with your Mauser?" I asked Billy. He scowled, clearly he did not want to stay in the tree line. "Without it we will have not coverer moving in."

"We should go in the back again." Pedro said annoyed.

"We used that way twice, if there is anyone left, they will have figured that out, an' they'll be ready." Billy spit on the ground. "We need to do bounding over watch to cross that distance. Pedro, you cover Bill an' I until we are set, then we'll cover you."

We both nodded, and drawing I breath and struggled to my feet. Billy and I crossed the first twenty five meters of open ground, then went prone and aimed in on the building and watched Pedro race past use to the edge of the parking lot. Once he was set he waved us forward.

We took up positions, behind a wrecked car, and waved Pedro forward. The smell of burning and decay filled the air. We abandoned our training and tactics, and stood by the burn barrel, there were no signs of life since the attack. The benches were still strewn everywhere, I swallowed hard as I approached the window that I had been accused of jumping through. There was blood on the broken glass, I felt ill.

I could see little through the smoky haze in the library. The door was easy to pull open, Pedro aimed his M16 down the hall, Billy slung his Mauser over his shoulder and drew his new 45, or one might say Tom's old 45. I stepped into the hall, I was right by the door we had thrown the Molotov's in.

Billy slowly pulled the door open, I aimed in, ready to engage anything in the Library while Pedro covered our backs. It was a nightmare of thick air, and back cinders, everything had been consumed by the flames. Blackened hulks of former bookshelves stood barely recognizable as what they had been.

The ash gave the feel of moon dust under my boots, the clouds of ashes kicked up gave the room and almost aquatic feel.

Like an icon in a pagan church the mural of Jump Wings with the word 'Airborne' still stood on the wall. There were no other signs, no bodies, several incinerated mattresses on the floor, until on closer examination I found a handcuff attached to an ancient looking heater near the airborne mural. One side was cuffed to the heater, the other hung open.

What had transpired here, I wondered. A prisoner of some kind I supposed, and wondered if his treatment had been as bad as our prisoner's. Of course I reasoned it might have been much worse. This might have been some poor girl, the coppery taste of fear rose in my mouth, what an end she would have met if she was handcuffed here when we attacked. Burned alive, but there was no body. Had someone come by and cleaned it up, or had we attacked an empty library, book burning, I thought with a shudder.

Clearly someone had made it out of here, perhaps they were the prisoner. "Hey!" Pedro called out from the hallway. "We have company!"

A toe headed boy of not more than ten years old was standing in the parking lot looking at us. "Don't shoot!" I yelled at Pedro.

"No shit." He responded,

Billy waved to the boy, the boy waved back. The boy came over and peered in through a broken window. "Ya'all in the Army?" He asked.

"Yeah," Billy answered, "Ya know what happened here?"

"How come he's got a machinegun and you don't?" The boy asked,

"'Cause I'm a sniper." Billy said coolly.

"But you ain't got a scope." The boy protested.

"Neither do you." Billy smiled, "Now what happened here?"

"There was a fire, an one of the gang that hung out here got burned up. "

"Was he tied up?" I asked.

"Naw, he was down there on the ground, we buried him just yesterday. " The kid answered calmly.

"What kind of people were staying here?" I asked.

"Bad people, they took everything from everybody." The kid said calmly. "They was mostly locals, but they had some guns, and was keepin' folks scared."

"What folks?" Billy asked.

"You know, folks in the town," The kids said climbing in through the window.

"You have folks?" Billy asked.

"Yeah." He answered like it was a stupid question. "I am stayin' with the Grandma. My Mom and Dad was in Atlanta when it happened, I don't rekon they made it out." His statement seemed so 'matter of fact' this was a tragedy that was nothing new, six months in the life of a child was a long time. I thought, six months does not sound like a long time, but that world, of six months before seemed forever ago. All we had seen, it was like we were on another planet, would this boy even remember the days before the world war when he was old and grey? Billy's kid would be like this, to him Atlanta Georgia would be as real to him as the lost city of Atlantis.

Billy dug some venison jerky out of his butt pack, and handed it to the boy. "What is your name?"

"Nathan, "He said hungrily devouring the jerky. "This is good! I aint had nothin' but dog or squirl in a long time!"

"Yeah it's venison." Billy said proudly.

"Billy we got to move," Pedro called out nervously.

More children had begun to gather around the school. "Hey mister! A little blonde girl called, "Give me something to eat!" Billy was digging around in his butt pack, a larger kid punch Nathan and took the second piece of jerky from him.

"Hey you little shit!" I yelled at him aiming my rifle at his face. He could not have been more than 14 with long stringy brown hair, and rat like eyes. He stared down my rifle chewing with his mouth open on the ill-gotten jerky. He showed no fear, like an animal, he was oblivious to danger. I found myself overcome with rage, "You little fuck! " lunged forward planting the compensator at the end of my rifle on his forehead with a thud. He tumbled backward and began screaming and crying. My stomach did a back flip, felt awful.

Billy saw the gather crowed and realized this could turn ugly fast. Begs turned to demands, and outstretched hand turned into grasping claws. We struggled towards the wood line, It was like a sea of filthy children appeared out of nowhere. A rock flew past my face, Billy fired a shot in the air with his 45, which put them off only a step, and soon we were sprinting.

The bushes were alive with movement, screams, and taunts, like a pack of feral humans, churned around us, just out of site. Rocks, stick and pinecones pelted us. Pedro was falling behind, "Wait he screamed." I took a look back and caught a chunk of brick in my right eye.

I staggered to Pedro who was white with fear, as irrational as it might sound now, there was something horrific about the screaming mass of wild things around us, like hyenas tormenting lions, they showed an insane irrational hatred, it was as though anyone who fell behind my be torn from limb to limb by these creatures. Oliver Twists as played by Satan himself I later thought.

I grabbed the suspenders of Pedro's H harness, "For Christ's sake keep up!" I shouted.

Billy was nowhere to be seen, "Billy God Damnit!" I shouted.

"Billy God Damnit!" The shrill voices mocked and laughed. "Billy Billy Billy!" They tormented.

"Rat bastard cock suckers!" Billy raged as he came into view his face bloodied, rifle slung across his back, pistol in hand. "God damn it, keep up!" He shouted.

By the time we reached the fence by the dead woman, the pack of children was slightly further back, I thought we were ride of them until a hail of rocks came from the orchard ahead. Once thumped me in the chest knocking the wind out of me. Pedro braced me with an arm over my shoulder and helped me forward.

Billy fired six times into the orchard with his pistol, and the slide locked to the rear, it was empty. He sent the slide forward, holstered it and unlimbered his rifle. A Shotgun fired ahead of us. Billy aimed in for a moment, until Jim Roberts waddled into view, waving his shotgun wildly. "Jesus Jim, we are damned glad to see you!" Billy called.

I was dizzy and could not yet draw a full breath, but we limped into the compound, chastened but alive.

Pat Miller was red faced "What the hell were you thinking?
"

"We had ta' see what was goin' on back there, for we knew

they was getting' ready to hit us again!" Billy shot back angrily.

"I understand that," Pat waved a dismissive hand, "But what about the Lord of Flies crew that you brought back on us?"

"What were we supposed to do?" Billy asked seeming as angry as Pat.

"Not get followed!" Pat pounded the table.

"We did find out that no one has been back there since we hit the place." I added trying to calm things down. "The locals buried at least one dead."

That seemed to placate Pat a little. "Any indication of who they were?"

"There was an Airborne dawning on the wall, but they seemed to have been holding a prisoner at some point, it may have been the guy in BDUs that jumped through the window when we hit." I said, thinking of the blood on the broken glass. "I think he was hurt."

"Why would they let him write on the wall?" Pat asked thoughtfully.

"Maybe he did it when they weren't looking." Pedro offered.

"Or maybe he was with them, and they turned on him." Billy thought out loud.

"Or he turned against them." Pat said darkly.

"Either way he was not on their side when we got there." I said feeling sick over the darkness I saw in Pat's comments. I think I was projecting that it might have been Bill, or perhaps it was because I was imagining the nightmare this paratrooper had endured.

"The real question is how did they get on your tail?" Pat said sitting down at the table.

"We were talkin' to a kid, "Billy started and Pat's eyes narrowed.

"Did you give him anything? Any food?" Pat asked.

"A little jerky." Billy answered sheepishly.

Pat looked deflated, "You are a good man Billy, but this is a real fuck up." Hearing him swear was startling, but his manner was almost fatherly. "They now know we have food, and where we have it. Before we can plant anything, we are going to have to fence in the orchard and anyplace we are going to plant, or they will steal it before it matures."

"What about them?" Pedro asked.

"We will have to increase patrols until the fence is done, probably some towers to." Pat said, but I knew that was not was Pedro was thinking, I was thinking of it to. What about Nathan and his Grandma? Were they supposed to starve?

The wall was completed on 16 June 1984, it was a string of sharpened logs, formed into pointed Jacks that where around six feet high, it was ragged and would have been east to crawl under, and not hard to climb over, but with a crescent made of 4 towers that were barely taller that the fence.

In order to man the gate and the towers, we did not have enough people to run patrols, and during construction we had been working from sun up to sun down, with one person in over watch with a rifle, and one person on guard at night.

When it was finally done I ended up on night watch, from midnight to four AM. I climbed the rickety tour, and for the first time was glad it had not been built higher. I settled in to the roughhewn bench we had built into it. The fact that we had not put a roof on this, or any of the other towers was a mistake, but everyone was so exhausted, that no one complained.

Looking up into the black sky, tortured with lightening I thought by the end of this shift, I might be the first to lodge that complaint. Like the whip of some pagan God lightening tore across the sky, the world seemed to bellow in pain and rage. I sat there watching this violent storm, it made me think of a piece of classical music, 'Wotan's Rage', and I could not place the sound, just the name. I recalled that the Norse God Odin was sometimes called Wotan, but what did that matter? Not only would all of that die with me, it was already dead. What good was it to remember the name of a piece of music and not the music?

Fat drops of rain began to pelt me, it was going to be a long four hours. My hands were raw, and muscles ached from the work on the wall, Billy, Pedro and I had done more than our share of the manual labor, a necessity of our youth. Several of the men had gone down with heat exhaustion, but not us.

Cold rain kept me awake, and shivering. I wished I knew what had happened to my poncho, but it was not in my butt pack. My teeth chatter and my mind wandered, the tree line was at least fifty meters away, on the other side of the dirt road.

The road was running like a river, I could not see it, but I could hear it. I wondered if that woman's remains would finally be washed away. If we were going to grow food here, it seemed that we would not want her rotting over there. Not that there was a lot left, but it was just a gruesome thought.

It was some time in the darkest part of the night, and I was sitting half asleep with my eyes closed, when a I snapped to alertness by the should of movement in the long grass. My eyes desperately probed the darkness but could see nothing.

The sound drew closer, and my heart pounded. I held my rifle at the ready, but it was no comfort, I had no idea where to point the damned thing.

The sound stopped, and my heart slowed. I wondered if I had imagined it, the rain slacked to a slow drizzle, and I went back to my losing battle against my exhaustion. When I heard movement again, it was from my right, I believed it was my relief, it was time.

I saw the figure of Pedro shuffling along the fence line. When he was close enough he called, "Hey Bill." With that the tall grass around him came alive with darting shadows, my heart seemed to jump into my heart. Pedro darted up the ladder, we sat precariously on the tiny tower.

"What that fuck was that?" Pedro asked terrified.

"I don't know!" I responded, just as panicky   "Where is your rifle?" I asked.

"I dropped it." He said solemnly.

"Shit!" I cursed.

"You are going to need to get it!" I said feeling green with fear.

"Fuck that I am not going down there." Pedro said desperately.

"I will cover you." I offered.

"Fuck it, I am not going." Pedro said sounding like he was going to cry.

"We will go together I said. "Just stay right behind me."

It was awkward to try to hold my rifle in anything close to ready, as I climbed down the rickety ladder. It seemed an eternity of tottering, on the verge of falling into the snarling maw of unseen terrors. Once I reached the ground I felt slightly better, Pedro behind me made me a little braver as I side stepped to where Pedro had been standing when whatever happened had happened.

It seemed forever I peered into the gently waving grass, and Pedro crawled around looking for his rifle. "Got it!" He said with joy.

"Thank fucking God!" I exhaled.

"I guess you are relieved, bro." Pedro said, and I faced the long dark walk back, alone.

It seemed to me that June of 1984 that we were experiencing a bizarre return to the 19th century, several of the men worked out a plow that could be pulled by a horse, and we spent the next two weeks tearing up the earth behind the fence. Billy, Pedro and I spent most of our time on Guard duty, we had three of us on during the night and just one during the day.   We all ended up planting by hand, it was back breaking work, step, plant, cover. Step plant cover….over and over. The winds had shifted again, and the sky was a cruel, empty blue, the sun beat down on us all day. On the night of 30 June I struggled up into the tower, my flesh seemed to throb with sunburn.

I collapsed into the seat in the tower, behind me where the rows and rows of planted seed, ahead the gloom of the woods. For the first time that I could remember since our time at sea I could see the stars. I am not sure I was providing much security as I sat there looking up at the stars. They seemed larger than before, 'before' I thought. Before the War? It did not seem like a war to me, it was like an act of God. Millions, tens of millions, maybe more killed in a single evening. Then what? Were there Armies and Navies still battling it out, out there somewhere? It seemed impossible in that world of the ever present danger of starvation and death.

The ship we saw explode made me think that perhaps there was still a war out there. What was between here and home? More wild dogs, and starving people, I supposed. Perhaps Bill was out there, bleeding and alone, deserted by his friends, deserted by me. Guilt raked my guts, some soldier, I thought.

What would be my fate if I could find the Army? I was a deserter in the time of war, wasn't I? I supposed they hanged deserters, but the unit had pretty much dissolved. It disturbed me beyond the fear of execution, had I done the right thing? I had started this journey, so that Bill would not have to do it alone. If he was not dead he was going it alone, I set my heart to it, that night, I would make it home.

Billy came over that afternoon to check a Pedro, we sat in kitchen, the air was thick with humidity, the blinds were closed to keep the sun out but it seeped in everywhere, as did the shrill voices of the rear guard of the army of crows that was polish off the last few morsels of anything edible. Pedro came out of the bedroom, bleary eyed from a nap. "How Ya doin?" Billy asked in a voice that was a tired specter of his former cheery disposition. Pedro shrugged, and sat at the table. "It's ok, not infected or nothing."

"Think you can travel?" He asked with excessive casualness. Pedro looked scared. "I suppose, if you don't need us to help with the harvest."
The words almost hurt, "There is not going to be a harvest, Pedro." I said as evenly as I could. "The rain washed everything away and the crows picked the place clean."

We ended up gathered around a AAA map of the Eastern

United States for most of the afternoon, it was like trying to give directions to the corner store on a globe, perhaps one that still had sea monsters, artfully inscribed. Billy spoke enthusiastically, I wistfully thought of him coming with us, but I knew better.

"Probably be safer to travel during the day, you are less likely to run into trouble," Billy mused.

"We are going to have to cut through the valley in broad daylight?" I asked.

"Fuck that!" Pedro said rubbing the stitches in his head.

"You keep messing with those they are never going to heal." I scolded.

"You can take the skeleton road." Billy offered. "Or get started that first night, put some distance in before sun up."

"Sounds like a big change of getting ambushed." I said, feeling ill again.

"I think the highway might be the way to go." Pedro said glumly. The thought of those woods at night filled him with terror. I could see deep in his eyes, the animalistic terror I recalled from when he awoke screaming. I struck me that he had ceased his night

359

terrors around the time of the beginning of the War. It was like he saw it coming, or more like felt it coming. They say the jungle knows, Pedro knows, I thought at the time, and wrote as much in Hugo's journal that night. Latter events would dissuade me from any thought of him as Pedro the Prophet.

"I hate to say it Billy, but can you really spare the horses?" I asked. "I told you they were yours." He answered firmly. "Set you off in style I said, 'and I will. Besides, I can't feed 'em."

"They could feed you." I said coolly.

"I can slaughter 'em I can't keep the meat good, we're low on salt." He straitened his back as a clergyman tempted suddenly reminded of his holy orders. "They are yours, I gave you my word. My kid ain't gonna have a damned Indian giver fer a Father!" I smiled, it was an odd bit of pride. They were times we still felt like kids playing soldier, but here was Billy the Prince, soon to be a Father, and heir to the throne of Sanctuary, this hard scrabble bit of Georgia clay that in the moment I was certain would endure these trials with dignity. My mind drifted across his tiny Kingdom to that skull, and the shrieking terrors waited in the woods. I chill went down my spine, and suddenly the time to leave this place could not come soon enough, I would latter torture myself with accusations of cowardice for such desertions, but in this moment these thoughts, and the thoughts of the obligations to Bill Collins' memory where distance unformed ghosts of thoughts, momentum was what sustained us. We planned our departure precisely because this was the plan. The plan, go home. Home must be gone to. It was Bill's plan, it was our plan. It made sense of the world.

The following morning I met Traveler, my horse. A brown horse, I knew nothing of horses then, and little more now. Billy showed me how to approach her without getting kicked in the head. He explained the basics, and we even took her for a test drive, it was not hard, though I had to admit to feeling I was going something wrong, it was not like 'in the movies."

Pedro's horse was named 'Lucky', I hoped that the two would make for lucky travel, and made that lame joke when we were dining on crow that evening. Billy wanted to ride to the entrance to the Appalachian Trail with us, but he would have had to come back alone, and we all agreed that to travel alone was insanity.

The found us a decent compass, and we talk at length about survival on the trail and all. I was the 27the of July when we finally decided that we were in out last day in Sanctuary. I slept that last night in the trailer, and I wondered at the world ahead of us. Pedro seemed to sleep just fine, I was up most of the night, in the morning we gathered at the barn, and made us we had everything we were going to need. Tammy ran up to us breathlessly, explaining she needed us right away.

Hector was on the floor of his trailer wailing wordlessly when we arrived. Estel had died in her sleep. We spent the day of the 28 digging her a grave down by the orchard. Uncomfortably close to where the blond woman's skull stood an eyeless watch on the tree line.   We said nothing as we dug. Tammy brought us some water, and he took a break in the shade. The sun was high in the hazy grey sky, when they brought her down wrapped in the sheets of the bed she had died in. We tried to make it dignified as slide her into the grave, but it was awkward. She landed crumpled, in a corner of the grave, I jumped down into the grave, and pulled her out strait. It simply seemed the right thing to do. When I tried to get back out I couldn't "Damn it Pedro!" I shouted a little more urgent than needed. He helped me out and I flopped onto the ground, vultures circled high overhead. Billy had already started filling the hole in. I was transfixed on those circling specters, what did the world look like to them? What did we look like? I thought of an old twilight zone episode where they could see the number of who would die next on their forehead. What number hung over my head? Over all of us?

I shook off the thought and went back to work. I slept well that night, and no one moved towards the grave until the afternoon when we all gathered and paid our respects. I took some comfort in the fact that we buried her deep enough that the vultures and the dogs could not get at her. I staggered back to the trailer and went to sleep without eating.

I went down to the barn and brushed Traveler, I tried to put the saddle on her, and found it a little more challenging that I thought it would be. I eventually got it on, and took her on a short ride around the orchard, it was terrifyingly high and wobbly. I know seems insane that someone who had jumped out of airplanes would be afraid of falling off a horse, but I was. After I made it back to the

barn and took the saddle off, I went back to the trailer and told Pedro

we needed to ride the next day, it suddenly seemed insane that I was

planning to rise a thousand miles on my first tip on a horseback.

Pedro found his trip around the orchard on Lucky even more

terrifying than my trip the day before. It took some time before I

could convince him to even sit up straight, as he was initially

clinging to the back of the horse like a baby chimp. Billy got a laugh

out of this, and it helped egg Pedro on to site up strait, suddenly I

seemed like a competent horseman.

That night the three of use eat together on the porch of our trailer.

We talked about survival on the trail, Billy seemed to have a lot to

tell us. He was worried. We both knew we would not have made it

this far without him. Now we would be on our own. Pedro asked

him a few different ways if he would come with us, but I already

knew he wouldn't.

The sun rose on that first day of August, and the sky was blood red.

Moister hug heavy in the air. The population of sanctuary all tuned

out to wave goodbye. It made leaving bitter sweet and a little more frightening. Only Hector was missing as we rode our horses down the steep hill for the last time. He came running waving a small canvas bag. "Don Quixote! Don Quixote!" He shouted. He almost knocked me off of my horse as the bag stuck me in the chest. "Save the damsels, Don! Save them!" He shouted.

His attention turned to Pedro. "Sancho Paza! Every faithful Sancho!" He bellowed, Pedro was wide eyed with fear, it was as if fear madness was contagious.

Billy grabbed Hector. "Let 'em be ya' crazy old Coot!"

My rifle was bandit slung across my back, I kept the reins in one hand and waved with the other. "You take care Billy! If you see Bill well him, you know."

"I will!" He said with a smile, restraining Hector with one hand while Tammy cling to his side.

The orchard faded all too quickly over my shoulder as I turned towards the Skeleton Road. Once more, into the wild, I thought.

The road spread out before us, looking endless. The sky was low and grey, the early morning mist clung to the trees, like a primordial fog. The sound of the horse's hooves seemed frightfully loud. The stomach knotted at the thought of what nightmares would be drawn to the sound.

The sides of the road were overgrown, as the wilderness seemed to be reclaiming the road, the cracks in the pavement sprouted green fingers, as if to tell us that the time of man was over. It looked as if a great civilization had died here a life time ago, not ten months.

As the fog left and the heat found us, our fears wilted, as did we. It was early afternoon when we stopped under a highway overpass. The horses with frothy with sweat, we flopped down on the pavement, my shirt was soaked in the sweat, I took a deep drink of water, looking up, I saw Traveler looking down longingly. I knew nothing of horses at the time, and little even now. Looking at that poor sweating creature, and I suddenly felt awful. I struggled to my feet and unfastened his saddle. "Pedro, you need to look after your horse." I said trying not to sound pissed. I was pissed, but not at him.

I was worried Traveler was not going to make it, I ended up pouring water into my hand and let her lap it up. There was no way she was getting enough to make up for what she had lost. We rested there a long while, and when we headed out we walked, holding the reins of the horses.

It was late afternoon when we found a pond by the highway. The horses drank deeply, and we collapsed onto the ground. My feet burned, blisters stuck my socks to my feet. I let them soak in the pond. Pedro fell asleep on the ground snoring.

I looked up at the blue sky and drifted off to sleep. I awoke to the blood red sun set, and realized how stupid we had been we were defenseless, "Pedro! Wake up!"

Pedro sat up wordlessly, and in a few minutes we had a small fire going and we laid or heads on our saddles.

I decided to take first watch, my heart was still pounding from that terrifying and guilty feeling of waking up unprotected out there. Between the packs of wild dogs, and the shuffling zombielike survivors on skeleton Road my mind was full of all the horse could of the fallen us as we stupidly slept there. Even with all of that staring into the fire, my mind drawn in to the visions of hell that one sees underneath the comfort of a crackling fire, my mind wandering through all of the horrors that I'd missed. I wondered if all the people that I had known, before Panama, before the Army, and before that day that millions of people died maybe tens of millions I wasn't sure, and I had just not been there. I had just not noticed, I wondered what kind of end those people had known. With these morose thoughts plotting through my head, my eyelids got heavy, poking the fire with a stick I knew I could just slouch over and fall asleep. The very thought stirred me to action, I painfully stretched placing my fire stick on the ground, and hefting my rifle I stumbled around her little campsite, were Pedro slept quietly, as did the horses. I staggered around as long as I could, and then I went to shake Pedro and let them know is his watch. When I touched his shoulder he recoiled in horror, "its okay it's just me", I said reassuringly "take it easy man to spook the horses."

He set up quietly, "I got this man get some sleep." I mumbled some form of gratitude and probably flopped down on my saddle drifting off into a very dark sleep.

It was one of those times it was so tired I did and even dream. When I woke the sun was fairly high in the sky and I set up with a bit of a start. "Pedro, what the hell did you let me sleeps so long?" Looking around I saw the fire was out, but still smoking. My horse Traveler, stood idly by looking at me with a kind of bored disinterest. Pedro and his horse where gone. My heart leapt into my mouth, I felt sick to my stomach, I glanced around his saddle, his weapon, and everything was gone!

My mind raced, my first thought was that something happened to him, but I quickly dismissed that, for no raider or robber was going to take him and his equipment and leave me unmolested. He must have left on his own, but for the life of me I couldn't think of why. I could not believe he would just abandon me out here, the more I thought about I decided he'd gone scouting for food or something with the thought of being back before I awoke. I kicked the ground it was so stupid. I wondered if you'd run into trouble if I would've heard the shots.

I quickly saddled Traveler, and started down the road, only to hesitate wondering if maybe gone in a different direction. Maybe gone back to sanctuary, but that seemed unlikely. If he tried to get off the side the skeleton Road to get too far ahead of them and never find them. He went far forward I would run into him coming back. In the end I went about a quarter of a mile and then just returned to her little campsite. My stomach knotted with doubt and concern, as much for my own safety is for Pedro's to be honest I sat there. I gave Traveler a break from his saddle, and rekindle the fire.

Traveler and I cooked under the overpass through the heat of the Georgia day. My mood swung between anger and fear on a moment to moment basis. I resolved saddle up and ride out after him and then thought better of it over and over again. It was around three in the afternoon when I finally did ride forward.

The hills were getting a little more noticeable around the highway. I climbed one of the more predominant ones, on foot leading Traveler by the reins. I made camp under some pines and tried to get a decent fire going hoping that Pedro would see it.

Long after dark, my eyes burning with the sting of pine smoke I ate some of the canned provisions that Billy had provided for us. I saved some for Pedro, and gave several handfuls of the oats that we had to Traveler. It was obvious that we did not have nearly enough food for men or horses. I wondered again it may be Pedro I decided he had a better chance on his own, or maybe he really had just scouted for food. At the time had no way of knowing.

In spite of the heat of the day the wind on that hillside was bitter cold that night. I kept the lonely vigil hunched over the fire, getting sleep moments at a time. When I woke in the morning, my legs were painfully asleep. I staggered and stumbled around the camp cursing. I cursed my loneliness, my legs, my fate, and all of the thousands of horrors that had become routine in my life. The newfound sense of purpose I mounted Traveler and we headed up the skeleton Road towards the Appalachian Trail.

It was before noon I saw the farm. There was no direct road to it from the highway, but there it was. I looked for a way to get down to it, I noticed that there was a culvert running under the highway several hundred meters ahead. Traveler reluctantly put on a little speed as we went forward to investigate. I dismounted and tied the horse to the guardrail and scouted around on foot. I found a narrow path down that led to the creek bed, my heart leapt when I saw the clear imprint of horse hooves headed towards the farm.

I led Traveler down the narrow path, cursing Pedro because it was far too narrow and dangerous to bring horse down, if his horse and fallen on him they would have both died, and I struggle to ensure I didn't do that. As if you punctuate precariousness of our situation I noticed a flock of the ever present circling vultures had found Traveler and me and they were watching eagerly for mistakes.

Traveler stopped for a long drink of the slow-moving water I was very unsure if it was safe, but it was clear that she was not going to be dissuaded. Once he finally slaked his thirst, I remounted and we headed along the creek bed. It was sometime later we came to the point where the trail was less clear. They had headed off in the general direction of the farm but was hard, if not impossible to be in their exact tracks.

I tied Traveler to a tree and unslung my rifle. I followed the trail the best I could, it was not clear until I came across a massive blood smear, my stomach sank, I wanted to run back to Traveler and ride away, I wanted to run forward and find Pedro. I stood there looking over the sights of my rifle, my heart hammering in my chest. I didn't know what to do. After what seemed like several eternities I crept forward, every rustle of leaves or grass seemed to be a thunderous invitation to bloody horrible death.

I picked up horse tracks headed toward the farm following them in terror I finally came upon the Iron Gate, a corpse hung from a noose on the gate. Pinned to his shirt with an arrow through his chest was s paper with the word 'Looter' scrawled on it. Looking up to the looter's face and I saw Pedro's dead eyes staring back at me. I ran as fast as I could, branches tore at my face, my heart was ready to burst.

I stumbled several times, when I burst through the bushes I startled Traveler, I dropped my rifle as I untied her. Bending over to pick it up the reigns slipped from my hand. I seized my rifle by the carrying handle and tried to get into get my foot into the stirrup. I fell onto my back, and saw Traveler trot off. I lay there on my back waiting for a storm of arrows to end me. As fear sank into despair, I thought to myself. I am alone. I am alone. I am alone. Pedro is dead, Bill is dead. I am alone. Fucking coward! Anger took me, I rolled over onto my belly and slithered into the bushes. I am going to go back to that farm and kill every last one of those Sons of Bitches.

I rose to my feet and began stalking toward the farm. Soon I was walking, then practically running. When I reached the blood stain, I stopped and kneeled. Listening to the sounds of the forest, the vultures marked where Pedro was hanging, I vomited and washed out my mouth from my canteen. My knees quaked as I went forward on my bloody task, the closer I drew the slower I went.

When my eyes fell again on Pedro's body, his eyes were gone, the vultures eyed me nervously but didn't leave. I aimed in at them, but realized it would alert my would be victims. Victims I thought, was that the right word? They murdered my friend they were going to die for it! The 'Looter' sign turned towards me as the vultures tore at him. Was he a looter to them? What would I be? Would there be woman and children there? Was I going to kill them too? Or just orphan them and leave them orphaned and alone in this nightmare to be torn apart by packs of God knows what? I fell to my knees and wept, I didn't care if I the arrows came, I didn't care about anything.

Time passed and death never came, tired to the bone I stumbled back to the blood stain and on towards the road. I found

Traveler waiting patiently near where I had tied her, I took his reigns and lead him back up to the road.

Once on the road I climbed onto Traveler and sat. I wanted to go back to Sanctuary, see Billy, tell them about Pedro, and maybe stay a while. How long? If I went back there I would stay, I would never see home again.

On the fifth of August I found the camp site at the entrance of the Appalachian Trail, there was a sprawling tent camp around it. Hollow eyed skeletons eyed me nervously as I road through, children clung to Mother's ribs, older children traveled in packs beside me hands outstretched begging for food. I encouraged Traveler to speed up, soon the group of children became a swarm, their begging turned to demanding, claw like hands dug at my legs, the saddle, everything they could reach. A pair of small black children pulled with all their weight on the reigns jerking Traveler's head to right. She panicked kicking her hind legs out smacking the girl the face with a sickening crunch. I fell hard into the crowd, they scattered like roaches, the wind knocked out of me, I stared up at the sky for a long breathless moment.

Adults joined the swarm of children as I struggled to my feet, a large black man brandished the bloody corpse of the little girl Traveler has kicked, he shook her ragged corps at me spattering me with her blood, shrieking obscenities at me. Hands tore at me from every angle, I unslung my rifle and brought the butt of it against a temple of a teen who hand me by the suspender, he went down hard. The howls of disapproval filled my ears, my thumb swept the selector lever to full auto and I loosed a burst of 5.56mm bullets over the heads of my tormentors.

I was suddenly alone, I chased after Traveler who was already headed out of the camp. Rocks and bottles filled the air as they pelted me.

I avoided serious injury, as did Traveler, aside from a need gash above her front right knee. It was near midnight when we stopped under a grove of pines. I found my saddle bags had been pilfered in the earlier melee. I drifted off to sleep hungry, and awoke shivering before dawn.

It was two days later that I finished the crackers that were there last of my provision from Sanctuary. I sat by a small fire wishing I had more food, I leaned on the saddle, I was worried that it had been wearing into Traveler's skin. She was laying on the ground not far away, I looked up into the stars where the smoke dissipated. Clouds churned though the sky, there were many nights when the stars where not visible. That night it was clear, possibly because of the mountain of blackness gathering on the horizon. I drifted off to sleep and dreamed of my bed in Panama and be feeling of not being alone.

August Sixth, Cold rain woke me before dawn, the fire was out, I figured it was best just to get going. Traveler wouldn't stand. The cut above her knee was swollen and smelled awful. I collapsed to my knees, the icy rain soaked us both.

I struggled to my feet, I didn't know what to do. I thought about shelter, but that wouldn't do Traveler any good. So I staggered off in search of food that was not toxic for men or horses. I found nothing, but my feet were hurting, my socks soaked through, immersion foot was likely, but I could not find anything to eat or anyplace to get dry.

I slogged back towards Traveler, my head bowed and my feet dragging. When I reached her it was getting dark, I chewed on some jerky that was to salty to be good, and wrapped myself in my poncho for a miserable night of shivering.

The rain continued into the seven August, I set out again looking for food, I found some cat tails growing in a swollen stream. I pulled them up from the muck barely rinsing them off in the creek before wolfing down the tender white inner stalks. Once the grove of cat tails was wiped out I stuffed my pockets full and headed back.

Climbing the hill toward were Traveler lay, the rain stopped and I found a moment of peace in the misty air among the pines, I suppose I thought that thing were going to be ok, that the pocket full of roots would feed Traveler and in a day or two we'd be back on the trail. I was sapped from my reverie by monstrous shriek. My blood seemed to curdle in my veins, I froze. I crept up the hill me knees trembling. My M16 gripped tightly, safety off.

The scene that unfolded before me was a nightmare, Traveler kicked desperately from her side at a German Sheppard that tore at her throat, another dog turned its bloody maw towards me barking and snapping. I shot it in the forehead it fell with a brief yelp. The other dogs seemed to suddenly disappear. Traveler lay there bloody making a sound of misery, her throat was ripped, as was her gut, I stood over her for a long time before I shot her in the head, slouched down the hill and trudged in the rain to the North.

I found a bridge to sleep under that afternoon and shivered through the night wrapped in my poncho. Three days later the rations ran out.

On 10 August I found a shelter set up for hikers on the trail, it was empty but it was nice to sleep indoors. Started regretting not cutting up that dog or Traveler for meat.

The last entry in the journal from the Appalachian Trail read "August 13 I shot a rabbit".

I slouched through the snow wrapped his poncho, poncho liner and a blanket salvaged from an abandoned car. Towels and garbage bags duct taped over my boots kept the snow out, I was out of energy and patience, if I stopped I would freeze, if I kept moving I would eventually collapse and freeze. This was going to be it and I just didn't care anymore. I walked down the middle of the snow covered road, no more snow plows anymore. A sign partially obscured with snow read 'Welcome to New York State, the Empire State. "

I laughed until I wept, I was going to die the night I stepped into my home State. To hell with that I said aloud as he staggered on toward a distant grove of snow covered pines. I imagined that I could smell a fire as a trudged on.

An empty parking lot and a green wooden building greeted my exhausted eyes, the sign outside said 'Starla's' smoke curled from the chimney. I pushed the heavy wooden door open nervously, there where tables and booths, a long antique wooden bar complete with bottles of liquor my eyes fell on a real horror he shouted with shock as I saw the emaciated scare crow staring back at him from behind a wild red beard. I laughed to the point of tears then I realized it was my own reflection that had so struck me.

A white bearded old man appeared, "Come one in Son." He said warmly gesturing toward the restaurant, "Take a seat anywhere. I bet you could use something hot, how about some soup?" I could not speak, or move for a long moment. I don't have any money I thought in a panic. I wondered if they'd take something in trade. I grabbed the magazine pouch on my belt and withdrew a 30 round magazine, the old man recoiled in fear. "No! For trade!" I blurted out.

The man laughed, and put a hand on my shoulder "Son, you scared the hell of out of me." He took the magazine out and withdrew three bullets, handing the magazine back "Since you are not going to rob me, I am not going to rip you off. This will more than cover a hot meal. "

The old man's name was Henry he was gregarious and chatty. I did not catch much of the details I was just happy to be talking to another human being. The one take away for me was that I should check my folk's cottage in the Finger Lakes an trudge the rest of the way to Rochester. I slept that night on the floor by the fireplace, it was the best night sleep of my life, and Henry took a single 5.56mm round for my breakfast.

Over breakfast I told Henry that the cottage in the Finger Lakes wasn't but 60 miles away and that I should be able to make it within a week. The scowled "Where will you sleep?" He asked.

"I find what I can, abandoned cars, under bridges, once you get a fire going it isn't that bad." I said enjoying my eggs.

He shook his head slowly from side to side, "That doesn't sound right."

I had to chuckle, he could not imagine what had happened over the last year since the world ended.

"I think it is in Galatians where we are told: Carry each other's burdens, and in this way you will fulfill the law of Christ." He sad returning to his gregarious demeanor, "So that is what I am going to, I will get you to your folk's cottage. "

"Well that's very nice of you Henry, but how do you intend to do that?" I asked genuinely hopeful.

"I have a little bit of fuel left, should be enough." He said in a low tone, like it was a secret.

"I thought all the vehicles where fried by EMP or something," I said my heart racing.

"I have an old pickup, it still runs." He said proudly. "You said yourself you were at your bitter end when you found us here. I think God put us in your path so we can do this."

The terrain that would have tortured me flew by, we could make almost 30 miles an hour in spite of the thick snow on the road. The crushing of the snow under the tires made an otherworldly sound. Henry was steadily preaching trying to save my soul, it wasn't that I was resistant, I was just so overwhelmed, I couldn't comprehend. I hadn't heard a word from another human being in four months and now I was overwhelmed. Though Henry's good natured rambling paled by the magnitude of the reality outside the window, I was going home.

Outside the town there was a roadblock made of a few trucks and 55 gallon drums. A Young man with an American flag baseball cap carrying an AR15 with a collapsible butt stock approached the driver's side window with caution. Henry rolled down the window, short of breath from the effort and perhaps some fear. "Good morning young man."

The kid looked us up and down, his eyes fixating on my M16 that I had placed across my lap. "What's your business here?" He asked.

"I am Bill McGill I am looking for my folks." I said stomach knotting for the confrontation I was sure was going to break out.

"Head up to the firehouse." He commanded "You know where that is?" He asked suddenly relaxed.

"Yes, I remember." I answered, and just like that we were on our way. The village was remarkably unchanged. We were the only vehicle on the road, but people were walking around, bundled against the cold, the same as every winter, there were even some Christmas decorations up.

When I climbed out in front of the firehouse, Henry shook my hand, "Good luck Son, God Bless you."

"You aren't coming in?" I said shocked.

"Naw the Wife is going read me the riot act as it is," As I was pulling my pack on and slinging my rifle it suddenly struck me that I had never seen Henry's Wife, or anyone else at Starla's. I thought of the rumors of the First Sergeant in Panama chopping up his wife and eating her, I immediately regretted this thought. "Take this." I said trying to pay Henry with a magazine. He just waved and drove off. "I will get my reward in the hereafter. Find Jesus Bill, trust me on this."

With that he was gone, I walked into the firehouse and was greeted by an enormous collage of notes and photos covering the walls. "Have you seen this boy?" "Sara we will wait for you at Grandpa's cabin,', "If you have seen or heard of this man, please tell...." I don't know how long I stared at that wall, the enormity of how broken the world was just washed over me. My eyes fell on a photo of a young paratrooper in a fresh beret, it was obviously an Airborne School Graduation photo. My eyes filled with thought of all my friends I would never see again. Pull yourself together man, I thought as I started to move on, and I caught a chill. The note said "Private First Class William McGill, Missing since the November 1983 Holocaust, anyone with information about his whereabouts should contact the McGills at 783 Honeywell Drive."

I pulled my picture down from the wall and looked around for someone to talk to, a rail thin man with an impossibly wild white beard, and a number of missing teeth was sitting at a desk with a sign in book, sipping coffee. He lept to his feet looking like he was going to hit me, I was shocked when he hugged me and wept. I hadn't recognized my own Father.

The walk to the cottage should have been familiar enough, I had spent many summers there as a kid, but I have never seen it in winter. It was less than a mile but it took a long time as Dad kept having to stop for coughing fits.

The Franklin stove in the kitchen was still burning, but was low. When I asked where Mom was I already knew. I had seen a grave out in the trees, I had noticed he hadn't mentioned her. "How did it happen?"

"She was blinded by the flash that hit Rochester. It took us weeks to get down here. She was sick "His voice trailed off. The rest of the day was quiet. He seemed always distracted, and coughing badly.

I collapsed on a real bed, and faded off to sleep. In the late hours of night I awoke and stripped off my tattered uniform, my feet where in terrible shape and smelled awful. I awoke in the morning unable to walk, when I put weight on my feet I collapsed on the floor with a crash. My Dad came rushing in with great effort hoisted me back on the bed.

He rushed off to get help, as I waited I peeled back my socks painfully, grey wrinkled flesh told me I had immersion foot. Eventually my Dad returned with the kid in the American Flag hat, who I later learned was Dan Bedard, and Dr. Weinstein, the Dentist.

Dr. Weinstein looked seriously at my feet immersion foot and frost bite, it was only going to get worse as it healed. The finger tips, earlobes were all in rough shape.

"Over the next few days you have redness and swelling in the frost bitten areas and will need to look for the flesh darkening, if that happens we are going to have to cut off that necrotized tissue before you end up with an infection. This isn't bad as it is, you might lose a finger or a part of a toe, but this could have been much much worse." Dr. Weinstein said solemnly. "I will be back tomorrow to see how you're doing."

"Thank you." I mumbled, lose parts of me sounded awful and the pain had already begun. After Dad and the Doctor left

Dan stayed behind. He had that CAR15 over his shoulder and looked younger than I had imagined. He seemed to want to talk and though I wasn't in the mood, I asked him his name. That opened the flood gates, he asked me questions about my M16, the Army, Panama, my theories on the War. I told him what I had heard down in the Keys about the war starting by accident in Germany. He seemed to think that nuclear attack was the first step in a Soviet Invasion, and this was a popular theory among many of the locals.

Over the next few days Dan came by and kept me company anytime he wasn't on duty, I found his hero worship of me a little bizarre, but I guessed this was what it was like to have a kid brother.

It was on my sixth day in the village we went to the town hall meeting, it seemed almost everyone was there. It was held in the American Legion Hall, at one end of the room was a stage with a half dozen chairs facing out over rows of folding chairs filled with restless people. Dan and I hung out in the back, my Dad had refused to come. Dan explained that the 'Emergency Committee' was formed in the days after the Professor Cornell was the Chairman, Dan didn't know where or what he'd taught, just that he was a University Professor who owned a cottage by the lake and was here when it all happened. The Vice Chair was Graduate Student of his named Kari something or other who he had essentially insisted on after the rest of the Emergency Committee was elected. The Sergeant at Arms was a Rochester City Policeman named Simonetti who had been in the village when the attack came. The head of the Town watch and Commander of the American Legion Post Commander was a Vet named Munroe. Mrs. Kelly was the Principal of the local school and was the newest member of the Committee since a Reverend that had held her seat died several month before. The Last member was my Dentist Turned Doctor, Dr. Weinstein.

The room quieted when Simonetti walked in, he wore a Rochester Police uniform, but would have looked like a cop without it; heavy set, mustache and all, and he trooped to the end of the stage and stood behind a chair. Kari was behind him, a short chubby woman with round wire glasses he carried an arm load of books and papers. Behind her came Professor Cornell a thin dignified figure with white neatly parted hair and threadbare sport coat. He was followed by Munroe a short twitchy looking man with an Errol Flynn mustache. Behind him Mrs. Kelly, a short woman with a bird like nose and weak chin, came out with her eyes downcast. Finally out came Dr. Weinstein short far and exhausted looking with his salt and pepper beard and hair projecting in every direction.

The Professor banged the table "Attention, Attention. The Fifty Third Meeting of the Emergency Committee is now called to order. Please be seated, Mr. Vice Chairmen what old business do we have to attend to?"

Kari shuffled through her papers nervously, "The motion to scrap the Legion Christmas food drive was tabled at the end of the last meeting." She said nervously.

"Table it all you want, it isn't being scrapped." Munroe snapped. "This community can take care of itself without being micro managed by this Committee."

"Mr. Munroe, you do not have the floor!" The Professor scolded.

"You probably hording food you're damned self." Simonetti taunted, he was easily a head taller and twenty years younger than Munroe.

Munroe turned crimson and the tow began shouting at one another incoherently and the Professor banged the table endlessly. After the din faded Kari spoke up "Mr. Chairmen I request the floor."

"The Floor recognizes Vice Chairmen Dunham."

Kari began nervously, "While Munroe rightly points out that this community is very capable of all manner of self-sufficiency in ordinary times. These are far from ordinary times, we remain isolated and food stocks are running low."

"Ending our food drive will change that?' Munroe chimed in ignoring procedure.

"Of course not," She said in a conciliatory tone. "The only problem with the American Legion Food Drive continuing is that takes away from our existing food distribution system, it will be far for effective if all food passes through the existing system run by the Committee."

"How is that more effective?" Dr. Weinstein asked.

"Please follow the procedure!" The Professor pleased.

"If the Legion is doling out food and we are as well someone could get food from them then turn right around and get some from us, getting more than their fair share." Kari said calmly. The audience exploded with shouts or anger. "I am not saying anyone would!" She recoiled.

"Yes you are!" An old woman shouted, "Calling everybody crooks!"

"How'd you get so fat?" Someone shouted, the Professor pounded the table "Sergeant at Arms have that man removed!" Simonetti signaled to two 'Officers' manning the doors and they escorted the man out. The 'Officers were in civilian attire but wore makeshift badges on their jackets. "If we cannot be civil I will close these proceeding to the public!" He pointed his gavel at the Committee member, "And as to the members of this Committee, I will tolerate no more breaches of protocol. We have these rules for a reason, for THIS reason. I will remove anyone who speaks out of turn."

"Mr. Chairmen point of inquiry." Dr. Weinstein spoke slowly, "What are the advantages to continuing having both systems continuing?"

"Mr. Munroe, could you care to address that?" The Professor asked cheerily.

"There are not two systems. We at the Legion accept what people donate to use and distribute it to whomever asks. The Committee is taking whatever is confiscated."

"Point of Order!" Kari shouted "We have never confiscated anything!"

"All that stuff that was collected from the stores and the empty houses when the balloon went up, whatever you wanted to call it. "Munroe continued "The point is that you have no right to dictate what people do with their own food."

"Point of Order. We are not trying to dictate anything, we are only try to ensure that what is freely given gets to who needs it the most." Kari said smoothly.

"Point of, "Mrs. Kelly started,"I mean request to make a motion."

"What is your motion?" The Professor asked smoothly.

"I move that the Legion Food drive continue with under the condition that the donated food be distributed through the Fire Station."

"Oh so you can decide who gets what?" Munroe snapped.

The Professor rolled his eyes "We have a motion on the floor, any seconds?"

"I second." Kari said immediately.

"Who votes in favor of the motion say Aye."

"What no debate?" Munroe squawked red-faced.

Everyone but Munroe and Weinstein voted "Aye"

"Who votes Nay?" Asked the Professor looking around casually. "I count 4 Ayes, two abstain, and Ayes have it the Motion carries,"

"Wait just a God Damn minute!" Munroe leapt to his feet, quickly the room erupted into chaos.

"Let's get the hell out of here, "I said to Dan. "My feet are killing me and this is pointless."

The following day Dr. Weinstein came by and told me I was healing nicely from the cold weather injuries but the immersion foot was still a concern, he wanted me to keep my feet in the open air and elevated until as much as I could over the next few days.

I slept and eat for several days my Father would bring me food to my bedside, he said very little, his coughing fits grew worse. I head his screaming at night, Vietnam nightmares I assumed, they were nothing new in our home, but my Mother's absence hung over the cottage, I kept expecting her to walk around the corner. More than a few times I heard him talking to her only to find him sitting alone. Dan came over to ask me if I wanted to come down to the Legion Hall will him, I was happy to do.

"You should bring you M16." He said to me which I thought was odd. "Why?" I asked expecting him to say something about the Russians being due any day, I could see that he was nervous.

"The security situation," He mumbled blushing "Is not as good as people think."

"Has something happened?" I asked pulling on my H harness.

"Munroe really should be the one." He trailed off.

"Look buddy, I will act surprised, but hook me up. I don't want to walk in there blind." I said shouldering my rifle and tentatively putting weight on my feet.

"We have had a lot of folks turning up dead around town. Outsiders, not townies, but people are freaking out."

"Alright, let's go talk to Munroe."

I hadn't been in the Legion Hall before, it seemed like a bar with a lot military paraphernalia on the walls. It reminded me of the Enlisted Club back in Panama, it also served as the town watch headquarter. Munroe sat by a wall map sipping coffee. He seemed twitchier than normal. He turned to Dan and me. "Danny finally got you in here I see." He stood and shook my hand. "Damn glad to have you here, I have had so many guys drop off the duty roster, I can barely keep two posts manned 24 hours a day."

"Am I drafted?" I joked.

He looked serious, "I need you to keep everything I am about to tell you under your hat, ok?"

"Yes Sir." I responded automatically.

"Mrs. Clark found a body on her front step this morning, half-starved irradiated, and probably frozen to death. Simonetti and his thugs took the body before anyone could make too much of a fuss."

"What's the deal with Simonetti, aren't you the town watch?"

"Yes, but we are only responsible for the perimeter and beyond, Simonetti and his half a dozen 'deputies' are responsible for internal security and law enforcement. Simonetti, prick though he is, is the only real Cop among them."

"How many folks do you have?"

"On Paper, eleven including your Father, but sickness and old age have taken everyone off the duty roster but, three Vets over sixty five years old, Danny and myself. "

"How about weapons?" I asked feeling a growing sense of dread that all of this was about to land on my shoulders.

"Two M1 Grands, an M1 Carbine, a few shotguns, and that AR of Danny's"

"Ammo?" I asked feeling ill.

"Not much, if we get hit we can't fight for long." He said flatly. "What's why we need to get off our ass and find out what is out there." These people that are stumbling into town are coming from somewhere. Where ever that is they are clearly starving, and if word gets out that we aren't they will descend on this place like a plague of locusts. "

"Any chance of some kind of a perimeter fence?" I asked knowing it was pointless.

"Everyone is too spread out, but we could fence off the village center and a sort of a Keep that everyone can run to in an emergency." He said almost wistfully, "But, of course the Council won't hear of it. Afraid it will scare everyone."

"Are you kidding me?

"You saw how they are!" Dan interjected, "they won't let the Legion do a food drive jest because they won't control it."

"Oh we can collect all the food we want, as long as we turn it over to them for distribution." Munroe said bitterly. Then he focused on the map. "You came up from the South," He tapped the area between the village and the Pennsylvania border, "Damned impressive too by the way."

"About 60 miles south of here there's a restaurant owned by a guy name Henry he help me get up here, he seemed to be doing some trading with other folks but he's the only person I actually saw north of the Pennsylvania border."

"I need you and Danny to find out where these folks are coming from, I'm afraid come spring we are going to get overwhelmed. Of course with the pace that seems to be increasing as much as it is I'm not even sure to wait till spring." Munroe said glumly.

"Yeah I can do that." I said suddenly feeling a little more nervous. "In fact I can just do the recon on my own." I can see by the look on his face that Dan was hurt. "Unless you want to go." I said knowing full well that he would. I'd made this so far by myself, I didn't want another Pedro situation, or Bill for that matter. The uneasy feeling in my stomach stemmed partially from what was ahead and partially from what it already happened. I come all this way and I was really starting to wonder why. I could've stayed in sanctuary with Billy. Hell I could have stayed in Panama.

Dan and I started our patrol before first light the next morning. The village was eerily quiet, the windows were dark in the streets deserted. The crunching of our boots on the ice seemed embarrassingly loud.

We walked silently along the ridge line that ran parallel to the Lakeshore. The snow-covered Pines seemed remarkably peaceful. It would've been easy to forget everything that it happened until we finally crested the hill, there was a park with picnic tables and barbecue pits. I had been to this park many times in summer when I was a kid and back then you can see the city of Rochester many miles to the north on the horizon. Looking up there now I saw the skeletal and twisted remains of buildings.

As we went down the other side of the hill towards the ruins they disappeared from view. It took us the better part of an hour to reach the throughway. As we came out of the woods we saw a sprawling maze of tents and shacks feeling the field in the parking lot of a truck stop.

We lay in the bushes for quite some time observing, there was smoke from many small fires and clusters of people shuffled back and forth across the camp. We relocated several times to see the camp from different angles and try and get a feel for how big it really was. It seemed difficult if not impossible to estimate how many people there were even attempting to count the number of shacks and shelters proved impossible.

We headed back to the village, not really sure if we'd accomplished anything but there had been no fence around the camp no security that we can see note guard towers there didn't even seem to be any organization to the place. When I briefed Munroe on these facts he did not seem encouraged. "Did anybody see you?" He asked nervously.

"No certainly not but there is a danger that somebody could follow our tracks in the snow." I said honestly. "I think we're going to need to go back up there and I think we're going to need to talk to those people."

"That's only can encourage them to come down here. There is no way we can support more people here we are barely making it through the winter as is." Munroe said nervously.

"What can we do? There's no way we can build an obstacle belt it's gonna keep them out of here." I said suddenly feeling very tired.

"We have a meeting of the committee tonight I want you to brief everyone I what we just talked about." Munroe said his eyes darting around the room nervously. "This meeting is not open to the public so don't tell anybody about it."

"The committee meets in secret?" Dan asked stunned. "When did they start doing that?"

"They've always done that the weekly meeting that's open to the public is mostly for show. Or to embarrass me, when they really want to get things done they don't like to have a whole lot of public scrutiny. The professor seems to subscribe to the public policy is like sausage analogy that Theodore Roosevelt used to use meaning you never want to see either one being made."

The thing that most surprised me that night when I went to the meeting was that they were still using the formal rules of order just like they had done in public. Kari brought the meeting to order and I gave them my report. Simonetti wanted to immediately draw everyone into the center of town and fence it off to keep everyone else out.

"People are not going to be willing to leave their homes." Munroe insisted "we should set up a defendable keep in the middle of town for emergency purposes but people are not going to want to be herded into some kind of a public accommodation."

"People just need to be made to see that they are better off with the safety in numbers that they will get here then if there spread out all over the place." Kari said insistently. The professor slowly shook his head "Mr. Munroe has a point as it do you Kari. No matter how much it might be in their best interest to be centralized people are going to be resistant to change. However if we set up the keep as a temporary measure people will become accustomed to it and over time more and more people will begin to use it as a full-time measure."

This line of thinking made me uneasy for the first but not the last time in dealing with the committee. It was clear to me that they knew that this was not what people wanted but they were going foisted on them anyway. I walked out of the meeting while it was still in progress either to give in my report I didn't think they needed me there anymore. As I walked back down to the cottage a sense of dread came over me wasn't really sure why, but when I open the door I knew. There on the kitchen floor leave the body of my father. I rushed to him and found that he had no pulse and was cold, I didn't attempt CPR I didn't think there was any point to it. I sat there on the floor next to him for a long time I just felt empty.

All that had come before now seemed utterly pointless. Dan came to the door later carry the body down the fire station we used a blanket as a litter. When I came back the house was cold fire had gone out I struggled to get another one lit in the stove. I said looking into the fire for what seemed like most of the night before finally drifting off to sleep.

I woke up shivering in the cold and dark, I thought of starting a fire I thought of crawling off to bed but I just couldn't move.

That's when I decided I was just done. I decided that was the day I

was going to die. But of course my father was still laying on a slab

down at the firehouse and for all of the differences he and I had over

the years I wasn't going to let him stay there. I'd at least get his

bones in the ground he deserved at least that much. We need fought

in Vietnam not because he wanted to, but because he felt he had to.

And then he spent the rest of his life going back there every night

when he fell asleep. I always felt that my time in the Army was a

cheap knockoff of what my father had done. I had been World War

III I supposed, but what I do I shot a kid in Georgia. I lost all my

friends, I walked up the Appalachian Trail it was all so pointless.

I staggered through the cold wet morning down to the fire

station the air didn't seem to move there was a heavy cold wetness to

everything. I got there Dan was the only person in the place, we

exchanged a few pleasantries and talked about what we're going to

do with Dad. It seemed appropriate that we bury them on the

property, the cottage that sort of thing used to be allowed to do, but

now that the world is over we can do pretty much what we need to

do.. I was a little surprised after Dan left they Kari walked in her glasses fogged up of course from the colder air outside the firehouse. She took her glasses off and placed a hand on my shoulder and asked if there was anything she could do. I told her in less that she had a bottle of booze there was really nothing left, I told her the Dan and I were going to put dad in the ground that afternoon, and then I kinda let the subject drop I hadn't change my mind and planning on shooting myself that night but I don't feel the need to tell her. Looking down into her soft round face I have to admit feeling us little spark of life, remembering a world that wasn't so full of horrors, but it only made me a little more sad.

Digging to the frozen ground was incredibly difficult and I had underestimated how wide the roots were of the oak tree we were going to bury next to it took Dan and I all day to get a grave that was at most 3 feet deep. It hurt my heart that I didn't get a full 6 feet but I just couldn't do it anymore and with the clarity of hindsight I have to say it was amazing that Dan hoped and worked all day without a single complaint. In fact in the time I knew him he was a much better friend to me than I ever was to him. When we were done even got the fire going in the stove to heat up the house and I can tell he wanted to stick around but I kind of shuffled them off and I felt a little selfish for doing it. But I knew in my heart of hearts I just couldn't take it anymore. I went through dad's room I found what little booze he had left and set to drinking it sitting by the stove. I just wanted to forget, there was a knock at the door I expected it to be Dan but I was more surprised when I open the door and there stood Kari with a bit of a smile she held up a bottle of Canadian hunter whiskey and said "I think I found you were looking for." I laughed and invited her in.

Before we know it we were drinking whiskey at out of coffee cups and she was chatting ever so pleasantly about her studies and the Village and all these of the things that I honestly wasn't paying any attention to I was just happy to be sitting there talking to a real girl.

When I woke in the morning to a knock at the door I was disoriented. Kari was snoring in the bed naked next to me and as I stumbled to the door I began to reconstruct the night before. Dan was at the door he seemed a little excited said that Munroe needed to see me down the Legion Hall right away. When Kari walked up behind me wrapped in a blanket complaining about how cold it was I saw wounded look on Dan's face. This was the first time I realized that he'd had a crush on Kari for a long time. Because as I said a good friend and he never held it against me although I think in the end it would give her leverage over him that could only do bad things. I got dressed of course got down to the Legion Hall.

Munroe was pacing back and forth by the bar smoking a cigarette, "six more he said six more came in last night Simmonetti is holding them downtown. But this thing is gonna happen a lot sooner than I thought, we're going to need to bill that keep starting today."

"How to even start?" Dan asked.

"How the hell am I supposed to know?" Munroe's face turned red "I was in the God damn Navy 35 fucking years ago how the hell I am supposed to know that?"

"Hey Munroe how about you take it easy on a kid for Christ sake." I said feeling maybe a little hung over. "Look I'll get down there we'll see what we can do but there's no point lose our heads over this." I didn't believe a word I was saying I was going to go down there I was in a try but I couldn't help but think of the skeleton road down in Georgia or the rioters when I first try to get on the Appalachian Trail. A plague was coming, the end of the world was coming. Actually the end of the world it already happened I thought I just had happened here yet but it was coming at was coming soon and in spite of my reprieve from the night before I didn't expect it to get any better and I didn't care. I do banded my thoughts of suicide, it just seemed to me that nature would take its course sooner than later and I did join all the dead and the missing I hoped there would be somebody left the could bury me under that oak tree by my dad. Not that I was that sentimental it was just the packs of dogs that I'd seen still gave me nightmares and the thought of my body being ripped apart by them was just too awful to contemplate.

Creating a keep and downtown proved to be a lot more difficult than it sounded. We ended up blocking off most of the roads with cars and trucks most of which we just had to put into neutral and push. But there was so much space between them and of course it's not hard to walk over the top of the hood of a car. So we ended up stacking furniture trash cans everything you can imagine and in the end it barely qualified as a perimeter. It certainly did not have the safekeeping feel that you would think of when you said quote the keep".

Simonetti joined us with an ancient looking and emaciated black man following behind him. The black man's name was Carter I didn't know that at the time of course but I later found out. He had wild gray hair and yellow looking eyes he seemed 1 foot in the grave. I saw his yellowy eyes darting around observing our defenses and I became angry with Simonetti. "What the hell are you doing with him here?" I hissed pulling Simonetti aside.

"Mr. Carter has agreed to go back to his people and tell them to stay out of our area. In exchange we've agreed to trade with them."

"We agreed?" I asked feeling a knot in my stomach "who the help you in charge, who decided you could speak for everyone?" He just ignored the question and the two of them walked off.

"I don't know, I just have a really bad feeling about this." I said to Dan.

"The committee is certainly not to like it." Dan said picking up his rifle up and putting it over his shoulder, "we probably need to go talk to them right now."

It was around dinner time we got the entire committee together. I expected there to be a lot of tension over the decisions that were made unilaterally, much to my surprise the argument that ensued had nothing to do with that and everything to do with what we would use to trade with the other refugees out there. When the entire crisis and started over a year ago the committee had taken every "bit of unclaimed property, every house that was empty and decided that it belonged to them it was "community property". Now they'd run out of almost everything and Kari thought they should confiscate luxury items that nobody needed specifically Mrs. Clark's jewelry.

I couldn't help but ask what right you have to take her jewelry.

"She doesn't need it it's just a luxury item." Kari said trying to sound patient.

"Luxury or not it's not yours." I said

"Well that's just selfish thinking." She snapped. "People really need to start thinking about other people's needs."

"You can have all the diamonds in the damn world these people are starving they're not going to have anything to trade that you can eat you know?" I said losing patience rapidly.

"It doesn't matter what they do and don't have we start taking other people's property just because we think we need it more than them then were no better than the communist that destroyed the damn country." Munroe said angrily. The professor leaned back in his seat brushed though straight white hair off of his four head for a moment "it wasn't Communists that destroyed the country Mr. Munroe it was people like you."

"What the hell are you talking about?" Munroe said red-faced and angry.

"Had your president Reagan not antagonized the Soviets none of this would've happened."

I could not help myself I had to ask "so the Soviets kill millions and millions of us and you blame us?"

"Look I know you're in the Army and they probably shaped your view of the world in a certain way. But you need to understand that the United States has not been a force for good in the world." Kari said condescendingly.

"What the hell are you talking about?" I asked "the Army doesn't tell you political shift they tell you how to shoot move and communicate on a battlefield how to march but they don't tell you how to think   ." I said not believing what I was hearing.

"Of course you would think that," the professor said calmly "but nationalistic indoctrination is been a part of military service since time immemorial."

"Oh really? And what branch of the service were you in" Munroe asked with a bit of a sneer. "No I didn't think so you never dirtied your hands with that sort of thing you and your people in academia for years been telling us that we needed to play ball to let the Soviets do their thing we do our thing and everything would be just fine. Well guess what professor things aren't just fine."

"Don't know it's not fine because we stopped living in let them live." Kari snapped at him.

"What the hell are you talking about? We didn't attack them, we didn't invade their territory, fact is you don't know what happened none of us know what happened.. We may never know what happened exactly. I believe that it was a mistake, I knew a Navy pilot who told me that he thought the thing they kick the whole thing off was a Russian pilot falling asleep in the cockpit and crossing into West German territory but it's just a theory." I said pleading "the thing is it's really not relevant anymore the question is how we can make it through the winter without starving to death"

"Mr. McGill has a valid point how are we going to get through the winter we don't have enough resources and I think the only rational thing to do," the professor said slowly and calmly "is we are going to half to bring all our resources together and divvy them out to everyone based on their needs."

Munroe scoffed "Oaks of from each according to their abilities and to each according to their needs?" He stood up and waved his finger at the professor "you have no right to take people's food and redistributed based on what you think is necessary."

"But isn't that the most compelling reason available?" The professor said seriously "life liberty and the pursuit of happiness start with the life and you need food for life don't you agree Mr. Munroe?"

"I find it amusing that you can use the Constitution as a justification to do the most wildly unconstitutional thing imaginable." Munroe shot back. "I'll say right now we are not going to do it. We are not going to become a confiscation force taking people's property just so you can play God."

"Internal to the village isn't the possibility of the town watch anyway." The professor said "Mr. Simonetti's police are responsible for enforcing rules inside the village. So you can take your moral objections right to the perimeter fence and keep a lookout."

Munroe stood up and stormed out. I followed him out and caught up with him halfway down the block. "Munroe," I asked confused "what the hell just happened?"

"We just lost the war." He said to me looking on most sad.

"How do you mean? We're still here or still alive, the enemy isn't at the gate, the Russians might be is worse shape than we are."

"Son, America's not a place it's not people America is an idea. And life liberty and the pursuit of happiness was a compromise of a revolutionary idea it was supposed to be a life liberty and property but they didn't go with property because the slavery issue was still out there and they were afraid if they would've kept it that way then the South would've always claimed they had the right to have slaves forever. You might be right about the whole nuclear war thing we may never know how it started but destroying American cities and military bases can't destroy America. What can is when we give up who we are and we become this collective experiment just like the Soviets, just like the Chinese, if the individual's life's work and property are the property of the community it's over. Mark my words young man this is going to turn into confiscation and control and when it's all over there won't be anything left."

I thought Munroe was nuts I went home and Dug one of the last cans of soup out of my pantry sitting there with it cooking on the stove I thought that perhaps Kari and the professor were right I was almost out of food there had to be more out there and I was almost out.

Kari came over that night she asked that I help the next day in doing what she called inventory which of course I agreed to. So she Dan and I went from door-to-door and wrote down a list of everything everyone had when we got to the Clark's house Mrs. Clark insisted we couldn't come in she was a frail small old woman who kept the chain on her door telling us to go away. Kari became irate and soon it turned into a shouting contest between the two and Mrs. Clark slammed the door.

"Well that was a bit of a bust." I said wanting to go home.

"That bitch has more than anybody else in the entire village and she just won't share." Kari spat

"You have a what are you gonna do? It's hers we don't have the right to go into her house categorize everything she has and decide what she gets to keep and when she has to give up." I said realizing that I was done and I was not to be a part of this anymore.

"You have to think about the good of the community." Kari pleaded "if some people don't get to keep everything they've ever had that's a small price to pay for the greater good."

"The Texas oil man and the showgirl." I said and both Dan and Kari looked at me as though I'd lost my mind but I'd remembered this jokes that my father used to tell and I didn't think I really understood it until about that moment. "There was his Texas oil man went to Las Vegas and the he sits down next to this showgirl and the he tells her. You're awfully beautiful why spend the weekend with me? The showgirl says, 'Sir or you don't understand I'm a showgirl not a prostitute.'   The Texan oil man said 'Well I understand that but you know I'm very rich and I'm a really nice guy it'd be fun you should spend the weekend with me I'll buy you a car and will give you $60,000.' And she says to him "Sir I'm a showgirl not a prostitute. So he said "I give you a car a give you $60,000 and I will give you a brand-new fur coat and a diamond ring." She kind of looks him up and down and ceases look sir that's very generous but "I am not a prostitute I am a showgirl, I am not going to do that. The oil man, looks thoughtfully and says what if I make it $100,000 and you just have to spend one night with me." She thinks about it for a moment she says you know I can do that why not? So then he puts his hand on her knee and ass "How about you give me a blow job right now for $50" and she gets offended says "Sir I am not a prostitute!" and that the Texas Oil man say "Young lady we've established what you are now, all were doing is negotiating over price". Kari this is not right, I am soldier, not a thug I am not going confiscate other people's property so you can play at your little social experiment."

I feel pretty good about myself as I was walking back to the cottage until I heard the shot ring out behind me. I ran back to the Clark's house the door was ajar with the lock shot off. Mrs. Clark lay curled up on the floor in a pool of blood. When Dan tried to shoot the lock off he didn't know it was going to hit the old woman behind the door. Dan was collapsed on the side walk crying apologizing. Kari was shouting at the old woman "Why didn't you just open the god damn door?"

"Shut the fuck up Kari. Just shut the fuck up don't you think you've done enough?" I said nearly slapping her. I'd never struck a woman before but coming that close to it frightened me. I stepped forward and kneeled next to Mrs. Clark I didn't know what else to do she was still breathing and sobbing slowly to herself, she had lost a lot of blood I took a towel from the kitchen and placed it against the wound she screamed. The Army always told us to put direct pressure on the wound but it just seemed to make things worse I had her hold the towel on the wound. "Come on Dan Let's go find Doc Weinstein and see what he can do."

I put my hand on Kari's shoulder, "Look I'm sorry, stay with her until we get the Doc here please." I took Dan by the shoulder and guided him towards town. I noticed he left his rifle on the sidewalk I thought about saying something but I thought better of it. "Look Dan I know it is not going help a whole lot but, honestly shit happens, you didn't want to hurt that old woman you were just trying to do the right thing."

By the time Dr. Weinstein arrived Mrs. Clark was already gone. By the end of the next day everything she owned was in the hands of the committee. And it turned out that she had a lot more than we realized, sets of jewelry, large amounts of cash under the mattress and in the freezer but she didn't have any food. We sent a runner up to Carter's people in the north to trade for food and of course they didn't have any food to trade. We sent a patrol to the south to find Henry to see if maybe we could trade with him but we found his place empty the truck was gone and there was nothing left. I went down to the American Legion Hall on New Year's Eve I found Munroe sitting there drunk and I noticed he had a 45 caliber pistol sitting next to I recognize that look, he wasn't planning on seeing the sun come up the next day I sat down next to him saying "hey sailor you got another glass?"

He smiled poured me a drink and said "We were living in trees when they met us. And they showed us each in turn that water would certainly whet us as fire would certainly burn but we found them lacking in uplifted vision and breadth of mind so we left them to teach the guerrillas as we followed the March mankind."

"Excuse me? I as to taking a drink.

"A poem by Rudyard Kipling. As it will be in the future it was at the birth of man there are only four things certain since social progress began as a dog returns to his vomit sow returns to her Meyer and the burnt fools bandage finger goes wobbling back to the fire when all of this is accomplished in the brave New World begins were all men is paid for existing and no man must pay for his sins as surely as water will wet us surely as fire will burn gods of the copybook editing with terror and slaughter return." He said sadly.

"I prefer the Tomten. On small silent feet moving about in the moonlight. Going between the building making tracks in the snow. Talking in a silent little language winters, winters go summers come in summers ago. Winters long and dark and cold winters come in winters go summers go soon the swallows will be here or something like that. "I said Munroe scoffed "it was a book my mom read me when I was a kid but an elf thing." We both laughed, we spent several hours talking about life, he encouraged me to write down the story of how I'd come home which quite obvious that I did. I had made it home, at least to the home or I'd spent my summers. But with my parents gone I found myself surrounded by strangers, or at least people that had been strangers when I arrived. It made me wonder why I kept going so long I could've made a life anywhere along the way. Had I not left sanctuary Pedro would still be alive, and had I not left Panama Bill might still be alive. Course I suppose Bill would not have stayed put in Panama really this was his journey not mine was supposed to be. I wondered at Billy's child, it going be born in a totally different world than the one I had been

born in. I supposed I'd never know, no letters, no telephones, and no

connections to the outside world anymore. Or so it seemed in that

last minutes of 1984 a year after the world had ended.

www.ingramcontent.com/pod-product-compliance
Lightning Source LLC
Chambersburg PA
CBHW060340260626
47160CB00006B/2150